Bernice Rubens was born in [...]
at the University of Wales, of [...]
Her novels to date include the 1970 Booker Prize-winner *The Elected Member*, *A Five Year Sentence*, which was short-listed for the same award, and *Our Father*, winner of the Welsh City Council Prize. Two of her books have successfully transferred into film: *I Sent a Letter to My Love* and *Madame Sousatka* – the latter directed by John Schlesinger and starring Shirley Maclaine. *Mr Wakefield's Crusade* was made into an acclaimed television series. Many of her novels are available in paperback from Abacus books.

Praise for Bernice Rubens and *The Sergeants' Tale*

'A novelist to be treasured' *The Times*

'A sympathetic chronicler of human weakness' *TLS*

'Rubens combines a sharply observant eye with a sympathetic psychological understanding . . . she writes like a dream' *Evening Standard*

'Rubens' skill lies in taking facts and turning them into a tale of real emotions, of ordinary men forced into extraordinary situations and families torn apart by differing political beliefs' *Irish Examiner*

'Serious, moving, and painful' *Scotland on Sunday*

BERNICE RUBENS

The Sergeants' Tale

An *Abacus* Book

First published in Great Britain in 2003 by Little, Brown
This edition published in 2004 by Abacus

A CIP catalogue record for this book is available
from the British Library.

ISBN 0 349 11730 6

Typeset in Galliard by Palimpsest Book Production Limited,
Polmont, Stirlingshire
Printed and bound in Great Britain by
Clays Ltd, St Ives plc

Abacus
An imprint of
Time Warner Book Group UK
Brettenham House
Lancaster Place
London WC2E 7EN

www.twbg.co.uk

For Paul and Maxine Goldberg

1

I have a story to tell. And tell it I must. I owe it to my great-grandfather, Avram Wertman. Or *Zeyda*, as we called him. It was he who started it, this storytelling. Though it was no story. It was the truth, and he enjoined his son to tell it to his children, and those children to theirs. Down the generations, so that it would never be forgotten. He told it to my grandfather, who told it to my father, who told it to me. So now I am myself obliged. I am pledged with a promise to keep.

But I have a problem. For I seem to be the last of that troubadour line. Because I am not of the marrying kind, much less a prospective father. And of my parents, I am the only issue. Sometimes I play with the thought of finding myself a wife and thus possibly a child, of whatever gender, for the sake of an ear, to listen to my tale. But such a thought is so entirely against my nature that it is easily dismissed. So I give it to you, dear reader, to whom my great-grandfather gave no blood, no gene of compulsive continuation. He wanted his story told, the story of his scruples, his doubts, his conscience and, some might say, his heroism. With good and honest telling, he wanted to secure his place in history.

Well, good and honest telling can vary, and over the years the story has been modulated according to the narrative style, the bias, and the imagination of the teller. You know how it is. The oral tradition is a precarious one and none too reliable. It is coloured by the fashion and the politics of the time of its telling. This personal editing is the entitlement of a storyteller, who, in any case, is a congenital liar. And I am no different from my forebears. Except in so far as I am of a different time. Let me explain.

My great-grandfather, for instance, told his story when it actually happened. In 1947, one year before the Israeli War of

Independence. So his political bias was clear. My grandfather's tale was loaded with the guns of the Six Day War in 1967. A proud time, when everybody wanted to be Jewish. Even those in the closet, those Johnny-come-latelys. All of them wanted to identify. So again, his bias was clear. My father had bad luck with his timing. It coincided with the Yom Kippur War of 1973, and apart from the gun-fire the only noise was a discreet closing of closet doors. His narration sat safely on the fence, rooted in ambiguity. As for me, in my time, I am up to my neck in the *intifada*, and thus I have a strange tale to tell.

I'll give you the bare facts of my great-grandfather's story. He was five years old when his parents fled from Russia, during the Kishinev pogrom in 1903. They made their way to Palestine and helped found the first Israeli kibbutz, Degania. The young Avram grew up in pioneering days. His childhood viewed the foundations of Tel Aviv and organised union labour. At the time the Arab population of Palestine was not too disturbed. Jewish immigration was sparse and presented no threat. But with the promise of the Balfour Declaration, the Arabs grew restless and there were sporadic raids on Jewish settlements. But when serious immigration staggered out of Europe after the end of the war, the Jewish need for independence was paramount. The prime enemy was the British occupation. Sundry underground resistance groups were founded. Amongst them the Irgun, ruthless and militant. My great-grandfather, *Zeyda*, though in his thirties, but still tough and athletic, and sweating with patriotic fervour, hastened to join the ranks of the Irgun and it was in this setting that his story took place.

Zeyda. It was he who helped kidnap the British sergeants. It was he who secured their hiding place. It was he who played a leading role in the sergeants' conspiracy. And he wanted his story told.

A potted history. But it will suffice for my tale – a tale open to sundry interpretations. Was *Zeyda*'s act one of heroism? Or one of extreme folly. Whatever.

I'll tell the story in my own way. No doubt I'll take outrageous liberties with chronology. Chronology, in any case, is very boring and lies in the dull province of historians and their obsession with facts. I'll give you the facts, though. They may have different names and be in the wrong place at the wrong time. My privilege. But, don't worry, I'll tell you all that you need to know. I'm concerned with the *nub* of my great-grandfather's story, and that I shall give you. I promise. For his sake as well as for my own.

My great-grandfather told the truth of his tale. My grandfather was influenced by the tenor of his times. My father likewise. And here am I, steeped in the *intifada*. A combination salad, this story. Leave the dressing to me.

2

The British Mandate rule in Palestine was not a benign reign. It was commanded by one Sir Evelyn Barker, a die-hard anti-Semite, whose avowed intention was to hang each resistance fighter from every lamp-post in Palestine. He did not keep his opinions to himself. He spread them among his men whose brutality reflected his hatred. His biggest headache, *Zeyda* used to boast, was the Irgun, led by one Menachem Begin, a number-one terrorist who later, shedding that label, would become Prime Minister of Israel. As indeed, years later, that old 'terrorist' Nelson Mandela became premier of South Africa. Labels oblige with the times.

At the time, *Zeyda* was living in Tel Aviv. He had married late, to Miriam, a girl from the kibbutz. After his parents died, he moved his family to Tel Aviv. He worked as a tailor, a skill he had learned at his father's workbench. When the family had fled Russia, they carried no luggage save for his father's sewing machine. Jewish baggage, due to the haste and terror of their flight, had to be portable, the wherewithal to make a living: jewellery, violins, farrier's tools, and the like. With his father's sewing machine, *Zeyda* was able to make a living. He sewed a fine seam, and he planted a neat bomb and, between the two, he reckoned he served his country well.

He had two children. Joseph, who would be the first inheritor of his tale, and Hannah, his favourite. Both children were resistance fighters, but they had joined the Haganah, the official self-defence organisation of the Jewish community. They disapproved of their father's group, and he of theirs, though their differences were never mentioned in the house. *Zeyda*'s wife Miriam ruled the silent roost and though she knew of every resistance move each one made, she feigned an ignorance, and, protected by that ignorance, she managed to keep the family together. The two movements were at loggerheads: the Haganah did not favour violence, while the Irgun saw no other way. An independent Jewish state was the aim of both, but for the Irgun, the means, however violent, justified the ends.

The war was over. But only for some. In 1946, in Poland, that time-honoured mothers' milk anti-Semitism still held sway. In the city of Kielze, Polish citizens stormed the Jewish Council House and murdered forty-two Jews, injuring many more. All because of a rumour that Jews were killing Christian children for ritual purposes, a medieval echo, not lost on Polish ears. And this, barely a year since Auschwitz. What Polish Jew could then safely stay in his homeland? Over the next three months, ninety-five thousand of them left the country, to join other displaced persons in camps in West Germany, thus boosting their number to a quarter of a million. The war was truly over. But not for everybody. For the displaced persons, the struggle had just begun.

The problem was where and how to place them. Some countries offered refuge, but to each offer a quota was attached. The only country that would welcome them, and without strings, was Jewish Palestine. But Ernest Bevin, the then British Foreign Secretary, refused such an immigration. Bevin was no lover of Jews, preferring an Arab alliance with its promise of oil. And so the 'illegals' began. Boatloads of them, and in any transport that was marginally seaworthy. And at the ports of Jaffa, Haifa and Tel Aviv the British soldiers, armed with guns and unbreakable orders, would be waiting for them.

Among them, on Haifa harbour, were two reluctant sergeants. David Millar and his friend Will Griffiths. They had been on such alerts before, and each sortie sickened them. From shorelines and jetties, they had watched and waited until the boats arrived, only to be barred entry. There was always resistance, many of the refugees drowned and some were simply shot for their presumption.

And often the boats were turned back to the hell from which they had sailed. The sergeants waited as night fell, and waited still until the dawn broke and the seas were smooth to the horizon. They smiled. Secretly they were pleased that the army had been conned; that information received, and clearly misleading, had sent them to the wrong bit of coastline. On their return to barracks, they learned that overnight hundreds of 'illegals' had quietly beached on the Tel Aviv sands and had landed without interruption. The Haganah movement had fooled them yet again.

It was this movement that concerned itself almost exclusively with the 'illegals', and Joseph and Hannah were active participants in these undercover manoeuvres. Shortly after their Tel Aviv success, they were called again to the same shoreline. They left the house when it was dark. Their mother did not ask them where they were going. She knew.

'Be careful,' she said. She might have been warning them to look both ways before crossing the road.

Sergeants Millar and Griffiths were ordered yet again to the site of their former humiliation. Both men hoped for another intelligence cock-up. Along with a patrol of about fifty other men, they had gathered in the coastal station of Herzlia. They were waiting for a signal from the watchtower. Sergeant Millar peered through the slats of the barracks' wall. The sea was calm and there was no boat in sight. He thought he saw a movement in the bushes close to the shore. And then a flickering flash. In its light, the bush was parted and he distinctly saw a woman's face peering out to sea. Her features registered clearly in his mind, and he thought he should report it. But for some reason he preferred to think he had imagined it. Quickly he closed the slats, and with the others he waited for the signal. And then it came from the sentry in the watchtower.

'Illegals,' he yelled. The patrol spilled out of the barracks, and the officer in command rounded them up. 'Spread out,' he said, 'and prepare for the trespass routine.'

To trespass was against the law, and arrest under the law was obligatory. 'Do nothing until they land,' he said. He looked through his field glasses. 'About fifty of them, I'd say. Manageable.' He was satisfied.

They watched as the boat neared the shoreline. A small boat, and clearly overloaded. What struck David Millar most was the total silence. The boat's engines had been cut, and its passengers, wary of discovery, made not a sound as they watched the blessed shore approach to welcome them.

The patrol moved forward, confident of their catch, until an explosion rocked the barracks behind them and, confused, they hesitated, waiting for orders.

'Now,' the officer roared.

But it was too late, a hail of smoke bombs had screened the whole shore. The soldiers, coughing and spitting, could see nothing and could hear only the rushing of the water, but not a human sound. They waited, knowing that their catch had escaped. In the distance, suddenly breaking the silence, they heard the roaring trucks as they pulled away from the shore, and as the smoke cleared they moved towards the water where the empty boat rocked in triumph.

'Haganah,' the officer muttered. 'Bastards.'

So it was back to headquarters to report their failure.

In the debriefing room, the Commanding Officer of Intelligence was spitting with rage. And around the room, about a dozen agents trembled.

'Call yourselves Intelligence?' the Commander barked at them. 'Fifty lousy illegals and four of our men killed. What in God's name are you lot doing out there! Drinking in market cafés? And with all your mint tea not one of you came up with a single lead.'

'But we found out they were coming, sir.' One of the officers dared to offer an excuse. 'We were waiting for them.'

'But you didn't find out about the Haganah, did you? And you must have had leads. Haganah or no Haganah, before they get in, *someone* must know they are coming, *someone* must know their route, *someone* must know their time of arrival. That makes

7

three "someones", not counting the someones who have to be informed, who have to arrange for their successful landing. It's not easy to keep such an operation quiet. And they're coming in by the boatload. We catch about one in ten. It's not good enough.'

There was no response from the group of agents in the room. They'd messed it up, and they knew it. They had no excuse.

'You know what I think?' the Commanding Officer said. 'I hate to say what I think, but it's an emotive issue, the "illegals". We all know what hell the buggers have come from. We know about the camps. We know about the gas. And maybe, maybe some of us feel that we should turn a blind eye. I confess, I've often felt like doing it myself. But it's our job to keep law and order here. And "illegals" are not law, and they're not order. Now bear that in mind, and you might get somewhere. Have any of you got anything at all to say?' he asked helplessly.

'If I might say something, sir,' one of the agents offered. 'If it were the Irgun or the Stern Gang, it would be different. But it's the Haganah, and almost every Jew here is on Haganah's side.'

'Then try the lousy Arabs, for God's sake,' the Commander said. 'And get out of here. All of you.'

When he was alone, he had to admit to himself that the agents were right. No Jew would rat on the Haganah. It was the backbone of the resistance movement – and the least violent. It was willing to debate with the authorities, to plead for concessions. It wanted dialogue. Unlike the Irgun which gave no quarter. To say nothing of the brutal Stern Gang. Between the three of them the Mandate authorities often found themselves helpless. The failure, the Commander concluded, was with his Intelligence agents. Somehow they so often got it wrong, and when they were right, it was usually too late. All his agents were officers and some of them were so polite, they were ineffectual. He would weed them out, he decided, and in their stead he would sprinkle a couple of rank and file. For some time, he'd had his eye on two sergeants.

3

David Millar and Will Griffiths were close friends and had been since their call-up posting. Neither had relished the conscription. Indeed, at one point, David had considered becoming a conscientious objector. Will was of the same mind and it was possibly this common factor that was the basis of their friendship. Otherwise they had little in common.

David was an only child and of a mixed marriage. His mother was Jewish and of an orthodox family who were in no way content with her choice of a Catholic husband. But after David was born, his grandmother, now widowed, had, at his father's invitation, come to live with them in their Bristol home. And it was she, that loving *bubbeh* of his, who nurtured and cared for him. It was for her sake that he was circumcised, and for his father's sake baptised. Thus he was comprehensively insured on all sides. It was his grandmother who organised the Seder table at Passover while David joined his father for Mass on Palm Sunday. It was *Bubbeh* who lit the Hanukkah candles while his father decorated the Christmas tree. David was a boy who had everything.

Will, on the other hand, had to take what he could get. He was one of six children, all of them boys, born in Ebbw Vale, a Welsh mining village. His father had been down the pit, and was now silicosis-retired, and he panted through life with the exertion of idleness. Will's mother took in washing to make ends meet. Will remembered being hungry sometimes. He loved school because of the dinners provided, and the mid-morning cocoa. He did well in his Higher Certificate and afterwards faced unemployment in preference to the pit, so that when the call-up papers arrived it was by way of a relief. It would take him out of idleness, even though he questioned its purpose. He was sent to Dorset for his training and it was in this camp that he first ran into David, and the casual exchange of men accidentally thrown together. Over the weeks of their training that exchange became less casual, more personal, so that by the time they arrived in Palestine they were inseparable.

Both of them shared scruples and discontent with their posting and their constant surveillance of the shores depressed them further. Together they decided to apply to Intelligence, a department that would at least exempt them from the shores, and those scenes of rage and rampage in the waters. They had little hope of success, though they knew that Intelligence was a department badly in need of an overhaul. Especially after the Tel Aviv fiasco. So they were little surprised, though highly excited, when they were summoned for interview.

They waited together in the anteroom. David was the first to be called.

'Good luck,' Will said.

Four officers were seated at a long table. David saluted and was told to sit down. He would have preferred to stand, for he was uncomfortable in officers' company. His friends were rank and file. Nevertheless, he took the seat that was offered him. He felt he was being watched intently as if his manner of seating himself might give them clues as to his reliability. He shifted in his chair as they waited for him to settle. But they never took their eyes off him, except for the chairman of the group, Captain Coleman, who was sifting through papers.

'David Millar,' he read out. 'Twenty-three years old. Joined Electrical and Mechanical Engineers. Posted to Palestine, July 1943. Born Bristol.' He stopped reading and without looking up, asked, 'For what reason do you wish to join Intelligence?'

'I'd like to help,' David said limply. 'I'd like to try.' It was the most honest answer he could give. He hoped that they'd at least be impressed by his candour. 'I've been here for some time,' he added. 'I think I know the country pretty well. And I've made friends here. Jews and Arabs. I feel I could be useful.'

A line of raised eyebrows greeted this display of confidence.

As far as the officers were concerned, no friendship could be counted on, either with Jews or Arabs.

The Captain returned to his papers. 'Mother,' he read. Then he allowed a pause. 'Jewish.' Another pause. 'That makes you Jewish too, Millar, according to Jewish law.'

'That's correct, sir.'

'But exactly how Jewish *are* you, Millar?'

'My grandmother lived with us in Bristol,' David said. 'She was orthodox and she saw to my Jewish education.'

'Apart from all that.' The Captain was getting impatient. 'What I mean is, how Jewish d'you *feel*?'

'As much as I feel Roman Catholic. Like my father.'

'Quite a mixed bag, aren't you?' the Captain said. 'Intelligence work can be dangerous,' he went on, 'and it requires holding your tongue. Especially on your Jewish bit.'

The 'bit' was offensive. 'Sir?' David asked. He pretended not to understand. He wanted the Captain to spell it out, loud and clear.

'You know very well what I mean.' The Captain appeared irritated. 'Just keep it quiet. You never know. It could get you into trouble.'

David gave a thought to all those thousands stranded on the shorelines who had got into exactly that sort of trouble. He wondered what kind of SS officer the Captain would have made. He was beginning to dislike the man. He stared at him, willing him to look him in the eye. He wanted to see that face, clearly, to record it, its every feature. But it was buried in papers.

Then another officer spoke, but at least he looked at him.

'You been cut, Millar?' he asked.

'Cut, sir?'

'You know, Millar,' the officer said. 'Your thing. Your Johnny.' A trace of a smile sneaked out of his lips and was quickly withdrawn.

'Yes. I'm cut,' David said, and almost proudly. He was a cut above those uncut officers around the table.

'Well, be careful where you drop your trousers,' the Captain said. And for the first time, he looked up from his papers.

David found his face was no surprise. It was mean overall, well-fed and unashamed. His nose was lightly veined as if it were familiar with the bottle. His little eyes were barely open and his mouth was lipless. A faceless face, and no doubt eminently suited to his calling.

'Take yourself to the briefing room,' he said. 'They will give you your instructions. And tell Griffiths to come in.'

David saluted and left the room. He dawdled his way to the anteroom.

'Your turn,' he said to Will.

'How did you do?'

'I made it,' David said. 'And so will you. They're desperate.'

'Thanks very much,' Will said.

David sat down and waited. He wondered why he felt no excitement. He had looked forward to the interview with such hope, crossing his fingers that he would be chosen. But now that he had succeeded he felt no trace of euphoria. He had not warmed to that cold panel of officers. In their role of authority, an authority laced with contempt, they sickened him. And the Jew 'bit', as they called it. That bothered him too. But it was more than that. It was the simple fact that, whatever his rank, he had landed himself in an army of occupation, and it was this description that had lately begun to offend him. He wondered what he was doing there in the first place, what right he had, with hundreds of others, to impose his rule on a people so justifiably inhospitable. There had been rumours that the British would soon pull out, a move that David would welcome. The Jews would be glad to see them leave. The Arabs too, although they had long been the favoured party. But both would be happy to see the back of them so that they could get on with their own wars with each other, without the interference of frequent army curfews and its continual surveillance. He wondered how Will was faring. He hoped he would pass as

12

easily as he had. His friendship with Will was one of the few bonuses of his posting and he did not wish Will back to the seashore.

Inside the interview room, Will, like David, was finding the panel faintly offputting. It was not its authority he resented. It was its simple ranking. Will hated officers. At one point in his army career, he had been offered officer training but he had refused because he didn't want to become like them, and it would make him an outsider in Ebbw Vale.

'You're a friend of David Millar,' one of the officers said. It was not a question. It sounded like the result of an investigation.

'That's right, sir,' Will said.

'In what way?' the officer probed.

'Well, we go out together. The beach. Cafés. Sometimes a concert. You know, that sort of thing.'

'That sort of thing?' The officer smiled.

His smile set Will on edge. He had an uncomfortable inkling of what it signified.

'Then we can assume that you are *close* friends,' the officer said.

But Will was ready for them. 'I have a fiancée at home,' he said. He recalled the homeless old woman who would wander aimlessly about the valleys. Phoebe was her name.

'Her name's Phoebe,' Will said. It was a name and it would do. 'We're getting married on my next leave.' He could not repress a grin as he saw himself beside Phoebe at the altar, surrounded by all her bags.

'Congratulations,' that same officer said. 'I hope it works out for you.' The smile again. But Will let it lie.

Then the Captain spoke head down, into his papers. 'You know about your friend's er – mother.' He looked up and Will stifled a shudder at the man's faceless face. 'About the Jew bit,' he said.

'Yes, sir, I know.'

'We're keeping quiet about it. And that means you too. You understand?' he almost shouted.

'Yes, sir.' He needn't have been told. He'd always kept quiet about it, knowing the complications that might ensue. And so had David. It was never mentioned between them.

The Captain returned to his papers. He was clearly uncomfortable with the human face. 'Report to the briefing room,' he shouted. 'They'll give you your orders. And no hero stuff,' he added. 'No risks. It simply isn't worth it.'

Now Will smiled. The Captain, like David, like himself and like the whole occupying army, all of them simply wanted to go home.

'Not too bright, either of them,' the Captain said when Will had left. 'Still, they're eager. And they'll learn. When they're ready, I'll start them off in Tel Aviv. See how they go. You never know. They might surprise us.'

4

It was rare that *Zeyda* and his family managed to gather together for a meal, but that evening the four of them sat around the table. Any talk regarding the resistance was avoided, since it always threatened disruption. However, each of them knew that something was in the air. In the air around *Zeyda*. All week he'd been in and out of the house, neglecting his sewing machine and his clients' orders. He'd been nervy too, and for no reason he'd often lost his temper. So neither his wife nor his children were surprised when he suddenly left the table.

'I'm going out,' he said. 'I'll be back tomorrow.' He was in no hurry. He knew he would be asked no questions. Miriam looked after him as he moved towards the door. After twenty-five years of marriage, she loved him no less than when he had courted her on the kibbutz. Yet she wished he had a mistress somewhere, one who could account for his frequent comings and goings. A mistress would have been safer. But he had nothing on the side. He had a wife, and it was not her. He was married to the Irgun. A marriage indissoluble.

So, 'Be careful,' she said. That warning, for big or trivial events, would always do. She didn't know where he was going or to what purpose. She would wait until the morning when she had no doubt that she would read about it in the papers.

But the news didn't break till midday. She was listening to the wireless. A woman was talking about the importance of trees to the environment. Suddenly the speaker's voice was silenced. Miriam stiffened and prayed that Avram, whatever he had been doing, had not been caught.

'We interrupt this programme,' the announcer said, 'for a news flash.'

Again she prayed, this time for the safety of her children. She thought she knew where they were. Teaching at schools in the suburbs of Tel Aviv. At least, that's what they did every day. But who, in such a climate, could be sure of anything? She shut her eyes as she listened to the broadcast.

'A huge explosion has totally destroyed the southern wing of the King David Hotel in Jerusalem. As yet, no organisation has claimed responsibility. Heavy casualties are feared. We will keep our listeners up to date with the news as it comes in.'

Then the tree lady took up where she had left off, as if nothing in the world had changed.

Miriam listened, but not so much to the subject of the talk. She was waiting for the silences that would break the woman's voice. She prayed for those breaks, but she dreaded them. 'Without the propagation of trees,' the woman was saying, 'man could not survive. There would be no life,' she said, and Miriam wondered whether, trees or no trees, there was life in any case.

A break again, and this time, almost all the details of the catastrophe were revealed. 'The Irgun has claimed responsibility for the outrage,' the announcer said. 'At least eighty people have been killed in the blast and many more injured. Irgun members, disguised as Arab porters delivering milk, entered the basement of the building. The milk churns were filled with explosives. One of the so-called porters was killed.'

Miriam uttered a prayer. For someone who had no belief in God, she wondered to whom she was pleading. But it was a relief to yell out her fear, even if only she herself was listening. 'The Irgun organisation,' the newscaster droned on, 'claims that a twenty-five-minute warning was given to the British Mandate authorities. Such a claim is categorically denied. We will continue with our bulletins as further information is received.' Then the tree woman, her tone offended by such constant interruption, continued to insist on the vital necessity of arboreal culture. Bugger the King David Hotel, she seemed to be implying.

Miriam heard the door of the apartment open, crash open, and she feared that they had already come for Avram. So it was

16

with some relief that she greeted her children. Two down. One to go.

'You're early,' she said.

'School's closed. There'll be a curfew,' Joseph said. 'Where's Papa?'

'Where d'you think?' Hannah said with contempt.

'One of them was killed,' Miriam said. 'It was on the wireless.'

They were silent then. Hannah put her arms round her mother's shoulders. 'He'll be all right,' she said. 'He always is.'

'How is he going to get back in the curfew?' Miriam whispered.

'He'll find a way,' Joseph said.

'Turn that damned radio off,' Miriam shouted. She was heartily sick of trees.

'Leave it,' Hannah said gently. 'There might be more news. I'll make some lunch.'

But none of them was hungry. They would not eat until Avram came home. His return – that was all that mattered. His solid form in the door frame and then they would let into him, with rage and fury – and not only him, but the whole bloodthirsty organisation to which he belonged.

'Check that the back door is open,' Miriam said. 'And the side window too.'

The lunch that Hannah had prepared lay on the table untouched. And untouched still through supper time. The wireless droned on all day but there was no fresh news, just endless repetition of the same facts.

'He won't come back before dark,' Joseph had said. But it was already dark and could not get darker.

'If anything had happened to him, we would have heard something.' Hannah tried to comfort her mother. But each of them knew that the Irgun was wary of communication, except by word of mouth and no words would dare break the silence of the curfew.

17

'We might as well go to bed,' Hannah said. But no one moved. The wireless still droned on and after its hourly repetition, announced that the curfew in Tel Aviv would continue indefinitely.

So they stayed up and waited. There was little conversation. Speculation about the bombing was pointless. Until Miriam whispered, as if she wanted nobody to hear, 'I don't want to know who was killed. I just want to know who *wasn't*.' And then she allowed her tears to fall.

'You must eat something,' Hannah said, but the food still lay untouched on the table. Under curfew, as it were, like the silent streets outside.

It was well past midnight. During curfew, they were allowed one hour in the morning to shop for food and essential medical supplies.

'He'll be back tomorrow,' Joseph said. 'During the curfew-lift.' But his voice lacked conviction. Much as he disapproved of his father's allegiance, there was no doubt that he loved him dearly, and now he began to regret the insults he had hurled at him regarding his militancy. 'I'm so sorry, Papa,' he whispered to himself, as if he was already mourning his passing.

But Hannah had no doubt that her father had survived, as he had survived countless sorties. Unlike her brother, she regretted none of the reproaches she had thrown at him. She was angry, enraged that he was causing his family so much pain. She would wait for his return and then she would give him what for.

They heard the squeak of the latch. They stood up, the three of them, trembling. It could be Avram, but they dreaded that it might be another of his group, breaking the curfew with terrible news.

'Hello?' they heard. A whispered voice. Avram's voice, whispered or not, like no other.

He stood in the doorway. Relief flooded the room, but anger, waiting in the wings, dispersed it soon enough.

Hannah rushed to confront him. 'Over eighty dead,' she hissed at him.

'And one of them Dov,' he hissed back at her. Dov Katz. His young protégé. Twenty-four years old. He brushed Hannah aside. 'Let me sit down,' he said.

Miriam went to embrace him. 'You must be hungry. First things first,' she said to her children. 'All of you eat. Then you can argue.'

And so yesterday's lunch was consumed. Avram ate very little. 'I must go to Dov's mother,' he said, 'when the curfew lifts.'

'D'you want me to come with you?' Miriam asked.

'That would be kind,' Avram said.

The meal was eaten in silence. In the face of their father's loss, there seemed no point in argument. He would have found their disapproval an obscenity. But still he felt he had to enlighten them.

'They were given warning,' he said. 'Twenty-five minutes before the blast. We told them to evacuate. The British deny it. No one phoned, they said. They're lying. They simply ignored the call. They thought it was a hoax. They couldn't believe that we'd dare attack the seat of Mandate government.' He looked into his children's eyes. 'We warned them,' he said again. 'Not one of them need have died. Believe me. We warned them.' They believed him, and there seemed little more to say.

Avram was shivering. He had clearly spent a rough night.

'I'll run a bath for you,' Hannah said.

He smiled at her. His girl. If not his comrade, his favourite.

'Does she know?' Miriam asked him, as she and Avram crossed the streets during the lift in curfew.

'No,' Avram said. 'I have to tell her. You don't have to come.'

'She needs another mother by her,' Miriam said. She hurried Avram along.

It took only a second, Avram thought, to say, 'Your son is dead,' but they had almost an hour in which to say it. He wondered how much he could reveal to Dov's mother. Dov had been one of the porters. He had rolled his churn at Avram's side. 'I'm Tevya the milkman,' he had whispered with a laugh. Those were probably his last words. When they had dumped the churns, they had run, all six of them. At the street corner they had hidden in a doorway, waiting for the blast. Then they had run for their lives. But not Dov. He had lingered, savouring the sound. Avram waited for him, afraid to call out his name. Then he heard shots above the blast and he had crawled back among the fleeing crowds. Dov lay in the doorway, his face and chest shattered. Avram folded him in his arms. He covered him with his own coat and, heedless now of capture, driven only by his despair, he ran towards their hideout. People stared at him with pity, thinking he was carrying a victim of the bombing, a passer-by, perhaps, in the wrong place and at the wrong time. Some offered help, but he ran, misted by his tears.

At the hideout, they laid him out on a bed and dared to look at him. 'His mother mustn't see him,' one of them said.

They would arrange the burial as soon as they could. Avram had offered to break the news to his mother.

He couldn't imagine how he could tell her. How he could soften the blow. But in what voice or language could 'dead' be a softened word? In what whisper or song or civil sigh could murder be a soothing tale? 'Only a little bit dead, Mrs Katz. Not much murdered.' But withal, Dov must be buried.

'She has suffered so much,' Miriam said. She was thinking of Mrs Katz's husband, Meir, killed two years before, in the same group and for the same cause. Dov was their only child, and Avram had been like a father to him.

Her door was open. They heard the wireless drone. She was sitting at the table laid with uneaten breakfast, lunch and supper. She was mouthing the repeated words of the announcer, having listened to them all night long. She was simply waiting for Dov to come home.

When she saw Avram and Miriam in the doorway, she knew that she was childless. She uttered a small sound. Avram didn't have to tell her. He didn't need any words at all. He simply held

20

her in his arms and together they wailed their loss. Out of her whimpering, there came a sudden scream. A sodden scream, drenched with her tears.

'I have given enough,' she shouted. 'The cause, the cause, the godforsaken cause.'

Miriam held her and sat her down. Avram opened a cupboard and found some brandy. He urged her to drink it. It would do nothing to assuage her grief, but it might stem her anger. Though he himself knew that that anger was her entitlement and for a moment he joined her in her loss of faith.

Miriam had always had her doubts. She could not help thinking of all the mothers, fathers, sweethearts, siblings, a long way away in England. They too were weeping, like Mrs Katz, and wondering about the nature of the cause.

'The funeral is in the morning,' Avram said. 'It's all arranged. We'll come to fetch you.'

'Can I see him?' she whispered.

'It was all over in a second,' Avram said. 'I witnessed it. He didn't feel anything.' It was the best and the only way he could tell her that Dov was no suitable sight to be remembered and mourned as her son. His curly black hair was all that was recognisable.

She accepted his non-answer. 'You must go now,' she said. 'The curfew.'

They wished her long life, kissed her and left. Once in the street, Avram broke down completely. He sobbed silently, refusing Miriam's supportive hand. It was nothing to do with Miriam. She was clean. It was *his* guilt, his own, and he would never forgive himself. The cause, the cause, he kept saying. Despite Dov's death, he was bound to it. Irrevocably. And now, more than ever before. The enemy would fail. And in the name of Dov he would kill them all.

The curfew was politely waived for the funeral, but the army was present in force. The soldiers had the grace to stand on the sidelines, while the column of mourners moved slowly towards the open grave. The Irgun was there as a body. No faces were masked as if they were asking for recognition from the enemy. Theirs was a defiant and proud visibility. And although the Haganah movement strongly disapproved of the hotel bombing, it had come out of respect for a comrade in resistance. *Zeyda* and his family led the mourners, supporting Dov's mother between them. There was no coffin: Dov's body, wrapped in a simple cloth embroidered with the Star of David, was carried by members of his group, all of them trembling with sorrow. As the body was lowered into the ground, it settled to the plaintive song of the rabbi's prayer, and a great pall of wailing chorused its burial.

Dov's mother sank to the ground. She was silent. She had been to this place before, and for the same cause. She had no more tears to shed. Let others weep for him now, she thought. Tears would not cleanse her. Her grief was a tattoo. Indelible. A grief that time would never heal. She would be, forever, inconsolable.

5

The two sergeants had undergone a month's vigorous training. They had studied the rules of espionage and their legal rights if captured. In staged situations, they had learned how to dissemble, how to feign friendship, how to lie with conviction and how, without scruple, to betray. Their tutor found them more than apt pupils, and recommended them for preliminary field work at the end of their course. For their cover, they were given posts as finance assessors at the English bank in Yehuda Street in Tel Aviv to which they had to pay daily visits for the sake of appearances. They would shed their uniforms for civvies, and take up residence in one of the flats owned by the bank, where they would stay until possibly transferred. They were given a couple of days leave to adjust and settle themselves.

The sergeants were excited, but nervous. Neither of them considered themselves adequately equipped for espionage work, and they wondered, in view of Intelligence's recent poor record, whether those others involved were equally unqualified.

'No more shore duty,' Will said, as they unpacked their kit.

'And no more uniform,' David added.

The two bonuses of their upgrading.

Their hair had been allowed to grow during their tuition time and had achieved a decent civilian length so that David, especially handsome, even in short back and sides, was now a regular Adonis.

On his first free day, Will decided to go to Jerusalem. He had friends there, musicians whom he'd met at the jazz café. He was no mean sax player, was Will. He'd been playing since he was a boy, first in the colliery band, and later in the miners' clubs. His friends welcomed him, his Jewish friends; but in their music-making that was irrelevant – together with his sergeant's uniform.

But tonight he would be in civvies and if asked why, which was unlikely, he would say that he was on leave. He packed his sax and looked forward to a good night's session. 'See you tomorrow,' he said. David, for his part, was happy to stay in the city. Although he knew Tel Aviv intimately, he'd never had the opportunity to wander its streets, move around without purpose as a tourist might, discover things that natives found too familiar to notice. He might even go for a swim. So he set out in his civvy-suit freedom.

It was a Saturday, the Jewish Sabbath, so many of the shops were closed. But that did not worry him. There was nothing that he wanted to buy. But some of the cafés were open on to the pavements and he made his way towards them. He would sit for a while and watch the passers-by. He spotted an empty table at one café and, as he approached it, he noticed a woman walking backwards in his direction. She was shouting greetings of a sort to another woman, also walking backwards. They were laughing, both of them. The second woman waved, turned and disappeared round the corner, and before the first woman could turn a lamp-post met her and she slumped to the ground. David ran towards her. 'Are you all right?' he asked. 'Come.' He lifted her gently. 'You must sit down,' he said, guiding her to the empty table. 'I'll get you some water.'

'Coffee would be better,' she said, smiling up at him.

He went inside and paid for two coffees. Then he joined her. 'All in one piece?' he asked.

'More or less,' she said. 'You're very kind.'

David looked at her, seeing her face clearly for the first time. But was it the first time? he wondered, for there was something familiar about her features. And disturbingly so. Of that he was aware. The disturbance. But he had no idea of where – or even if – he had seen her before.

'My name's Hannah,' she said, and put out her hand. He took it formally.

'I'm David.'

24

'That's a good old Jewish name.'

'It's pretty common in England,' he said, 'among Catholics, which is what I am.'

His first half-lie. Out of the army, in another country, he could have owned to being Jewish. But not here and not now. Though since his arrival in Palestine he had felt more Jewish than at any other time, even at his grandmother's loving knee. He thought of her and smiled.

'What's funny?' Hannah asked.

'Just a happy memory,' he said.

'What are you doing in my country?' she asked.

He was careful not to react to her possessive. Any Jew in this country would have said the same.

'I work in a bank,' he said. 'Very dull, I'm afraid. And you?'

'I'm a teacher. Kindergarden.' She sipped at her coffee and once again he studied her face. She was without doubt beautiful, and unspoilt, as nature had intended. For she wore no make-up and her long black hair, tangled at the ends, had clearly not seen a brush for a long while.

'Are you married?' he dared to ask her.

She laughed and her face wrinkled with the laughter. 'Of course not,' she said. 'I've lots of things to do before I think of settling down.'

He joined in her laughter, relieved that she was uninvolved.

'And you?' she asked.

'I've too many things to do before settling down,' he mimicked her.

'Then we have something in common,' she said.

'And what are all those things you have to do? Apart from running into lamp-posts?'

She laughed again. 'I see friends,' she said. 'The cinema, theatre sometimes. There's always something to do in Tel Aviv. And you? What do you do when you're not counting bank notes?'

'Well, I'd play chess if I could. But I can't find anybody to play with.'

25

'How long have you been in Tel Aviv?' she asked.

'Almost two years.'

'Two years and you haven't discovered the chess café?'

'Is there such a place?' He grew excited.

'On Herzl Street. My brother – he's a champion – he plays there most Sunday nights.' She paused and looked at him. 'I go with him sometimes.' It was an oblique invitation to another meeting.

'I'll certainly try that,' he said.

She put down her coffee cup and framed her face in her hands, cathedral-like, the tips of her fingers meeting at her forehead and her hands curtaining her cheeks. And then David knew precisely who she was, and why he knew he'd seen her before. That small face, triangled by green bush leaves, as he had seen it through the slats of the barracks. On that disastrous night on Jaffa beach when the shoreline was flooded with vapours, and the 'illegals' had vanished in its mist.

He was shaken. As far as his new posting was concerned, Hannah was a find. And a find that could lead to the opening of a monstrous can of worms. A find that could lead to the Haganah itself, and the total destruction of the 'illegals' operations. And all this on his first day when he was not even supposed to be working. Suddenly he wished he had never set eyes on her, that it had been another beautiful girl who'd collided with a lamp-post. Because he had taken a liking to Hannah and he very much wanted to see her again. He couldn't pretend he had never seen that face in the bushes, but he would not act on it. No one need ever know he had forfeited such a chance. No one. Not even Will. Then perhaps he could see her again and pretend it was only for the second time. But now he wanted to be on his own. He had to consider what he should do. How he should proceed. He could never bring himself to use Hannah in any way. Yet he was supposed to be in Intelligence and to pass up such an opportunity was a kind of betrayal. And then he wondered where his loyalties lay.

He looked at his watch. 'I have to meet someone,' he said.

'Where'd you live in the city?' she asked.

'In Yehuda Street. A flat that belongs to the bank. I share it with a friend who works with me. Will. He's gone off today to Jerusalem. Plays the sax at the jazz café. Will and his sax, and me and my chess.' He was anxious to include Will in his next encounter with Hannah, as if to proclaim a protector of sorts. For his own benefit. A friend, but one in whom he dared not confide. For Will would tell him with little hesitation where his loyalties lay.

He rose from his seat and smiled at her. 'Perhaps I'll see you one Sunday,' he said.

'Maybe. And thanks for the coffee.'

Slowly he walked away from her, his mind in a turmoil. As he turned the corner of the street he caught a familiar melody, one he'd not heard since his grandmother's time. His ears watered. It was the closing hymn of the Sabbath service. *Adon Olam.* He hummed it to himself, overwhelmed by a terrible sadness. Yet another betrayal, he thought. He felt his grandmother's hand in his as she kept him by her, upstairs in the women's section of the synagogue because he was too young to join the men downstairs. And he missed her sorely. He was tempted to go inside, but he had no head cover and no *talith*. He would be turned away as an outsider, one who had no business there, and perhaps they would have been right, though in his heart no one had a greater right than he. He turned away, and it was not until he felt the hot tears on his cheeks that he realised he was crying. Quickly he made his way to the beach. Once there, he could go into the sea, and with the camouflage of water he could weep his heart out.

Afterwards he lay on the beach, becalmed as if after a storm. He would see Hannah again, he decided, and as if he had never seen her before. And one day he would find a *talith* and go to the synagogue and declare himself to himself.

* * *

27

In Jerusalem, Will found himself in a similar dilemma, and one he had no intention of sharing with David. He was welcomed in the club, but with a little surprise. His friends had never seen him in civvies before. That could be explained by a short leave. But it was his hair that puzzled them. Where was the short back and sides they had so frequently mocked him about? 'You look like a deserter,' Gabby joked.

'He looks like us,' the pony-tailed Ariel said. 'And no bad thing. I was never comfortable playing with short back and sides.'

They were teasing him, he knew, but he realised that he had made a terrible mistake. He should never have come. They knew him as a uniformed sergeant, and they would never think of him as otherwise. A uniform was now forbidden him. The civvies were easy – a few days leave. But the hair. He had no excuse for his new style, and a return to the old was equally forbidden. He would ask David for advice. But then he realised that he could not confess to David that he had put himself at such risk. He comforted himself with the thought that his musician friends were not interested in politics. Neither were their fans. They were indifferent to the Mandate. Jazz was their whole life and took priority over everything else. Yet still he had to explain the hair.

'I just thought I'd try it,' he said. 'Until somebody bawls me out. But so far, and it's almost a month now, I've got away with it. So take a good look, fellows. It may be your last.' And it certainly would be their last, Will thought, for he dare not come to the club again. But for now he would play his heart out.

As always, the café was crowded. Will recognised most of the faces; a loyal and regular following. Jazz buffs, who appreciated each rhythmic nuance, each audacious entry, cheering any impromptu soloist. They didn't care whether he was tinker, tailor or soldier. But could he depend on every single one of them? He couldn't take that risk. This night would certainly mark his last appearance.

They played well into the early hours. There was no transport back to Tel Aviv. In his uniformed days, he could always pick up an army truck on night patrol. But long-haired as he was, that was no longer possible. Uri, the bass player, offered him a bed for what remained of the night. He had no option but to accept, but he was loath to become more embroiled in their company.

Uri lived on his own. He'd been married at one time, but only for six months, for his wife had left him. She couldn't compete with his bass, and it is possible he didn't even notice her absence. When he could tear himself from his instrument, and in order to earn a pittance, he worked as a piano-tuner, a self-employed job that suited him. There was no shortage of work. A piano in a Jewish home is almost a given, if not to serve the manifold prodigies of expectant parents, then to take care of the display of bar mitzvah, graduation and wedding portraits of a proud family. Uri unfolded the put-u-up in his living room. Despite the early morning hour, neither man was tired.

'Don't you ever get lonely?' Will asked.

'Never,' Uri almost shouted, over-protesting. 'I've got the band, the band and the band. How could I be lonely?'

'Is that enough?' Will asked.

'Well, it has to be. As long as this occupation lasts. It tides me over. Afterwards it will be different – for all of us.'

Will was nervous. He sensed a surprise turn in the conversation. A political turn that he had never associated with Uri, or with any of the band. He said nothing.

'When are you lot going home?' Uri asked. He smiled as if he didn't want his question to be taken seriously.

But Will knew that the smile was just a cover. They'd learned the uses of a smile in their training course. Uri was serious. He wanted information. It was possible, Will surmised, that he worked in the underground.

'Nobody tells me anything,' Will said, and he too smiled. 'I've got to get some sleep,' he pleaded. He wasn't tired. He simply wanted to end the conversation, fearful of where it might lead. He could not possibly play with the band again, but at the same time, he was aware that he was forfeiting a God-given avenue of

Intelligence. But these men were his friends, and for that reason alone he must not see them any more. He was anxious to return to Tel Aviv, to feel safe in David's company, even if he could not share with him the cause of his fear.

Uri went to his room. Will heard him pacing about for a long while. Then he heard the front door slam, and wondered where Uri was going. In the morning, he found a note on the kitchen table. 'Will,' he read. 'I had to go out. See you next session. Good luck with the hair. Uri.'

Will dressed hurriedly and rushed out into the street where the Egged bus to Tel Aviv was approaching its stop. He took a seat at the back and listened to the non-stop wireless that blared from the driver's bench. No reports of raids, bombs or illegals. The curfew had been lifted in Tel Aviv. Police were still hunting the bombers of the King David Hotel. For a moment Will wondered whether Uri had been one of them. Before last night it would have been a preposterous idea, but slowly it was gaining credence. In his new position, everybody was suspect – it was his job to think so. But not Uri. Not that laid-back pony-tailed bass player who suddenly wanted to know when the British were pulling out. Any Jew or Arab in Palestine at the time could have asked the same question. All of them were entitled to an answer. But nobody knew. Not even the army or the British authorities themselves. What was known was that everybody wanted to see its end, no matter what chaos might ensue.

The Tel Aviv streets were crowded with shoppers. Will hopped off the bus to buy food for breakfast. But when he reached the flat, he found breakfast already prepared and David waiting for him. Both men had looked forward to seeing each other, to sitting quietly together and to withholding that which was untellable.

'Did you have a good day?' Will asked.

'Yes,' David said. 'I met a girl.' There was no harm in telling Will about Hannah. She was just a girl and no more. 'She bumped into a lamp-post and I picked her up. We had coffee together.'

'Promising?' Will asked.

'Very,' David said. 'She told me there was a chess club on Herzl Street. Her brother goes there every Sunday to play. He's a champion, she says. I might go.'

That was all that Will needed to know. Hannah and the club. Both innocent.

'Well, thank God I won't have to listen to you whining for a partner any more. And I mean a *chess* partner. Though who knows?'

'She's just a girl,' David said. 'And you. How did you get on?'

'The usual,' Will said. 'A great session. Lasted almost all night.'

There was a silence then between them, a silence that could well have been a prologue to secret-sharing. Will sensed that David was holding back, and sensed too that David suspected his own reserve. It was David who broke the silence.

'You know,' he said, 'when you were gone, I thought maybe it was a mistake. After all, they know you as a sergeant. They've only ever seen you in uniform. For one time, you could be in civvies. You could explain that. But every week?'

'You're right,' Will said. 'It occurred to me too.'

'And the hair. What about that?'

'I got away with it. Said I was daring the authorities. But you're right,' he said again. 'I won't be going back.'

'I'm sorry,' David said. 'What will you do about playing?'

'I'll blow my heart out in my bedroom and I'll drive you up the wall.'

They both laughed with relief, for their secrets were half told, and that was a beginning.

They decided to spend the day at the sea. Work would begin tomorrow and their timetable had been organised. David would idle on the streets of Jaffa and in the marketplaces. He'd been given a contact, Abu, a fruit-stallholder, unashamedly in British pay. Will had been ordered to stay in Tel Aviv. There had been hints of another group of 'illegals' arrival. He was given no names. He had to mosey around and pick up what he could. But today

31

there was time to spend on the beach and then a good night's sleep. Both men looked forward to their first day at work.

The beach was crowded. They laid out their towels and settled down.

'Can't deny it,' Will said, looking about him. 'Jewish girls are pretty attractive.'

David agreed. He thought of Hannah, recalling her face, obliterating that curtained image in the bush. He heard her laughter and he very much wanted to see her again. Perhaps one Sunday. Will, lying by his side, was thinking of Uri, his sudden questioning and his unexplained disappearance. He wished he could share his suspicions with David but no relief would come from such sharing. He just prayed that Uri, whatever he was doing, even if it was nothing, he just prayed that he wouldn't get caught.

They left the beach at sundown. The cafés were already crowded but they found a free table at a small bar in a side street.

'You know,' David said, 'I don't think we're cut out for this job. Either of us. I like this place, and I like the people, and I don't want to shop anybody.'

Will smiled. It seemed as if David had read his mind. 'But we must be seen to be trying,' he said.

6

The next day they went to the bank together, and arrived at opening time. Following orders, the sergeants entered through the front door, made themselves known, and after a short stay went out through the back entrance. Then they parted, wishing each other well and giggling a little, both finding their roles faintly ridiculous.

If one followed the beach road one could walk to Jaffa, and David chose this way. He was in no hurry. Abu would be trading in the marketplace most of the day. He had been supplied with a description. Abu would look very much like any market-trader, except for his multicoloured head-cover, which singled him out from the others. Abu himself had been apprised of his new contact and given a rough description. They should have no problem in recognising each other.

It was a fine humid-free day, and the sea breeze tempered the heat. He recalled the last time he'd been to this shoreline and the vapour of smoke bombs that had shrouded the coast. And Hannah. He recalled her with affection, imagining her face and hearing her laughter. He'd had only a few girlfriends in his time, and none of them had hinted at any permanence. He was green and shy, like his father. He thought of him now, and of his mother, sharing his letters, missing him and wishing him home. As he did himself, or at least had until he met Hannah, and he marvelled at how that short meeting had turned his mind around.

He reached the outskirts of Jaffa. It had been a long walk and he sat on a bench to rest himself and to prepare for his encounter with Abu. Opposite him, near the shoreline, he saw the rock to which, according to Greek mythology, Andromeda had been chained before Perseus dared to rescue her from the monster. He remembered that story from his schooldays and how his father had bought him a book of Greek myths. And, as if to restore the balance, his grandmother would tell him tales from the Bible, stories of the Maccabees and heroes of the Holy Land. And here he was, he thought, in that very place where both storytellers would have found a common ground.

He walked into the town and towards the marketplace. He stood, hidden for a while, scanning the stalls. But there were so many of them: vegetables, fruit, souvenirs, furniture, carpets, all of them jumbled together. He would have to walk through the aisles to find his quarry. He dawdled at some of the stalls, viewing the varied crafts. He spotted Abu's headgear from afar. It was not easy to miss, for its garishness yelled its difference. David waited for a while and observed him. His stall looked pretty bare of produce. Some apples, oranges and aubergines were all that was on offer. It was clearly a cover. He had no customers and he stood looking about him, obviously expecting the new recruit. David ambled unhurriedly towards him. At the stall he stopped. He wondered whether he ought to buy something, simply for form's sake. He pointed to an orange. Abu put out his hand. David handed over a few coins and at the same time showed his identity card. 'Abu?' he asked.

Abu looked round furtively. Nobody was in eavesdropping distance. In any case, little could have been heard above the din of the marketplace.

'I have information,' he said and he held out his hand.

'Information first,' David said.

'Citrus House,' Abu said. He pushed his hand out further.

'When?' David asked, knocking the hand aside.

'Thursday night,' Abu said.

'What time?' David persisted.

'I don't know. They don't tell me everything.' Once more he stretched out his hand. David greased his palm with the money he'd been given and then turned away, disgusted. It was true he had scored well on his first day at work and he would report immediately to headquarters. But Abu and his like, and presumably

there were many bribed in Haifa, Tel Aviv, Jerusalem and elsewhere, deeply offended him. The notion of loyalty never occurred
to them and they were not even troubled by it. He thought of
home and of the separate faiths in which he had been raised. There
had never been a conflict between them, and loyalty was freely
given to both. Until Palestine. Concealing his Jewishness was close
to denying it. And failing to report Hannah was a defection of
sorts. So what about his own loyalty? But at least, unlike Abu, he
was burdened with a conscience, and such a conscience disturbed
him.

He made his way out of the marketplace, and from a distance
he once more looked back at Abu's stall. He had no customers
and he was sitting on a stool, openly counting his money. Had
David stayed longer, he would have seen a man approach the
stall. He was dressed as an Arab and he did not bother to buy
anything. Abu stuffed his money into his pocket and held out
his hand for more.

'What did you tell him?' the man asked.

'I told him exactly what you told me to tell him.'

'And what was that?'

'The Citrus House. Thursday night.'

'Is that all?'

'That's all you told me.'

More money then greased Abu's palm.

'How are you going to earn a living when the British leave?'
the man asked.

Abu laughed. 'They'll never leave,' he said. 'This is a job for
life.'

David took the bus back to Tel Aviv and so did the second
palm-greaser. His name was Gad. He greased on behalf of the
Irgun and, like David, he was on his way to his own headquarters to report his findings.

The British HQ was open to the public. Any interested party, Jew
or Arab, was allowed to make enquiries there. They were screened,

of course, and allowed inside by the main entrance. It was this access that David used. He could have been any decent citizen. Once inside, he made his way to the debriefing room. There was only one officer present, a Lieutenant Westrop whom David had met before. He did not look up when David entered. He seemed intent on his crossword.

David saluted. 'Sir?' he said.

Westrop glanced up. 'Ah', he said, smiling, 'the new boy. Don't tell me you have something already.'

'I met with Abu in Jaffa,' David said. 'He gave me information.'

'What d'you think of him?' Westrop asked. He seemed none too eager for the information.

'Not very much, to be honest. I don't like his sort,' David said.

'It's not your business to like him. Nobody likes him. But he's useful. He's been very helpful in the past. When he proves to be wrong, it's not his fault. He's just been misinformed. So you don't have to like him,' he said again. 'This business of ours is riddled with rogues like Abu, without any sense of loyalty. We need them. So you might as well get used to it.'

'He says there'll be a raid on Thursday night. The Citrus House. He didn't know the time.'

'Jesus!' Westrop exploded. 'Irgun again. They're after guns. Citrus House has quite an armoury.'

'Will that be all, sir?' David was anxious to get away.

'Well done, Millar,' Westrop said. 'We'll get on with it. Watch out for fireworks on Thursday night.' He seemed excited by the prospect. 'We'll nail those buggers once and for all.' He put his crossword aside. 'On your way, Millar,' he said. 'I have a lot of work to do.'

It was barely lunch-time but David felt he had earned his keep for the day. He wondered how Will was doing. He'd been given no contact – he'd been told to wander, to check up on cafés, to take note of any suspicious groupings. David doubted that Will could come up with anything. He thought he might do a little wandering himself. But *he* wasn't going to wander, for he knew exactly where he was going. He was going to make for that café in the side street where he had taken Hannah. He wanted to make it *his* place, to reserve it as it were, and hopefully for Hannah as well.

Will was sitting in a café on the other side of town. It was the sixth such location he had visited and, with little pleasure, he was sipping his twelfth cup of coffee of the morning. He had gleaned nothing. Out of one group on a coast café he had picked up the Hebrew word for 'illegals'.

Most of the army personnel knew that word. And he had picked up 'Haifa' to go with it. There might have been a connection between the two words but he didn't think it was worth reporting. In any case, he was restless. He couldn't keep his mind on his work. He was worried, worried about Uri. The band would wonder why he never came back to play with them. Uri above all, especially if he had underground connections. And he would make it his business to investigate. There was only one solution. He would pretend to have left the country so that they could forget about him and write him off. He would send Uri a letter. In it he would state that he had been granted compassionate leave because his sister had died. Will had no sisters so the lie could be written without fear of the wrath of God. He would add that as his tour of duty was in any case nearing its end, it was unlikely that he would be returning to Palestine. He would express his thanks for all the happy hours he had spent in their company and hope to meet them again in more peaceful times.

He took out his letter-case, and began 'Dear Uri'. When he had finished, he felt relieved. He just prayed that he would not run into Uri again. He would avoid going to Jerusalem and he was pretty sure that Uri seldom visited Tel Aviv. Jerusalemites held Telavivians in contempt. To them they were parvenus, *arrivistes*, and so was the nature of their show-off city. They allowed that much more was going on in Tel Aviv than in Jerusalem but that nothing in that city built on sand could be taken seriously. However, he was aware that he was taking a slight risk. If he ever came across Uri, he would have to make sure Uri didn't see him. He would not tell David about the letter. He had not told him of his suspicions about Uri so the letter would make no sense to him. But he was glad that it had been written. He sipped the last of his coffee and decided to call it a day.

7

Gad stayed on the bus until it stopped at Jerusalem. With respect for his appearance, he made his way through the Arab quarter, then quickly down a narrow cul-de-sac. Halfway along, he paused at a doorway and, facing the street, he rapped a rhythm of taps on the wooden panel. Shortly after, the door opened, and he backed into it; then he ran up two flights of stairs and into a windowless room, lit by a paraffin lamp.

Three men sat there, expectant, clearly waiting for Gad's arrival. The cream, if one could call them that, of the Irgun. Menachim Begin, their leader, Avraham Pinsker and Giddy Dror.

'It's done,' Gad said. 'They've been told we're going to the Citrus House. That's where they'll be waiting.'

'So let them wait,' the leader sneered.

Begin was an ugly man. Nature had not been kind to him. Even if one had delved beneath the skin in search, perhaps, of a passable soul, such an investigation would have been fruitless. Begin was ugly through and through. He looked like a caricature of a Jew in Streicher's magazine, *Der Sturmer*, a portrait which would have required no parody. Begin was a Jew who was not good for Jews, nor ever would be.

His companions were equally unprepossessing. With their leader, they shared a sallow colouring, as if most of their adult lives were spent in this windowless room and they ventured outside only when the sun had set.

'Are the costumes prepared?' Begin asked.

'Yes,' Gad said, 'but wearing a British uniform makes me feel ashamed. Always.'

'It's in a good cause,' Dror said. 'And don't worry. You won't wear it out. Soon they'll be gone.'

'And Arab kits. A dozen,' Begin said. 'We'll meet and change here. All of you. The truck will wait outside. Uri reckons the whole operation should take no more than fifteen minutes, and he's always been accurate. Take what you can in that time.' He turned to Gad. 'Well done,' he said. 'If it weren't such a risk, I'd go over to the Citrus for the simple pleasure of seeing them make a fool of themselves.' Then he smiled for the first time. But it wasn't a smile of pleasure. It was a smile of oneupmanship, and one he had used often before. Then the men left singly, each to destinations unknown to the other.

Begin was the last to leave. When he reached home, he covered his head and prayed for the safe return of his men.

For the next two days, David and Will went about their business, achieving nothing. Each day David went to the café where he'd met Hannah, and sat at the same table. He was very much looking forward to Thursday night and the fireworks that had been promised him, as well as confirming that his information had paid off. He would take Will to the Citrus House with him. He had no idea what time the raid would be mounted. Certainly after dark, so just before eight o'clock he and Will left their apartment for the firework display.

There was no obvious army presence at Citrus House. Apart from the sentries who were always there on duty, no other soldiers were visible. But that was not a surprise. 'They're already inside,' David said. 'Waiting for them. This is going to be an easy one.'

So they waited, as Begin predicted they would. And waited. At midnight, David gave a thought to Abu, and began to hate him.

The direct route to the British army camp at Ramat Gan would pass the Citrus, and though tempted to view the fruits of their deception, Gad avoided it and instructed Benji, who was driving, to make a detour. At eight o'clock they were in sight of the barracks and its profitable armoury. Inside the truck, the men were silent. Two dozen of them, half in Arab attire and loosely handcuffed, and the others in British army uniforms. Through the windows they could see the fortress and, as they expected, it was ringed by defence posts, each manned by machine-gunners. Two armed guards stood idly on the roof. Gad ordered Benji to pull in on to the forecourt. 'Wait for my signal,' he said. 'Then bring them in.'

Gad got down from the truck. He looked very smart in his First Lieutenant's uniform, which gave him an air of authority, and with supreme confidence he marched into the forecourt, acknowledging the salutes of the gunners in his sights. There were two duty officers at the desk.

'I've got a dozen Arabs outside,' he said. 'Caught robbing the food canteen at Tel Litvinsky.' Gad had a monkey talent for languages and his English was impeccable.

'Did any of them get away?' the duty officer asked.

'Caught red-handed. All of them,' Gad said.

'Then bring the buggers in.' The officer rose, prepared for their reception.

Gad went outside and signalled to Benji. He looked at his watch. Uri had said fifteen minutes and he would honour that timing. He watched Benji as he lowered the tailgate of the truck. Six mock British corporals, Uri among them, were the first to alight and after them, the 'Arabs', heads down and frightened. The 'corporals' pushed them roughly into line, then led them towards the fortress. Gad was waiting for them, and when they were assembled, he led them inside.

The duty officer looked at the prisoners. 'Typical,' he said. 'Scum, the lot of them. We'll lock them up first,' he said to Gad. 'The particulars can wait,' and with his second-in-command he led the way down a long corridor. The prisoners, flanked by corporals, shuffled behind them. We're in, Gad thought and he was relieved because he had not expected such an easy entry. It was a good omen. As they shuffled along, the prisoners took off their handcuffs, and from under their Arab dress, they pulled out their Stens and revolvers. They were ready.

They reached the lock-up and the second duty officer swung

open the door. Then both officers were set upon, gagged and bound and threatened with guns. They were roughly shoved into the cell and locked up with their own keys. For a moment, Gad looked with some amusement at their astonished faces and the puddle of urine that their fear had released. He glanced at his watch. 'So far, so good,' he said. 'Ten minutes to go.' Then he handed the keys to Uri who led the men back down the corridor.

'Follow me,' Uri whispered. Uri knew the ins and outs of the fortress. He'd studied a map of its layout, a map that the Irgun had managed to steal. He lost no time in reaching his target. For a moment, he studied the lock and then his bunch of keys. At his second attempt, he pushed the door open. A treasure trove gaped at them. Quickly, and in precise order, each man collected as much ammunition as he could carry. Guns, ammo and Stens. Gad knew that the final stage of their mission was the most dangerous. He assembled all the men in the entrance hall. Each 'soldier' was told to shelter each 'Arab' and ordered to go out in pairs. Through the window, he checked that Benji was waiting at the truck tailgate. Then he gave the order for the first couple to leave.

They did not hurry and they reached the truck without hindrance. It was when the second couple were halfway to the van that Gad heard a yelled shout. 'Irgun!' It came from the roof from which the guards started to fire. Benji, at the tailgate fired back and Gad knew there was no time to lose. 'Go', he shouted to all those of his men remaining. Now the sentries were trigger-happy, but so were his boys. He saw one guard fall. He and Uri were the last to leave. Uri sprinted ahead and Gad watched as his partner, as if in slow motion, slithered with grace to the ground. He dared not tarry to help him. He crouched under the gunfire and crawled to the van. Within seconds he was inside it and the truck was off. 'Uri's hurt,' he said. 'I think it was his leg.'

'They'll take care of him,' Benji said. 'One prisoner.'

'God help him then,' one of the men whispered. They had

lost men before, wounded men and those caught in escape. They had been tried and no quarter had been given. In accordance with British justice, they ended on the gallows. Apart from a murmured prayer, there was silence in the truck. They were already mourning. Again, on their return, they avoided the Citrus House and the truck crawled like a hearse to Jerusalem.

David and Will waited till well after midnight. Then they saw the Commander exit from the house, his face a blaze of fury. Slowly the troops followed him, hangdog almost. They'd been humiliated yet again.

'Those bloody Jews,' one of them shouted, and no move was made to silence him.

'It wasn't your fault,' Will said, as they turned to go home. 'Your Abu is a double agent, or else he too was conned.'

'But I still blame myself. I can't help it.'

Early the next morning, David reported at the debriefing room.

'Not your fault, Millar,' the Captain said. 'At least you found out there'd be a raid. And on an armoury.'

'I don't understand it, sir. Abu was a tip-off from CID Headquarters in Jaffa.'

'That was before the Irgun got to him. They pay more than we do. Don't blame yourself. We've got one of them anyway,' the Captain went on. 'Uri Berger by name. Known to us. He's wounded but they say he'll recover. Then we'll hang him. Teach those bloody Jews a lesson.'

'But there'll be a trial, won't there?' David asked.

'Oh there'll be a trial all right. British justice and all that. Must be seen to be done.' He smiled. 'Anyway,' he added, 'he'd better recover. He'd better be fit to stand trial. I need a healthy neck to hang him with.'

David felt ill. He excused himself and hurried away. He made his daily visit to the bank, then went straight home. His work had begun to sicken him.

He found Will slumped over the newspaper. 'What's the matter?' he asked.

'They got Uri.'

'What's Uri to you, Will?'

'He's the bass player at the jazz café. I stayed with him at his place. I can't believe it.'

David picked up the newspaper. The raid had been reported and the captured prisoner was named. 'Uri Berger,' it said. 'A piano-tuner from Jersusalem.'

'He'd be insulted at that,' Will said. 'He was a bass player and a fine one. Piano-tuning was just a way to earn a living.' He was clearly very upset. 'What will they do with him?'

'He'll go to trial,' David said, and made a point of saying no more.

Will thought of the letter he had sent Uri. In view of what had happened, it had been unnecessary. He hoped he had been away from home and hadn't received it. But he didn't care about the letter. He cared about Uri and what would become of him.

'They'll find him guilty, of course,' David said. 'He was caught red-handed, you know. On the forecourt of the fortress. He was carrying guns.'

'But what does guilty mean, for heaven's sake. Or innocent, for that matter?' Will said. 'Uri was acting on his rights. And he has *rights*, hasn't he?'

'The Arabs have rights too,' David said.

'The Arabs didn't go to the gas ovens. You know,' Will said after a pause, 'sometimes I wonder – well – you with your Jewish mother and grandmother, I wonder whose side you're on.'

David had wondered the same for a long time. And especially since his new posting. As a simple soldier, his doubts had troubled him less. He could smother them under his sergeant's uniform, and he could feel on the British side. But now his scruples nagged at him. 'To tell you the truth,' he said, 'I don't *know* which side I'm on. But I'm truly sorry about your friend. I'm sure of that.'

'I'll go to his trial,' Will said.

'Is that wise? His friends and yours will be there. And they'll see you still in civvies. And with your hair even longer.'

'I'll tie it in a pony-tail. Like Uri. Don't worry David. I won't let myself be seen. One thing, I'm not working today,' he said. 'Bugger the Mandate.'

'I'm with you on that,' David said and, taking his arm, he led him out of the flat and to his very own café table. The thought of Hannah cheered him a little and he wished that Will could find an equally loving focus to lessen his burden. And to his boundless delight, Hannah was sitting in that very café, at that very table, and in the place he had reserved for her. Her table too.

He steadied his pace towards her. 'No school?' he asked.

'Morning off,' she said.

He was glad that Will was with him. He needed the presence of a third party to temper his excitement. He introduced him. Hannah gave Will her hand. 'The sax player,' she said.

He could have done without such a reminder, so he gave her a feeble smile. 'I'll get the coffee,' he said.

'You didn't come to the club on Sunday,' Hannah said as Will left them. 'I was expecting you.'

'I'll come if you'll be there,' he felt bold enough to say.

'Next Sunday, then.'

He put his hand over hers on the table. She turned it over and held it in her own. A partnership sealed. He was almost sure of her.

She left soon after the coffee arrived. 'Work to do,' she said. 'I'll see you on Sunday.'

'Very pretty,' Will said, when she had gone.

'She's a lot more than that.'

'She's really got to you, hasn't she?'

'It feels like that.'

'Nothing can come of it,' Will said. 'You know that. In time, maybe soon, we'll be out of here.'

'But I could come back.'

'Here?' Will asked. 'Here, of all places?'

'I like this place,' David said. 'And since Hannah, I like it more and more.'

'You're crazy.'

They both laughed.

'I wonder who Abu's conning now,' David said.

'Forget him, and refuse to use him again.'

'What about you?'

'I've been given a contact. At last. Someone in Haifa.'

'I hope he's not another Abu,' David said.

'Some you win, some you lose,' Will replied. 'And, quite frankly, I don't bloody well care either way.'

'I'm beginning to feel the same,' David said.

They got up from the table. David put his hand on Will's shoulder.

'Our little secret,' he said.

8

On Sunday evening, David made his way to the chess club. Will had opted to go to the cinema. He couldn't play chess and he would have felt out of place – as did David when he first arrived. There was no sign of Hannah and very few people were in the café. Those couples who were, were playing at the tables. What struck David as he entered, was the silence of the place in contrast to the noise and bustle in the street outside. He took a seat at an empty table by the window and stared at the inlaid chessboard in front of him. He hadn't played a game for a long while, and the sight of it excited him. He felt awkward, sitting there alone like a wallflower, and he wished that Hannah would come with her brother and there would at least be a chance of a game. While he sat there, idling, staring out of the window, he was aware of company seating itself at his table. He looked at the stranger, an old Jew, bearded and with a *yarmulka* on his head. The man touched David's shoulder, then spoke to him in a language that was foreign to his ear. It was neither Hebrew nor Arabic, both of which David would have recognised. But he knew from its intonation that the man was asking a question. He presumed he was asking him if he wanted to play. So he nodded, and the old man shuffled to the counter and returned with a box of chessmen. He laid them out on the table, then he took two pawns, one of each colour, and hid them behind his back. He shrugged each shoulder in turn, indicating that David had a choice. And it was black that David chose, so the old man made the first move. It took only four turns before David was mated and immediately the old man relaid the pieces, placing white on David's side.

'You're too good for me,' David said.

Whether he understood or not, the old man smiled. Then he waited for David's opening gambit.

And so they played on. The second time, David held out for a little longer. He was enjoying the game, and almost forgot why he was there in the first place. The old man was a challenge, and with a little more practice, he felt he could master him. Now he himself relaid the table, and as he did so, he felt a tap on his shoulder. He looked round. Hannah. She was alone. 'Joseph couldn't come,' she said. 'Finish your game. I'll wait for you.'

She went to sit at the counter and ordered a coffee. The old man made the first move. Now David found it difficult to concentrate. He was looking at Hannah as she leaned towards the counterhand and whispered in his ear. He wanted to get her away from there, away from secrets that she could share with others. He recalled once more that face veiled in the bushes on the Jaffa shore. He lost the game quickly, then rose. He thanked his partner, and mimed that he had to leave. He took the man's outstretched arm. 'Shalom,' he said. Everybody knew that word, that word for Hello and Goodbye. But for either, it meant 'peace'.

'Shalom,' the old man said. It was probably the only Hebrew word that he would allow, for he, like everyone else, wanted an end to the conflict.

'Who was that old man?' David asked when they were outside.

Hannah took his arm. 'Let's walk,' she said. 'We'll go to the river and I'll tell you.'

They said little to each other. Often they had to separate to negotiate the crowds that thronged the streets.

'Where's your brother tonight?' David asked in one of those moments when they were linked.

'He had to see somebody,' Hannah said.

David wondered whether her brother too was in the Haganah and whether that somebody he was seeing was in the Haganah as well. Again he was aware of the profit that could be gained from a close relationship with Hannah, but once more he dismissed the idea. He thought of Uri and he knew that, trial

48

or no trial, Will's friend would go to the gallows, and he shuddered at the thought of the risks Hannah was running.

They reached the river Yarkon. Although David knew the area, and had often walked along the river bank, he had done so only in daylight for it was known as a favourite haunt for lovers when the sun went down. He was flattered that she had taken him there but nervous, too, because he didn't know what would be expected of him. As they walked, their arms now safely linked, they passed many couples sitting on the bankside, all whispering to each other as if in conspiracy. Even Hannah caught the tone.

'Come,' she whispered, and she pointed to a willow tree, the branches of which hung over the water. She found a spot beneath it and motioned him to sit by her side. David was happy for her to take the initiative. He knew that as soon as they were settled, she would take his hand. He knew too that she was attracted to him, and he didn't know why. As far as she was aware, he was not of her people, and he had no intention of enlightening her. And soldier or not, he was still an Englishman, and part of that nation she saw as her oppressor. In view of her Haganah connections, was it possible that she hoped in time to gain some useful information from him? He was suddenly wary, and he withdrew his hand.

'Is anything the matter?' she asked.

'Nothing,' he said. He could not temper his feelings for her, but he knew he had to tread with caution. He didn't want to tell her about himself, nor did he wish to know more about her, so he settled on a third party who held no threat.

'Tell me about that old man I played chess with,' he said. 'Or at least tried to.'

'That was Moshe. Moshe Rostov. He's unbeatable. My brother has tried often enough.'

'What language was he speaking?'

'Yiddish. His mother-tongue. He doesn't know Hebrew. Refuses to learn it.'

'Why?'

49

'He's a refugee. Came here just after the war. Alone. His wife and three children went to the ovens. He doesn't know how he managed to survive and he wishes he hadn't.'

'But why the Yiddish?'

'He says it's what they spoke as a family, and that if he forgoes that tongue, he forgoes their memory. At least, that's what he says.'

'D'you understand him?' David asked.

'Most of it,' she said. 'It's my parents' mother-tongue too. They talk in Yiddish about things they don't want us to hear. Over the years I've picked up quite a lot. And now, sometimes, we speak it openly.'

'Where did your parents come from?' David asked.

'Same little Polish village as Moshe. But they came here when they were young. Went on a kibbutz at first where Joseph and I were born. Degania.'

David had not asked for personal details. He was still wary of them, and the intimacy that they entailed. But she was volunteering them and he thought he might as well encourage her in order to avoid talking about himself.

'What does your father do?' he asked.

'He's a tailor. And a very good one. Like his own father.'

'But not your brother.'

'No. Joseph is a born teacher. That's all he wants to do.'

He took her hand again. He felt less wary.

'Shall we walk a little?' she asked.

He took her arm and guided her along the river bank.

'It's beautiful here,' she said. And then she was silent.

She seemed uninterested in asking him about himself, and her silence gave him confidence. He wondered if he dared kiss her. He stopped and faced her. 'May I kiss you?' he asked.

She stroked his cheek, and reached towards him.

He held her for a while, then gently stroked her lips with his own. 'You're lovely,' he said. Then he urged her forward, and in silence he took her home.

At her door, he asked if he could see her again.

'I hope so,' she said. She gave him her telephone number. 'Be in touch.' Then, after a pause, 'Please,' she said. She ran into her building and he stood there for a long while. He was reassured. She had not wanted to know anything about him. Perhaps it was possible that she liked him purely for himself. He thought of his grandmother and wished her alive so that he could share his happiness with her.

'Hannah is the girl for you,' she would have told him.

9

The following week, Will went up to Haifa. His contact was neither Arab nor Jew. He was a Christian, a lowly curate who plied his trade in the church of St Stephen.

A meeting had been arranged in the graveyard that circled the church. Will was early, so he ambled around the head-stones reading their legends. All were written in English. Some dated from the eighteenth century, their inscriptions illegible. He strolled for a while and suddenly felt very tired, as if he had walked for miles. But in cemeteries one moves not through distance but through time, and it was time that had wearied him. He sat on the bench to rest, and waited for his informant. The man was not to be given money. He was on a regular payroll, but on whose account, Will didn't know. And he was to ask no questions. Even before meeting him, Will found the man offensive. The very principle of 'shopping' offended him, and when he spied him, slithering lizard-like between the head-stones, he saw no reason to change his mind. He did not stand. He waited for the cleric to approach him. Even when he stood before him, Will did not rise.

Without invitation, the curate sat down beside him. 'A lovely day,' he whispered. He clearly fancied himself as a master spy. Hence the whispering in case the graveyard was bugged for the eavesdropping of the dead.

'What do you have for me?' Will asked. Almost shouted because he didn't want to play the spy game.

But the curate still whispered. 'Four thousand,' he said. The number slipped through his lips, laced with his saliva. It was a goodly number and worth every shekel of his hire.

'Four thousand what?' Will shouted.

But the curate insisted on the whispering. 'Illegals,' he said.

'Where?' Will demanded.

'Here. Not a stone's throw away. Haifa harbour.'

'When?'

'Next Wednesday.'

Will stood up. 'Anything else?' he asked.

Then the curate too rose. 'You're greedy,' he said and he turned away, shuffling back to his parish.

Will watched him go. He appeared to shrink as he neared the church. As a spy, he seemed much taller.

Will returned to Tel Aviv straight away to report his findings. In the debriefing room, Captain Coleman complimented him and offered him coffee. He seemed available for a chat.

'Enjoying your work, Griffiths?' he asked.

'I find it puzzling,' Will said.

'Any questions? Fire away. Anything you want to know?'

'Well, this curate, for instance,' Will said. 'What's his source? How did he find out about the illegals?'

'Don't you worry,' the Captain said. 'He has a very reliable source. Between you and me, he has a parishioner in his flock who looks very Jewish. I'll say no more. Now off you go, Griffiths. We'll be in touch.'

Will was not flattered by the Captain's bonhomie. He did not want to be his friend. The Captain would undoubtedly play a part in Uri's trial, and there was no question about his verdict. Uri played on Will's mind constantly. Despite all the evidence to the contrary he could not envisage Uri as a member of the Irgun. To him, he was a bass player. And a fine one. And, above all, a friend he was in danger of losing. He wanted desperately to go to Jerusalem and to talk and play with the band. But he dare not risk it. Perhaps Uri had received his letter and had told the group that their sax had gone back to England. But he had to see Uri again, even if he couldn't talk to him. He had to see him in the dock. Then he would have to believe that the Irgun had claimed him.

It was still early in the day, and he decided to go back to the flat. He hoped that David would be at home. He needed to talk to somebody about the curate and his findings.

'David,' Will called out as he entered the flat.

'In here.' David's answer came from the living room. He was at his desk filing his dead-end reports for debriefing. The contact he'd been promised in Herzlia had not shown up. Someone else had probably offered him a better deal. He'd hung around the cafés and eavesdropped with little result. Haifa seemed to be the buzz word, but he could discern little connection. Will made it clear.

'You're right,' he said. 'It *is* Haifa. Next Wednesday. Four thousand illegals. I'm assured it's a reliable source. A man of God no less. A slimy curate from St Stephen's church.'

'And what's *his* source?' David asked.

'It's a secret. But Captain Coleman told me. Apparently there's a worshipper in his parish who looks very Jewish. Make what you want of that one.'

Will noticed that David had suddenly gone quite pale. 'You feeling OK?' he asked. 'You don't look too good.'

'Caught too much sun, I think.' David improvised. 'It'll pass.' But it was not a touch of the sun. His pallor was due to thoughts of Hannah. On no account must she go to Haifa. He had to find a means of keeping her in Tel Aviv. He would phone her. But not from the flat. Their calls were probably monitored. He would go to his café and phone from there.

'I don't suppose you want to come to the beach,' Will said. 'I could do with a swim.'

'You go,' David told him. 'I'm going to stay out of the sun for a while.'

As soon as Will had gone, he scanned the newspaper to see what film was playing at the Moograbi. It was *Casablanca*. He'd seen it before and enjoyed it and it could certainly bear a second viewing. It was four o'clock. By the time he reached the café, she would be home from school. He was excited at the thought of hearing her voice. Even after the few days that had passed since their last meeting, he could still replay the kiss they had shared on the river bank.

The sun was still high, and he walked at his leisure. On his way he rehearsed what he would say to her. She might claim another appointment and that would worry him, for such an appointment would mean Haifa. He sat at the table and ordered a coffee. He would take his time. Perhaps she would pass by. So he waited. But after a while, he was impatient to talk to her. He dialled her number. A man answered the phone. A deep voice. Probably her father.

'Can I speak to Hannah?' David asked. He was relieved that the man did not ask for his name. He heard him calling Hannah, as if she were a long way away. In time she came to the phone.

'David here,' he said.

There was a pause. 'Hello,' she whispered gently. 'I was hoping you would call.'

'Look,' he said quickly. 'I'm free on Wednesday night. And there's a good film at the Moograbi.'

'I can't,' Hannah said, and with no hesitation. 'I've got a school meeting. Can't get out of it.'

'Could I see you afterwards then?' he tried.

'They tend to go on very late,' she said.

A school meeting. David thought. A pretty euphemism for Haifa. 'Another time then,' he said helplessly.

'I'm free on Thursday,' she said. 'We could go then.'

If you're not caught, David thought. 'I'll meet you at the café. Seven o'clock,' he said.

'Our table,' she laughed.

'Our table. As you say.'

He was glad he didn't have to talk further. Now he was worried about Will and his presence on Haifa harbour. If he should catch sight of Hannah there, Will would shop her. He would consider it an act of loyalty to his friend. Somehow he had to stop Will from going.

But that turned out to be no problem. At supper, Will volunteered his decision to avoid the harbour. He'd had his fill of shore duties, and didn't yet again wish to witness the violence and inhuman indifference they entailed. He had little hope that the information would turn out to be misleading. The cleric had been so full of confidence, and no doubt he would be on the harbour himself, relishing the efficiency of the Mandate authorities for whom he probably felt responsible. Will could actually see his smirking face as the wretched cargo was turned away. No. He would not go to Haifa, he told David. He would listen to the news to check whether or not the curate's information was reliable. David would listen too, but for reasons of his own.

The following Wednesday morning saw a strong detachment of militia on Haifa harbour. They were taking no chances. The *Knesset Israel* or the *State of Israel*, as the boat was hopefully named, could arrive at any time. And they would be waiting. The army authorities did not expect a struggle. That had already taken place. The army had been informed of the plan to intercept the boat in the Mediterranean when the 'illegals' were in praying distance of their goal. There would be no resistance. The refugees would already have been overpowered by those soldiers who had boarded the vessel. Other ships lay in the harbour, prepared for the refugees' deportation to Cyprus, where they would be housed in army camps. All was prepared. There was no reason why it should not be a peaceful transfer.

But they were mistaken. As soon as the *Knesset Israel* docked, the rioting began. The 'illegals' were not going to be deported without a struggle and the glaring presence of the world's press with their flashing cameras gave them courage. In sundry languages their protests thundered and their message was unmistakable. 'Let us in. Let us in.' They ignored the soldiers' orders to disembark, so they had to be pushed and shoved into disorderly lines. In the confusion, families were separated and women could be heard screaming for their children. Some of the older and more frail refugees simply fainted in their despair. Others collapsed on the decks in the hope perhaps that a feigned illness would save them from deportation. For a while, the disembarkation was halted so that orderlies could carry out those who had fallen. Some were able to walk, others were put on stretchers but ambulant or not, they were dumped on board the ships bound for Cyprus. The resumption of disembarkation orders did not quell the rioting or the screaming protests. Young men fought with the soldiers. But there was no contest. The travellers were tired from their long and nightmarish journey. They were hungry too and weakened. So they were beaten into line, an action done with relish, for the soldiers had had more than enough of 'illegals' and they had to be taught a lesson. And finally that lesson reached home, and within a few hours of their arrival, four thousand refugees, broken in body and spirit, were on their way to Cyprus.

David and Will listened to the news bulletin. Will's information was confirmed by the event, but he took no pleasure in it. David was satisfied that there had been no mention of the Haganah. Hannah was safe and he looked forward to seeing her on the following day.

In the morning, on their daily visit to the bank, they received an invitation to a dinner to be held in honour of the bank manager who was due to retire. Lounge suits were requested. Headquarters informed them that they were obliged to attend. The problem was clothing. But not for Will, who for some reason had packed his black chapel suit into his kit-bag. It would need pressing. His father had insisted on it. 'You never know,' he had said. 'Where you're going, you might be called upon to wear it.' He probably had funerals in mind. It was Will's best suit and he only wore it on occasions. Both he and David had been provided with suitable 'bank' attire.

'My black suit will have to do,' Will said. 'It *is* lounge.'

But David had no such suit. His entire wardrobe was army issue.

'I'll have to have one made,' he said. 'Hannah's father's a tailor.'

'It'll cost,' Will said.

'I need a decent suit anyway. Never had a proper one,' David said.

'Well, it's one way of getting to know the family,' Will said with a laugh. 'You can ask him for Hannah's hand while he's measuring your inside leg.'

'I'll have to ask Hannah first,' David said.

'You're not serious.'

'Who knows? It's early days.'

'But you hardly know her,' Will protested.

'I'm learning,' David said, though he knew a lot more about Hannah than Will could guess at.

That evening he called for her as they had arranged. She didn't feel like a film, she said. She suggested they go down to the beach and sit on the sands and watch the changing face of the sea. He was happy to agree. He took her hand, more bold now, and during their stroll to the shore he gathered the courage to put his arm round her waist. She stopped and turned towards him.

'You know,' she said, 'I can't wait for the British to leave. We'll all be glad to see the back of them. Arabs too. But some I'd like to stay. One especially.' She smiled.

'I don't understand you,' he said. 'I'm flattered of course. But why me?'

'You're different from the men here. They're fighters, most of them. And they're not gentle.'

'But when the British leave, won't they change?'

'It's a long road to independence,' she said. 'The war will go on.'

They had reached the sands, and they sat down by a small dune.

'How was your school meeting?' he asked. He noticed that she hesitated, puzzled by the question. 'Your meeting last night,' he said.

'Oh that,' she said, suddenly in the false picture. 'All right. As usual. Boring. And what did you do?'

'We listened to the wireless, Will and I. About the "illegals" who were sent to Cyprus.'

'They'll be back,' she said. 'As soon as the British leave.'

'D'you have friends in the resistance?' he dared to ask her.

'Not that I know of,' she said. 'I'm not involved in that sort of thing. I'm not all that political.'

She lied so prettily, David thought. She was no doubt well practised. He sealed the lie on her lips. 'I'm getting too fond of you,' he said.

'Does that disturb you?'

'When and if the British pull out, the banks will go too.'

'You don't have to go with them,' she said. 'You're not under army orders.'

'There'll be no job for me here. And I'll still be British.'

'But not an occupier,' she said. She kissed him again, and he lay back on the sands. He wanted to touch her, to feel her limbs, her body shape, the curve of her hip, the swell of her breasts. But although there were few people around, it was still a public place, and that fact tempered his ardour. He thought talking might help, so he told her about the dinner at the bank and the suit he had to find.

'My father will make one for you,' she said. 'He's at home tonight. Come back with me and he'll measure you up.' She started to rise.

Even though it had been his idea in the first place, he did not expect such a rapid outcome.

'Are you sure he won't mind?' he asked.

'Of course not,' she said. 'It's time you met my family anyway.'

He wondered what she meant by that. Was it a token of her intent, her intent of a serious relationship between them. He was excited at the prospect, but nervous too. One day he would have to tell her who he really was, that his mother was Jewish, but despite that he was her enemy. But all that would have to

59

wait. All that knowledge must shuffle uneasily in the wings until his love for her, and hers for him, had endured beyond destruction.

She led the way to the apartment. It was part of a small block, on the first floor. The front door was open. 'Papa,' she called. 'I've brought you a customer.' Then she was in the living room with David hovering behind her. Joseph and her father were playing chess at a table, while her mother was polishing silver at one end. A happy domestic family scene, peaceful, non-terrorist, apolitical.

'This is David,' Hannah said. 'Works at the bank. He needs a suit. Joseph, my brother,' she went on. 'And Mama.' Hands were shaken all around.

'We'll finish the game, then I'll measure you,' *Zeyda* said. 'It's almost finished,' Joseph laughed. 'In case you haven't noticed, you're in check.'

'You're too good for me.' *Zeyda* shoved the board aside. He rose. 'Follow me,' he said. He led David into his workroom at the far end of the apartment.

'What kind of suit?' he asked.

'Something lightweight,' David said. 'Single-breasted, with vents.' He was envisaging his father's best suit, the one he wore to church on Sundays and holy days. It was a dark brown. David opted for a lighter colour, but of the same cut.

Avram offered him a swatch of samples.

'What d'you think?' David asked, bewildered by such a choice.

'This is a good one,' Avram said, picking out a pale grey. 'Good for our climate,' he said. 'And smart.'

'It has to do for England too,' David said. 'We might all be going home,' he tested him.

'Not my concern,' Avram said. 'I don't mix with politics. I'm a simple tailor. Like my father was. Now stand up.'

He unrolled his tape measure. A notebook lay on the workbench, and on it, a pencil, much lead-sucked in its time. It was probably his father's, David thought. *Zeyda* picked it up and licked it. A speck of blue tinted his lips. 'My father's pencil,' he said. 'My grandfather's too. Together with the sewing machine.' He was inviting David into his family, and David wanted to hug him for his seeming innocence and he wondered whether he had any idea what his rebellious daughter was up to.

'David what?' Avram asked as he poised the pencil on the paper.

'Millar.'

'David Millar. Recommended by Hannah,' he wrote, speaking it aloud. Then he started his measurements.

'How d'you know my daughter?' he asked.

David volunteered the lamp-post incident. Nothing sinister about that. 'Then I ran into her in Dizzengoff Street and we had a coffee in one of those bars. She told me that you were a tailor. So here I am.'

Avram seemed satisfied, for he probed no further. In silence he continued his measurements, sucking his pencil before writing down each one. When he had finished, he commented, 'You're almost stock size. A little shorter perhaps. But you could buy off the peg.'

'I prefer handmade,' David said.

'Come for a fitting next Wednesday evening. With luck you can have the suit at the end of the week.' He waited for David to leave. And he smiled. Though not unfriendly, David thought Hannah's father was faintly cool. Perhaps with a Jewish client, he might have been more forthcoming. But as David was leaving, he said, 'What d'you think of our country?'

David noted that he didn't use Hannah's possessive.

'I think it's beautiful,' he said. 'If only it were at peace.'

'It's what we all wish for,' Avram said. 'I'll see you on Wednesday.'

An innocent, David thought, and felt sorry that he seemed so ignorant of the dissent within his own family. He paused at the living-room door, in order to say his goodbyes.

'I gather you're a chess man,' Joseph said. 'We must play some time.'

'I've heard you're a master,' David said. 'Certainly too good for me.'

'I lose sometimes,' Joseph laughed.

'I'll take my chances then,' David said.

Hannah had gone. 'I'll tell her your goodbye,' her brother said.

'Thank you.' He made for the front door, wondering whether Hannah's departure had been deliberate. Whether she had wanted to feign indifference in front of her family. He hoped he would see her on Wednesday.

He made a detour to pass by his café and their table, and there she was, as if waiting for him.

'I knew you'd come,' she said. 'And you knew I'd be here.'

She stood up and he took her in his arms. 'I hoped for it,' he said. Then he kissed her, uncaring that it was a very public place, and Hannah made no move to withdraw. He felt it as a declaration of sorts. That whatever the adverse circumstances, they were a couple. And for the first time he seriously considered asking her to marry him. He could wear his new suit for the wedding.

10

'You're rather keen on that David fellow,' Joseph said.

He and Hannah were alone in the living room. Their mother had gone to visit Mrs Katz, and *Zeyda* was at his sewing machine.

'Does it show?' Hannah asked.

'It's pretty obvious to me,' Joseph said.

'You sound as if you disapprove.'

'I don't want to see you make a mistake.'

'Why should David be a mistake?'

'Well, first, he's not Jewish. And second, he's English, and third, he'll soon be going home. Three pretty good reasons for disapproval, I would imagine,' Joseph said.

'I think I'm in love with him.'

'That's what worries me, Hannah.' He put his hand on her shoulder. 'I don't want to see you hurt,' he said.

They were close. Always had been. Ever since their childhood.

There was but a year between them, but Joseph, being the elder, had always acted as his sister's protector. They worked together in the Haganah, and on seashore raids he was always by her side. But now he could sense she was heading for disaster.

'Not all the English are bad,' Hannah said. 'And he's not even in the army. In any case, he doesn't have to go back home. He wouldn't need permission to stay.'

'You've dealt with two of my objections. But you've avoided the first,' Joseph said. 'And that one's the most important.' Hannah did not respond, for she too was troubled by that obstacle. It represented a chasm between them, a cultural and historical gap that was unbridgeable. She knew. She didn't need Joseph to warn her of that. Intermarriage, at any time, and in any place, was frowned upon by Jews. But in Mandate Palestine,

63

where the Jews were under constant threat, intermarriage was considered tantamount to treachery. Not only her parents would be appalled, but the whole resistance movement to which she belonged. Yet she loved him and instinctively she knew that that love would endure, whatever its consequences.

'You're young,' Joseph was saying. 'He's your very first boyfriend. He'll go home. There'll be others.'

'I wish you'd get to know him,' Hannah said. 'Do it for my sake.'

'I'll audition him,' Joseph laughed. 'But only for your sake. I promise.'

And this promise he kept on the following Wednesday when David came for his fitting. Hannah was not at home, as David had more or less expected, but he knew where he would find her. He made straight for Avram's workroom. *Zeyda* greeted him cordially and with little conversation. His lead pencil hung at attention from his mouth as he went about his fitting. He seemed satisfied with his work and there was little alteration to be done.

'How d'you like the colour?' he asked.

'I've never worn grey before,' David said. 'Except when I was in school and in short trousers.' He hoped to give Hannah's father a possible opening for a little conversation. He was making himself available for questioning, questions about his background, his schooling, his qualifications, his future plans. In other words, his eligibility for his daughter's hand. He was prepared to tell it all, all, that is, except the knowledge of his mother and grandmother. But that knowledge he knew to be crucial, for it would tip the balance of her father's blessing. And that knowledge he could not divulge. At least, not until the British went home. But *Zeyda* showed no curiosity as to his client's schooldays or anything thereafter. He simply stated that he was satisfied with the fitting and that the suit would be ready on Friday. He was so reticent, so indifferent, that David began to suspect him. It was as if he showed no interest in others because he himself didn't want to be known.

He could of course have been a simple and silent man, but such men, David had learned from his training, were often dangerous. He had a strong suspicion that this simple tailor, like his daughter, was part of the resistance too. But he dismissed the thought. He preferred to think that the tailor was simply shy and nervous in any company other than his own family. He reminded David of his own father in that respect.

He left the workroom, and made to pass through the living room to reach the door. Joseph was reading the paper. He looked up as David entered and smiled. 'How's the suit?' he asked.

'Looks good,' David said. 'It'll be ready on Friday.'

Joseph put his paper aside. 'Feel like a game?' he asked.

David knew that Hannah would be waiting for him at the café. But he was tempted. Besides, Joseph had already brought the chessboard to the table, so David could hardly refuse.

He sat down. 'I must be asking for punishment,' he said. 'Hannah tells me you're very skilled.'

'I just like playing,' Joseph said. He set out the pieces. 'Take white,' he said, giving David the opening move.

They played for a while slowly and silently. It was Joseph's move and he was dawdling. David had the impression that he had lost concentration and that his mind was elsewhere. At last he made a move, and then for the first time he spoke.

'You're fond of my sister,' he said. He had been wondering how to broach the subject but could think of no oblique way, so he went straight to the point and David now realised why he'd been invited to play. The game was not meant to be finished, but he already felt in check. He had been called to account.

'I'm very fond of her,' he said. 'And I dare to think that she is fond of me.'

'I don't want to see her hurt,' Joseph said.

'Why should that be?'

'Nothing can come of it. You know that.'

'I want to marry her,' David said. He hoped that the declaration would allow for no further argument.

'Have you asked her?'

'Not yet. But I intend to.'

'She will refuse, you know.'

'How can you be so sure?' David asked, though he knew the answer.

'It's simple,' Joseph said. 'You're not Jewish.'

His mother and grandmother itched on David's tongue. He recalled his interview with Intelligence and Captain Coleman's warning. Hold your tongue on the Jewish bit, he had said. So he was silent. He could think of nothing to say.

'Shall we finish the game?' Joseph said. He had spoken his piece and he was satisfied that his point had been taken.

It was David's move. He made it with little thought. He wanted to lose, and quickly. Hannah would be waiting for him. It took Joseph two more moves to mate him.

'Sorry,' he said, and David knew that his apology was not for his loss of the game.

He rose. 'We'll have to see,' he said.

'See what?'

David went to the door. He felt helpless. 'Everything,' he almost shouted.

Hannah was waiting for him at their table and though he was happy to see her, his anger had not yet abated. He was angry because he knew that Joseph was right. He was right, but he didn't know the truth, and there was nothing David could do to enlighten him.

'What's the matter?' Hannah asked. She could see that he was disturbed.

'Nothing,' he said. He didn't want to tell her about Joseph and how he had so neatly shattered his dreams. 'Can I ask you something?' he said.

'Anything.' She took his hand.

'Do you . . .?' He was afraid to ask.

'Do I love you?' she asked for him.

He nodded.

'Yes. Of course I do.'

'Enough to marry me?'

'You've been talking to Joseph,' she said.

'Yes. He doesn't approve. He told me that nothing could come of it.'

'Don't judge him harshly,' she said. 'It's because you're not Jewish. He cares deeply about such things.'

'And you?'

'They matter to me too,' she said.

'But you say you love me. You wait here for me. You go out with me. Why? Tell me why?'

'It's *because* I love you,' she said. 'I can't help myself.' She squeezed his hand. 'What will become of us?' she whispered.

'We can still see each other,' David said. He was suddenly hopeful. There would come a time, perhaps sooner than he dared to hope, a time when he could fully declare himself and thus erase all objections to their union. He clung to that hope and prayed that the army and all the Mandate paraphernalia would go back to where it came from.

'Let's go to the river,' Hannah said. 'Let's just be with each other.'

He took her arm. She was right. Until he could free his mother from the army's internment, they would simply have to be with each other. And to stay together until that amnesty.

11

The following morning, after his regular visit to the bank, Will went to headquarters, ostensibly to enquire about available contacts. But, in truth, he went because of Uri. He wanted to know about the progress of the investigation, and the possible date of his trial, and all the while he would feign indifference. But short of asking a direct question, there was no way he could find answers.

'How's life?' Captain Coleman asked.

'Fine,' he said. 'But I'm idle a lot and I could do with more work.'

'It's very quiet,' the Captain said. 'No leads. And it's a bit worrying. I think that the Irgun are hanging fire until the Ramat Gan trial.'

He had given Will an opening, a justification for a direct question. 'How's it going?' he asked. 'Has a date been fixed?'

'Not yet. We're still questioning Berger. But the man won't open his mouth. Except to yawn. He treats us with utter contempt.'

Will suppressed a smile and a sigh of admiration for his friend.

'We can't get a single name out of him,' the Captain went on. 'And we've tried all the usual practices. He's brave, that Berger. I'll give him that. He doesn't flinch, and we give him plenty to flinch about.'

Will could not suppress a shudder. He knew about the 'usual practices', and how prisoners, after long silences, suddenly began to talk, and didn't stop talking, giving out names, places, plans, more information than had been asked for, any word on earth that would halt the usual practices. But not Uri. He would sooner die than open his mouth.

'So there's no trial date?' Will asked.

'We'll push him as far as we dare go. We need him alive, if only to hang him. In a couple of weeks, I'd say.'

He rose and went over to where Will stood. He put his arm around Will's shoulders. 'Don't upset yourself, Will,' he said. 'It's part of our job.' Then he tousled Will's locks, and smiled. 'It suits you, long hair,' he said.

Will did not shrink from his touch, and he wondered why it did not repel him. He actually smiled at the Captain, then instantly regretted it. He turned and made for the door.

Now Will knew all that he needed to know, and much that he could have done without, and he left the office empty-handed and with a heart full of foreboding. He felt utterly helpless. There was no way he could visit Uri, or his Jerusalem friends. As far as they were concerned, he was back in the Welsh mountains attending the obsequies of his fictitious sister. And indeed, he wished he were home, away from the bleak sadness of this place, and inside a life that was warm and familiar, one without disturbance. But he knew that wherever he was, and however comfortable, thoughts of Uri would haunt him for the rest of his life.

He went back to the apartment hoping that David would be there. But it was empty. He couldn't bear the thought of being alone at this time and having nothing to do but brood about Uri, so he went to David's café where he was sure to find him. He spotted him from a distance, alone, but smiling his Hannah thoughts, and Will felt a stab of resentment at his friend's well-being. He felt belligerent. He wanted to rush to the table and bombard his friend with his fears for Uri. He wanted to punish David for his happiness.

'They're going to hang him,' he almost shouted, even before he sat down.

David put his hand on Will's shoulder. 'Take it easy,' he said. 'Sit down.' He signalled to the waiter for an extra coffee. 'Now tell me what you heard. Slowly.'

'I saw Coleman,' Will said. 'I didn't ask him, but he told me about the trial. They're questioning him and Uri won't say a word. They're torturing him. As long as they dare, Coleman said. They want him alive to hang him. Those were his very words.' Now it was out. All of it, and Will made no effort to send the tears back where they came from. David was shaken. The news itself did not surprise him. But its effect on his friend troubled him, and he dreaded the outcome.

'I'm sorry, Will,' was all that he could say. Then, after a silence, 'It's all part of this rotten deal we've been landed with,' he said. 'We're bound to pull out soon, and you'll be home. You won't forget about Uri, but it will ease with time.'

Will grabbed the coffee that the waiter placed on the table and drank it, scalding hot, as if it could burn out his sorrow.

'I hate this bloody place,' he said.

Before Hannah, David might have agreed with him. Now he was torn. But he could not discuss that conflict with his friend, especially as Will so needed his support. 'I have to see the Captain myself,' he said. 'Report all my non-findings. All my blind alleys. Do you want to come with me?'

'I'll wait for you here,' Will said. 'I've seen enough of Coleman for one day.'

David wanted an excuse to find out more about Uri's impending trial, in the hope of discovering something with which he could comfort his friend.

'Good man, that colleague of yours,' Coleman said as soon as he entered the debriefing room. 'But he gets easily discouraged. Tell him from me, he's doing a great job.'

'He told me about the Uri Berger trial,' David went straight to the point. 'Is it such a foregone conclusion? His hanging, I mean?'

'No doubt about it,' Coleman said. 'He could appeal, of course, and that would lead to a reprieve. But he won't appeal. It's a principle with the Irgun never to appeal. They don't recognise our court, so an appeal is irrelevant. We've sent enough of them to the gallows and, whether you believe it or not, we don't enjoy it. Apart from everything else, it leaves us in bad odour. It gives us a bad press. An appeal and a reprieve. That would save our faces. But without an appeal, we can do nothing.'

A ray of hope, David thought. A glimmer that he could convey to his friend. 'Does he have any visitors?' he asked.

'Just the one. His mother's allowed to see him. She's a widow. Poor devil travels all the way from Jerusalem every Monday and Friday. Can't help feeling sorry for her.'

David was anxious to get away. There *was* something he could do for his friend.

Quickly he reported his non-findings, and eagerly asked for further contacts.

'As I told Will,' the Captain said, 'it's a quiet time. They're waiting for the outcome of the trial.'

David left hurriedly and made straight for the café where Will was waiting. He reported all that Coleman had told him, stressing the necessity of an appeal and a possible reprieve.

'But he refuses to appeal,' David said.

'Then we must persuade him.' Will was suddenly hopeful.

'Not we,' David said. 'His mother. She visits him twice a week. Lives in Jerusalem. I managed to get her address. I'm going to see her.'

'I'm coming with you,' Will said.

'No.' David was adamant. 'I'm going on my own. I'll say I'm a friend. He tuned my piano. Something like that. She doesn't know me. But if you show your face, she'll describe it to Uri and the whole of the Irgun will be after you. I'll go alone. I'll find her. I'll be back some time tomorrow.'

Will had to accept that David's arguments were sensible. 'Do your best,' he pleaded. 'He's too young to die.'

'So are they all,' David said. 'The British too.' His loyalty irritated him. It was inconvenient and he looked forward to a couple of days on his own, hopefully to disentangle his priorities.

He took the bus to Jerusalem. He would spend the night

there in a pension under an assumed name. Then he would pay Uri's mother a visit.

In all his time in Palestine, David had spent little of it in Jerusalem and he welcomed the opportunity. The city retained its biblical air. At that time it housed a large Arab population and David made his way to the souk and its sundry stalls. He gave a thought to Abu and his wily deception. He paused at a stall that displayed a range of embroidered skull caps. He picked out one of the plainer ones, and tried it on for size.

'You look like a Jew,' the stallholder laughed.

That's just what I want to look like, David thought. The cap would do for a *yarmulka*. The 'Abu' stated his price, and was surprised that there followed none of the customary haggling. David paid what he was asked. You didn't bargain over a *yarmulka*.

He found a room in a hostel and registered under the name of Richard Davies. There was no point in concealing his nationality. At the desk he asked for directions to Mrs Berger's street.

'Poor Uri's mother,' came the immediate response. She lived not far from the hostel itself. It was too late to call on her, so he roamed the streets for a while before returning to his room. There he rehearsed what he would say to her. He tried to imagine her despair, yet he could not help thinking of that same agony of hundreds of British mothers whose sons had fallen in the Holy Land. But being killed in battle was redolent of a kind of honour. The gallows was different. It was more deliberate, more callous, and certainly more unnecessary. British mothers did not have to wait for their children to die. They lived in hope until the bodies were found. But Mrs Berger waited. And without hope. The body had been delivered even before its execution. He was suddenly sickened by the futility of it all, by the Haganah struggle, the Irgun, the Mandate. There was no question of loyalty in his mind. Every death, from whatever motive, was pointlessly heartbreaking and he was mourning them all.

He slept fitfully, fearful of the morning's encounter. He was anxious to get it over. But at six o'clock when he awoke, it was too early for a visit. He walked the streets again, and took his time over his breakfast. At nine o'clock, he made his way to Mrs Berger's flat.

She lived in a four-storey walk-up block, on the top floor. As he climbed the stairs, he thought of how she made that hopeless climb each post-prison visit. He felt her breathless despair, and mounting sorrow. He paused at her door, and once more tried to rehearse. But the words had gone. Perhaps when he faced her, her presence might prompt them. He touched the *mezuzah* on the door-jamb, and he thought of his grandmother and how on each arrival at and departure from their house she would stroke the *mezuzah*, confirming its hidden affirmation of faith. And he longed, not so much for home, but for its truth, that truth that could embrace Hannah.

He rang the bell and waited, hoping for a little time to find the right words. Hoping even that Mrs Berger was not at home. But after a while the door was opened. She had the look of one who lives alone, that cautious look through a barely opened door. And the sadness too of that look, empty of expectation or surprise.

'Mrs Berger?' David asked.

'What do you want?' she whispered.

'I'm a friend of Uri's,' he lied. 'I'd like to talk to you.'

'You're very brave,' she said through the crack in the door. 'He has many friends, I know, but they dare not come here. There are soldiers everywhere and they are afraid. What makes you come?'

'I'm not in the resistance. I'm not even Jewish. I'm just a friend.'

She started to cry. 'Come in,' she said. She led him inside. The curtains of the living room were drawn and she switched on the light. 'Would you like a cup of tea?' she asked.

'Thank you, no,' David said. 'I just want to talk.' He caught sight of a picture on the sideboard, set lovingly in a silver frame.

It featured a young man with a pony-tail, standing behind a double bass. It had to be Uri. He went to the sideboard and studied it.

'I used to nag him,' Mrs Berger was saying, 'over and over again to get his hair cut. Now he has no hair at all. They've shaved it all off. He looks terrible.'

She motioned David to sit down. Then sat down herself at the table. 'They've tortured him,' she said. 'He's all covered up, so I can't see any marks. Except on his neck. His neck,' she repeated; that word that was his visa to dying.

David put his arm round her trembling shoulders until they were still.

'He has to appeal,' he said. He spoke sharply as if giving an order. 'It's his only chance. The Mandate would welcome an appeal. I know some people in authority. They don't want to hang him. An appeal would save their face. They could grant him a reprieve. He *has* to appeal,' he almost shouted. 'Very soon the British will leave. Everyone knows that. Then he will be freed and go back to his playing and his tuning. And his pony-tail,' he added. 'You have to persuade him,' he said.

She waited for him to finish and calm himself.

'I've already done so,' Mrs Berger said. 'I do nothing else. Every second of my time with him. But he is adamant. That's exactly what they want, he tells me, and I won't give them that satisfaction.'

'What stops him, d'you think?' David asked.

'The Irgun. Who else?' she said with contempt. 'They don't recognise the court, to start with. So in their eyes an appeal would be just as illegal. They are a cruel bunch.'

'But once he is free, he could work for independence. Isn't that what the Irgun want?'

'Of course,' she said. 'We all want that. But the Irgun want martyrs too.'

Then there was silence between them; David could do nothing more.

'I'll tell him you came,' she said after a while. 'Give me your name.'

'Richard Davies,' he said. 'Though he probably wouldn't remember me. He tuned so many pianos. That's how I met him; he came to tune mine. Just tell him that you met someone in the know and that's what they advise. Beg him, Mrs Berger, to change his mind. He owes the Irgun nothing.'

'Except his life,' she sobbed.

David rose. He put his arms round her and kissed her cheek. He could not give her hope. He could only wish her strength and courage.

Helplessly he returned to Tel Aviv. He had little to report to Will, and that little offered no hope. He found him in the apartment anxiously awaiting his report. And when it came, Will was not surprised.

'They're bastards, those Irgun,' he said. 'I bet that swine Begin never puts himself on the line. He sits smugly in his quarters and sends young men to their deaths and never gives them the right to survive. What makes a man like Uri follow such a monster?'

'They call it idealism,' David said.

'What can I do?' Will asked.

'Nothing,' David said. 'Nothing at all. As Captain Coleman put it, it's all part of a rotten deal.'

'His poor mother,' Will said.

'There are hundreds of them like her,' David said. 'And what for? For nothing. When will it ever end?'

12

The lull continued and the quiet was unnerving. No soldier walked alone. They moved in groups of three or four, wary and cautious. No one believed that peace had come at last. The eerie silence served only to generate fear. Will spent the time writing letters home. He found letter-writing difficult but it helped take his mind off thoughts of Uri. So apart from his parents, he wrote to his brothers and cousins, aunts and uncles, all safely nestled in the Welsh valleys. There was little to write, and nothing he could divulge, so the letters were repetitive to each recipient. And while writing them, he longed for home. He thought of that sister he'd never had, that sister he had gone home to bury. The obsequies were over, and it struck him that there was now no reason why he shouldn't return to his unit.

'Uri, I'm back,' he shouted into the empty room. 'I've come to visit you.'

He rushed to headquarters. Captain Coleman was delighted to see him, and he walked towards him as he entered.

'It's my favourite eager beaver,' he said. 'Ever hopeful. No news, I'm afraid. Not even rumours. But sit down anyway.'

'I've come with an idea,' Will said, as he took a seat.

'We're short of those,' Coleman said. 'Tell me.'

'I know Uri Berger,' Will said. 'I've known him for a long time. Ever since I've been here. I play the saxophone, and most weeks on a Friday night, I've been going up to Jerusalem to play in a combo. Uri Berger plays the double bass. I've stayed in his flat. I had no idea who he really was or what he was up to. As far as I was concerned, he just played the bass and tuned pianos for a living. I looked upon him as a friend. I know that the authorities want him to appeal so that they don't have to hang him. I'd like a permit to visit him. In uniform, of course. Perhaps I can persuade him.'

'An excellent idea,' Coleman said. 'Why haven't you mentioned it before?'

'To tell you the truth, I was shocked. I hated him for his deception. I didn't care if he was hanged,' Will lied.

'You would do us a service if you could persuade him,' Coleman said. 'I'll make out a permit. And get your hair cut.'

Will tried to hide his excitement. He would be seeing Uri once more and he would not leave him until he agreed to an appeal. He rushed back to the apartment and, unwilling to waste time, he cut his hair himself. He'd learned the craft from his mother who was the regular family barber. Once in his uniform, he felt legal and entitled to the privileges of the Mandatory power. He did not relish them but they would ease his passage. Like the car and driver that Coleman had provided to take him to and from the prison.

On arrival he presented his letter of permit. Although its envelope was open, he had not read it, but clearly it must have stated that the visitor was on urgent business and was to be brought to the prisoner without delay. Will was greeted respectfully and led through a maze of corridors. He was struck by the silence of the place, though each cell was occupied. It was a death-row silence of abandoned hope. Each cell was barred. Will was reluctant to look at the prisoner inside but a quick glance told him that each one was alone. There was no other with whom to share despair, or hope, or to question the cause and its outcome. Above all, no one to whom one could whisper the obscene word 'appeal'. For all were Irgun prisoners, denied that final human right.

At last, the warder stopped in his tracks, and Will trembled.

'Visitor for you, Berger,' he shouted through the door. 'An important visitor,' he added. 'Stand to attention.' He unlocked the cell door and motioned Will to enter. 'I'll wait here for you,' he said.

'You don't have to wait,' Will said. 'I may need some time.

I'll ring when I'm ready to leave.' He didn't want eavesdropping, much less overseeing. He didn't know how much time he would need. Perhaps a minute would be too long, and a week not long enough. The cage door was open, yet he hesitated. He tried to still his trembling. He took off his beret, hoping to appear less formal and, with his short back and sides, to confirm that he was no more than a regular soldier. He went inside and heard the gate click behind him.

'Will,' Uri almost shouted, and his face cracked into a smile of pure joy.

Will stared at him and could do little to hide his horror. His friend's head was shaven. His face was hollow, and the tears of happiness that fell from his eyes, bounced on the ridges of what were once his cheeks. He had that gaunt look of one who has been deprived of food – or perhaps he himself had refused it. Either way, his friend smelt of mortality.

'Uri,' Will said, and he went forward to embrace him. He noted that Uri hung back a little and he attributed his reserve to shyness.

'You wrote that you'd gone home,' Uri said.

'But I came back. After the funeral.'

'I'm sorry about your sister,' Uri said.

Will regretted having deceived him. 'It was expected,' he said. 'She'd been ill for a long time.' He hoped to lessen Uri's need to console.

Uri led him to his cot, and they sat side by side.

'I was staggered when I heard,' Will said. 'I had no idea that you were Irgun.'

'Neither did the others in the band,' Uri said. 'I don't know what they're thinking.'

'I'll tell you,' Will said, his voice firm. 'They want you to live. We all do.'

'I don't have any choice,' Uri said. 'I was unlucky. I was caught.'

'But you do have a choice,' Will insisted. 'You can appeal.

They'll commute to life. They don't want to hang you.' The word stuck in his throat, as if he felt the rope about his own neck. 'They don't want to hang you,' he said again, as if he needed to get used to the word.

'I wouldn't give them that let-out,' Uri said. He was silent.

'Listen,' Will said after a while. 'They'll give you life, but the British will soon leave. Everybody knows that. And sooner than you think. Then you'll be absolutely free. Free to work for independence. Isn't that what you all want?'

'Others will carry on the struggle,' Uri said. 'In any case, I can't appeal. Appeal is against Irgun principles.'

'Fuck the Irgun,' Will shouted. He rarely swore, but now he was filled with a sublime hatred for the group that was so cosily sending his friend to the gallows.

Uri smiled. 'It's good to see you,' he said.

'I want to see more of you,' Will said. 'More and more. And so do your friends. You're a musician, for God's sake, and a bloody good one.'

'You're wasting your time,' Uri said. 'I know that you mean well. But the gallows is part of the deal.'

'You want to be a martyr,' Will whispered.

'Every good cause needs martyrs,' Uri said.

Again there was silence between them. Will knew that his mission had failed. But he tried once more.

'Think of your mother,' he said. 'Think of all the mothers who are mourning their sons. Their lives are shattered, once and for all. Your mother lives alone, I know. You are her only child. What will become of her? Picture her, Uri, I beg you. How can you do this to her? How can you rob her of what little life she has to lead? You are murdering her too. How can you be so cruel?'

Uri wiped a tear from his eye. 'That's the hardest part of all,' he said.

Will was hopeful. Perhaps thoughts of his mother would lead him away from the gallows. 'Her heart would break,' he persisted.

'Enough,' Uri said. 'She will survive.' He took Will's hand. 'I'm glad you came.'

Will felt he was being dismissed, but he stood his ground. He was angry. He recalled Coleman's phrase, the 'usual practices'. 'You don't have to give them names,' he said. 'You just have to put in an appeal.'

'That's just the same as giving names,' Uri said.

Will embraced him once more, and as he clasped his back Uri gave a howl of pain. Then Will knew that it was not shyness that had held Uri back from the first embrace. It was pride.

'They've tortured you, haven't they?' Will said. He turned him roughly around and lifted up his shirt. Uri's back was striped with red furrows. He had been flogged. What struck Will was the meticulous symmetry of the lines, how parallel they were, how deftly designed.

'My poor friend,' he said.

'You people do a thorough job,' Uri whispered, but without bitterness. He even smiled.

'I'm not one of them,' Will said. 'I'm on your side. Believe me. Stay with us, Uri, I beg you.'

Uri led him to the door and he himself rang the summoning bell. 'Thank you for coming,' he said. 'You are a worthy friend.'

For some reason, Will felt faintly insulted. A truly worthy friend would not have visited at all.

He was anxious to get back to Tel Aviv, desperate to rid himself of his shameful uniform, to burn it even, and to don those innocent civvies that had nothing to do with the flogging. His mission had been a failure. He would see Uri just one more time. At his trial. And then he would have to mourn him.

David was not at home when he returned and Will was glad of it; he needed to be alone. Eventually he would tell David of his visit, but he did not trust his voice to relay the flogging.

David had taken himself to Hannah's to collect his suit. The streets were emptying. People were at home preparing for the

80

Sabbath. At the door of Hannah's apartment, he could smell the hints of that preparation. Fresh bread, no doubt the Sabbath *chollah,* and the baked fish and simmering compote. Those Friday-night smells of his childhood, and he longed for that time again, a time when there were no choices to be made, when one faith lived beside another in equal harmony.

He pushed the door open, and went inside. 'Hello?' he called.

'Come right in. It's ready.' It was Avram's voice calling from his workroom.

Hannah was laying the Sabbath table, and setting the two candlesticks at one end. Her mother was at the stove, stirring. Joseph was shredding horseradish, his eyes streaming. That used to be *his* job as a boy, every Friday night, and his grandmother would reward him with a humbug, his favourite sweet. For a moment he felt as if he had come home, and looking at Hannah he knew that once he could declare himself nothing on earth could impede their union.

He muttered greetings as he crossed the room. Miriam and Joseph did not leave off from their work. But Hannah looked up and smiled at him.

He moved into the workroom. Avram was chalking a piece of cloth on his workbench. A new suit order. A headless dummy stood in the corner and on it was draped David's new suit. He stared at it. He viewed it as if it had been ordered by somebody else. But it pleased him. Its colour was gentle, modest, and its first-class tailoring had managed to achieve a casual look.

'Let's put a head on it,' Avram said, rising from his bench. He slipped the jacket off the dummy. 'Try it on,' he said. He returned to his bench and his chalking, while David began to undress. He turned his back on Avram as he dropped his trousers. In this room he had to be especially careful.

The new trousers first, and they fitted like a glove. Then the jacket, which draped comfortably in place around his shoulders. Although there was no mirror in the workroom, he knew that it was a good fit and that it looked well on him. He stood before the bench for Avram's approval.

Avram looked up from his chalking. 'It's good,' he said. Then he went to open a cupboard, the door of which was lined with a mirror. 'See for yourself.'

David regarded his reflection. He was pleased with what he saw. It would do for the party at the bank. It would do for any formal occasion. But that was not its purpose. It was specifically bespoke for the synagogue, and that is where he would air it the following morning. He changed and paid the bill that Avram offered him. He shook his hand and thanked him. As he passed through the living room, he noted that the Sabbath table had been prepared. At the door, he turned. 'Good Shabbos,' he said, echoing his grandmother. Miriam murmured a puzzled response and in a blur of bewilderment, David left the apartment.

He found Will in a mood of deep despair. He had to badger him to talk, and at last his news tumbled out. In dribbles at first, and then in a spate of words: Uri's feelings, his silences, and his sheer bloody-mindedness. Then the accidental discovery of the flogging and finally Will's own failure.

'You did all you could,' David said.

'It wasn't enough.'

'It wasn't just Uri you were trying to persuade,' David said. 'It was the whole of the Irgun. And they are intransigent. The cause is all.'

'I'll never forget the sight of his back. *We* did that, David. *Our* lot,' Will said. 'Was that *our* cause?'

'You did all you could,' David said again. He noticed the crumpled uniform lying on the floor. It had been trodden on, and spots of mud lined its creases.

'You'll have to tidy that lot up,' he said. 'You'll need it for the trial. And I'm coming with you.'

13

The next morning Will went to headquarters to report his failed mission. David put on his new suit and made for Allenby Road. He slipped his Arab skull cap over his head as he entered the synagogue. He had no *talith* but if questioned, which was unlikely, he would invent some excuse. Before seating himself he lingered at the back of the hall. The synagogue was crowded and he wondered whether he had happened upon a festival of sorts. And then he understood, as a young boy was led to the *bimah*. He watched him as he climbed to the platform and placed himself nervously before the awesome Book of Law. It was a bar mitzvah celebration and David was shipped right back to his boyhood: to the synagogue on the Bristol road, in his new grey suit with his first pair of long trousers. Slowly his chosen portion of the Law came to his lips and he recalled it word for word. Even those phrases that he was able to sing. And looking up at the women's balcony, he saw his mother and grandmother sharing pride, then below, in the front row, his father *untalithed*, but as legal as the rabbi by his side. Never in his life had he been so sure of who and what he was. Ambiguity was not his problem. It was a puzzle for others like the army Intelligence Board. He was a Jew, by Jewish law and Jewish disposition. And as a Jew, he would marry Hannah and make his home in Palestine.

He stayed until the young boy had finished, had earned his right to be called a man. Had earned his right to more fountain pens than he could ever use, books, cheques and shaving-kits. And he would go to his party and knock about with his friends. As he himself had done over ten years ago. He wanted to leave before the service was over. He knew of the hospitality of Jews during festive times. No doubt as a newcomer he would be invited to share in their celebrations. It would be too complicated. He was not ready to come out so openly, so he left while the streets were still relatively empty. He made his way back to the apartment.

As he was changing into his civvies, the phone rang. It was Headquarters and he was ordered to report immediately. His first thought was that something dreadful had happened to Will, that during the course of his Uri report, he had collapsed in despair. He rushed to Government House, and through the maze of corridors to Intelligence. The room was crowded and noisy and his entry wasn't noticed. He looked around quickly and was happy to see Will, alive and well, sitting in the front row. There was an empty chair beside him. David rushed to take it.

'What's going on?' he whispered.

'The Officers' Club. Jerusalem. A dozen killed.'

'When?'

'This morning. About ten o'clock.'

He'd been in the synagogue. Their Sabbath, and undeniably his. Never before had the Irgun struck on a Sabbath. On the whole they were an orthodox bunch, but they'd certainly taken advantage of the surprise factor. The Mandate authorities had always regarded Saturday as a day off.

Captain Coleman called for order. 'I don't know what you lot are doing out there,' he shouted. 'I know it's not what we expected on a Saturday, but it turns out they don't seem to have much respect for their faith. There must have been a leak somewhere.'

There was not a sound in the room. An embarrassed silence.

'You've grown complacent, the lot of you,' Coleman said. 'You were duped by the lull. You thought nothing would happen until after the Berger trial. So you let down your guard. Let this be a lesson to you. Never trust a breathing space. It may explode.'

'Permission to speak, sir,' came a voice from the front row.

'Go ahead, Lewis,' Coleman said.

'There doesn't seem any point now, sir, in delaying the Berger trial. Why don't we just get it over and done with?'

'That's an obvious deduction, Lewis,' Coleman said, 'and the Judiciary no doubt will waste no more time. But God help us when we hang him. So keep your eyes and ears open. Dismiss,' he said.

The room began to empty. Will was reluctant to leave. Perhaps he had it in mind to plead for further delay. But David knew that Uri was sentenced to death even before his trial. He took Will's arm. 'Let's go,' he said.

Will allowed himself to be led out. 'What now?' he asked.

David had nothing to suggest. Except the sea, which might offer some solace. Stopping off at the apartment, they turned on the wireless. Apart from the report of the assault on the Officers' Club, there were reports of attacks on British camps throughout the country. Heavy British casualties were feared. It was indeed Irgun's bloody Sabbath.

'The Mandate days are numbered,' David said. 'What's the point of our being here? Nobody wants us any more than we want to stay.'

'Bugger Intelligence,' Will said suddenly. 'From now on I'm going to lie low. Whatever we do, win or lose, people die. Innocent people. Jews, Arabs and British.'

But David knew, that despite his sundry labelling, Will was talking about Uri. He dreaded the trial. He feared that Will would break under the strain. He feared too for poor Mrs Berger who surely could not survive the agony of her son's sentence.

'I don't think you should go to the trial,' he said after a while. 'It will be too upsetting for you.'

'I have to go,' Will said. 'He's my friend I must stand by him. And bugger the Mandate,' he said again. Then he put his head in his hands and wept unashamedly.

He's in love with him, David thought. Uri is Will's Hannah.

He went to him and put his arms round his shoulders. 'I'm so sorry,' he said. He had no words of hope and it was pointless to tell him that time would heal. An eternity would not heal such a wound.

It's possible that Will didn't understand it himself, or what the pain was all about. But it astonished him, shamed him even, and he didn't know why. It gnawed at him, locking his nerves in a cramp. He wondered what was to become of him. He thought of his aunties, Gwen and Blodwen, and of his uncles, Dai, Gareth and Gwyn. He dared not think of his mam and dad, but he saw them all in the chapel pews and he shuddered. And suddenly, and for the first time, he didn't want to go home.

For a while, they sat together in silence. Neither of them had an appetite for the beach. In any case, escape would not now be possible, for they heard the rolling trucks outside, and the tannoy announcement of a curfew until eight o'clock the following morning. At nine o'clock, the curfew would be resumed. Indefinitely. There was now no possibility of seeing Hannah that evening. In the morning, she would surely take advantage of the free hour and go to their café.

He rose early, even before the day broke. He checked that Will was still asleep, his sole defence against his unfaceable reality. At the stroke of eight, he left the apartment and made straight for the café. The streets were crowded, not so much with food shoppers, as with marchers, protesting as usual against the Mandate presence. 'British Out,' they shouted, over and over again, in enraged repetition. There was a heavy presence of soldiers on the street, but they did not interfere. It was a peaceful march, and the soldiers stood aside as spectators. Even though he was not in uniform, David felt accused.

Because of the march he could not get across to the other side of the street so he had to dawdle a while and watch the procession from the side-lines. Amongst the protesters, conspicuously carrying a banner, he recognised Joseph. His presence in the march did not surprise him but he was relieved to see that Hannah was not by his side. No doubt she too wanted the British out, and he nursed the hope that she had abstained from the protest because there was just one whom she wanted to stay. He was impatient but the march seemed unending. Even those who had used the curfew break to buy food now joined the march. The women and their children brought up the rear, and in time it was possible to cross the road.

He hurried to the café. Hannah rose when she saw him and ran towards him. He held her in his arms.

'I've missed you so much,' he said.

'But we're together now,' she caressed his cheek, 'if only for a while.'

They walked to their table and ordered coffee. While waiting, he leaned across the table and held her. 'We'll be together for always,' he said.

They had little time before the curfew would resume. David was anxious to tell her about Will, hoping perhaps to glean some more information about the trial. Although the Haganah and the Irgun were at loggerheads on the nature of their resistance methods, they knew of each other's tactics.

'D'you know Uri Berger?' he asked.

It was a question out of the blue and it surprised her.

'Why do you ask?' she said.

David noticed that she was on her guard. 'He's a friend of Will's,' he said, 'and he's upset about it all.'

'How does Will know him?' she said.

So he told her about the combo in Jerusalem, and of their weekly meetings.

'I've heard Berger's a very good musician.' She was giving nothing away.

'D'you know anything about the trial?' he asked.

'What's to know? They'll hang him. Like they've hanged all the others. And they're going to be very sorry.'

'What does that mean?'

'The Irgun have had enough. They won't take any more hangings. They'll get their revenge. And it'll be a big one.'

She clearly knew more than she was revealing.

'In what way?' he asked.

She smiled at him, squeezing his hand. 'I'm so glad you're

not a soldier,' she said. She leaned towards him, and cupping her face, he kissed her.

A sudden curfew hooter shattered their embrace and David, his lips still pursed, met a void. She had gone, and he glimpsed the back of her, diving through the crowds, panic in her heels. With her resistance connections, she could not afford to be detained on a minor curfew-breaking offence. He sat for a while, drinking the two coffees that the waiter had brought. The café was empty now and he sat alone.

'Curfew,' the waiter reminded him. He dared not claim his immunity, so he paid and left. He didn't want to return to the apartment and the pall of Will's depression. He wished that the trial date had been set and that it was all over and done with, and Will could begin to mend. He recalled Hannah's relief that he wasn't a soldier, and he was frightened at his deception. He'd been tempted at that moment to come clean. And totally. To tell her of his Jewish mother, to reveal his Intelligence ranking. But he was British, and a soldier in the British Army, and such revelations would have been tantamount to treason. Yet he didn't know how much longer he could maintain the lie. He prayed that the British would pull out soon, so that he could opt to stay and once again become his own man. He would join the Haganah, and fight by Hannah's side.

But he knew that before that, they would have to hang Uri – and God knows how many more. However he was heartened by the rumoured murmurs from Whitehall that the Mandate had failed. The pull-out could not be delayed much longer. Even so, there would be time, alas, to hang Uri Berger.

14

As Captain Coleman had foreseen, the Judiciary sprang into action. The trial was set for the following week. Had General Barker had his way, he would have lost no time at all. There had been no appeal, and nothing had been heard of a case for the defence. Indeed, Berger had refused a lawyer. A couple of days at the most, then Berger could go to his Maker. Try him, sentence him, and hang him, Barker favoured, and all before the Irgun could organise demonstration and protest. And even to keep the execution itself under wraps for as long as possible, until, after sundry delays, his visiting mother would have to be told that it was all over. But British justice had to be seen to be done.

Nevertheless, Coleman insisted, as far as he could, in keeping a low profile on the trial, and to this end he forbade the attendance of army personnel at the hearing, except for those directly involved in the testimony.

When Will heard of this veto, he flew into a rage. 'I'm going,' he shouted, 'And no one's going to stop me.'

David was equally enraged, but not so much by the veto itself – indeed for him it was a relief – but by Will's reaction.

'You'll be caught,' he said. 'You'll be court-martialled. You'll be sent home with a dishonourable discharge and you'll never get a job. Think about it.'

Will said nothing. He knew that David was right. But the thought of never seeing Uri again curdled his heart. But like David, he had to admit to a certain measure of relief. He had been dreading the trial, and what would be his last sighting of Uri, knowing his irrevocable sentence. He would prefer to remember him plucking his bass, his pony-tail swinging. But for that memory, he had to block out his prison visit and Uri's shaven head, his sunken cheeks and his voracious appetite for martyrdom. Those images were indelible.

'It will all be broadcast,' David said. 'We can stay here and listen.' Though he dreaded that too. He would sooner persuade Will to a day on the beach, though he knew that even there the wireless would be blasting. For the interest in Uri's trial was nationwide. Not so much in the trial itself, which carried its own foregone conclusion, but with the reaction of Irgun and the revenge it had in mind.

And for this reason Will and David and the whole of the Intelligence unit were put on alert. Every day they reported to headquarters, and were given leads, which sent them up and down the country and which came to nothing. Both men were grateful for being given something to do, even though the purpose of their quests related to the fate of one they didn't dare think about.

On the opening day of the trial, they holed themselves up in the apartment, and glued their reluctant ears to the wireless.

From very early in the morning, buses had rolled through the streets carrying Irgun supporters and others on their way to the north. Similar transport rolled out of Jerusalem and Haifa. The Irgun could not save its martyr, but it was publicly going to honour him. The sun was half rising as the transport pulled up at the prison gates. The prison guards had been told to expect them and to marshal them into some kind of order. By law, they could not be kept out of the courtroom, but the chamber was too small to accommodate them all. Only thirty or so could be allowed an entry, and the choice was in the power of the guards. A random choice, and hopefully a way to sort out the trouble-makers. But one of them managed to get through. Avram Wertman, my *zeyda*, wearing a look of benign innocence, flavoured solely with a simple curiosity. The rest were marshalled on to the foreground of the court and there they set up their banners. Some of them read, 'Free Uri Berger', others, 'We want no British justice here', but most of the banners blazed, 'British

Out', and this shouted plea was more optimistic, tinged with possibility and it was chanted by most of the protesters with fervour and hope.

It was a solemn assembly. Some of its members were praying, huddling together in supplication. It was still early and they did not let up on their whispered protest, nor did those with the banners and their raucous requests. At about nine o'clock, the press contingent arrived. They had been alerted by the Irgun, much to Captain Coleman's dismay and his faint hopes for a low profile. It was bad enough having to allow the press inside the chamber.

The freelance photographers set up their cameras around the forecourt and covered the demonstration in long shot and close-up and from a variety of angles. After a while, having exhausted their coverage, they idled on the fringes, waiting for something to happen. It was not until shortly before ten o'clock that a photograph, highly worthy of publication, presented itself. Mrs Berger had arrived – 'the grieving mother' was the headline – together with another woman who turned out to be her sister. They were sorry figures, and they tried in vain to shield their faces from the greedy clicking cameras. A path was made for their passage. As they passed through the crowd, there was a sudden cessation of protest as if a silent wave of sympathy had stilled their voices. A sentry came forward to meet them, and gently he ushered them inside.

When Mrs Berger and her sister entered the courtroom, they were acknowledged by murmurs of greetings. People moved to make room for them, and they noticed a signal from Avram to sit beside him. He had often met Uri's mother in the past and he respected her. When she had settled, he took her hand. She had the smell of Mrs Katz about her, Dov's mother, that sickly smell of unfair bereavement. He could think of nothing to say to her. Later, when it was all over, he would visit her in Jerusalem, and still he would find nothing to say. He squeezed her hand. 'Be brave,' he heard himself mumble.

Outside, the photographers and reporters withdrew. They expected nothing more of interest until the verdict, and then they would be back in force.

The clock struck ten, the hour that the trial would begin. The protesters sat themselves down on the cobblestones or on the cushions they had brought with them. They kept their silence for a while, hoping perhaps to overhear some of the proceedings, but the forecourt echoed only with the sentries' footsteps, to and fro across the entrance. Soon they began chatting to each other, but in whispers, and the mood of the crowd remained sober.

Inside the court chamber, the spectators were silent but fidgety, as if their silence was a bottled one that could erupt into anger at any time. When the president of the court entered, followed by three stern judges, they all stood up, though such a gesture had nothing to do with respect. Colonel Fell, the president, was an object of their hate. He was well practised in sending men to the gallows. And he seemed to relish it. He sat down and called for silence. Pointlessly, because there was no murmur in the courtroom. He clearly anticipated trouble, and thought to scotch it from the very beginning.

'Bring in the prisoner,' he said.

Uri's arrival was heralded by a jangle of chains, a cacophonous prelude to his appearance. When eventually he stumbled into the dock, there was a communal gasp from the chamber. And a mew of weeping. This was not the Uri they knew and loved. Where were his cheeks, to start with? To say nothing of his famous pony-tail. But at least he had retained that proud look, laced now with a dressing of disdain.

Colonel Fell stared at the prisoner in the dock. And stared for a long time. Uri met his gaze without flinching. But after a while, he shrugged and turned his face away, in a gesture of contempt for all that his judges stood for.

'I'll hang you, you insolent bastard,' Colonel Fell said under his breath. Then, 'Read the charge,' he bellowed. The prosecutor stood and read from his papers. He read it automatically for he knew that it would fall on deaf ears. 'Uri Berger,' he said. 'You are charged that you were the leader of the group that stormed the armoury at Ramat Gan. Do you have anything to say in your defence?'

Uri turned to face the Colonel and looked at him with abject contempt. 'Nothing,' he said. 'Because I do not recognise this court. Nor your right to try me.'

There was a sudden cheer from the spectators' well. It was not prompted by surprise. The Irgun contingent expected no less. They were simply cheering their man's courage. Colonel Fell hammered on his gavel and, when silence resumed, Uri continued. 'Yours is a regime of oppression,' he said, 'and we shall fight against it, and overthrow it until you leave and return this land to its lawful owners.'

'Thank you so much, Mr Berger,' the Colonel said with infinite sarcasm. And he smiled. 'We are no doubt obliged to you.' He was delighted. The trial was virtually over. With luck he could even make lunch with friends in Haifa.

'Mr Berger,' he said patiently, 'we are trying to give you a fair trial. And in such a trial, you are entitled to a defence. You have refused to invite anybody to speak on your behalf. So it is now up to you.'

'I have already said,' Uri addressed the court in general 'that in my eyes this court is illegal.'

'But not in *my* eyes,' the Colonel shouted. 'And if you refuse to offer a defence, then all that is left, according to British law, Mr Berger, is to pronounce sentence.'

A terrible hush embraced the chamber like a shroud. Everybody knew that it was all over. Suddenly a shrill cry, a heart-broken plea of 'Uri', broke the silence. It came from his mother. It might have been a voice for his defence, or it might have been a simple scream, lodged for so long inside her, that had finally broken its proud bonds. Avram put his arm round her and there was silence once more.

'The court will adjourn to consider its deliberations,' the Colonel said. 'Take the prisoner down.' He rose and was followed by the three other judges who sat on the bench beside him. The audience listened to Uri's chain-orchestrated exit, and fell quiet in its echo. There was nothing to talk about, no hope to be shared, and mourning, so predictable, still lay in waiting. From outside, the strains of 'Hatikvah', the Jewish national anthem of hope, filtered through the chamber. They listened, too late to be inspired.

Eventually the judges returned and Uri was recalled. Again the rattle of leg-irons and the silence when he was settled.

The Colonel rose and reached for his black cap, though the ritual was unnecessary. No sign was needed. The sentence was abundantly clear.

'Uri Berger,' he said. The 'Mr' had at last been dropped. 'Whether you recognise this court or not, it is my duty to pass sentence and to see that that sentence is carried out. The court has decided that you shall be sent from this prison to a place of execution, where you will be hanged from the neck until dead. And may God have mercy on your soul.'

The sentence was listened to in silence. Most of the audience had heard it all before. The same words. Some even mouthed them with the Colonel as they had mouthed them before at the sentencing of many of their comrades who had been hanged as indifferently as the Colonel hung his flypapers.

But Uri did not hold his tongue. 'Long live Israel,' he shouted from the dock, and the audience too then broke their silence with loud and prolonged cheering.

'Take him down,' the Colonel yelled.

The cheering was heard by the crowds outside and it was possible that it was taken as a sign of acquittal. And they too cheered, their hopes fulfilled. But when the gates opened and the press reporters rushed to their cars, it became clear that their cheering had been misrouted.

'Gallows,' one reporter shouted, and another, 'What did you expect?'

The crowds moved out of the chamber and into the forecourt. But Mrs Berger stayed behind. Avram took her arm as she walked across the room to the clerk of the court and asked him if she could see her son. The clerk's face clouded with inside information, and he told her to wait while he made enquiries. He left the chamber, but shortly returned.

'Not now, I'm afraid,' he said. 'We must abide by visiting hours. Ten o'clock tomorrow morning.' He touched her arm. 'I'm so sorry,' he said.

Avram led her away. 'Where will you sleep tonight?' he asked.

'I have a friend in Haifa,' she said. 'Though I don't expect to sleep. I shall see him tomorrow and say goodbye. Then I shall sleep and hope to sleep for ever.'

He kissed her and held her for a while. Then he left. He had to get back to Tel Aviv to see Begin.

The protesters boarded the coaches. The banners were carefully stacked. They would no doubt be needed for further demonstration.

It was a silent return journey. They thought of Uri in his cell and marvelled at his courage. But some among them, especially the women, began to question its value, and as a corollary of that, to doubt the very purpose of the Irgun. Many of them lost heart. The Haganah was less violent, less punitive. And certainly not lacking in courage. It was on such a return journey, and there had been many from Acre prison, with the gallows shadowing its path, that faith was frayed and doubts would surface. Until the next trial, when they would demonstrate once more and return in mourning.

Uri's mother did not sleep much that night. She dozed a little and was suddenly woken by the midnight bell. Her head seemed to spin, just once in swift circle and infinite pain. Then, as quickly as it had begun, it subsided into calm and stillness. She fell asleep again, and woke up weeping.

At ten o'clock precisely, she presented herself at the prison gates. A sentry guided her through. He seemed nervous. He was anxious to get away, and as soon as he had delivered her at the superintendent's lodge, he fled.

'I've come to visit my son,' she whispered through the grille.

'Name?' the officer asked.

'Uri. Uri Berger.'

The man stared at her, and with a key he opened the grille. Then he took hold of her hand.

'Did they not tell you?' he asked gently.

'Tell me what?' she said. Though she knew. She knew why her head had spun in the night. She felt in pain again, and heard the midnight bell. 'Tell me what?' she asked again.

'They hanged him at midnight,' the man said.

'But they told me,' she protested. 'They told me to come. They . . .' Then she let out a curdling scream, one that echoed through the corridors and cells, a scream that would never cease even when she was urged to silence. And in that silence she screamed her way back to Jerusalem and screamed, inside herself and out, until only death in its own time could quieten her.

15

One of the guards at Acre prison, an Arab in the generous pay of the Irgun, lost no time in informing them of Mrs Berger's morning visit and of Uri's behind-the-back execution. And the Irgun lost no time in broadcasting the deception on its illegal radio. According to their informer, Uri Berger had gone to his death singing, and others on death row had chorused him to the scaffold. Those who heard the broadcast, and there were many, were outraged. None more than the British authorities themselves. Their ruse had been rumbled, and such a trick was shameful. The Mandate's reputation was one of corruption and dishonesty, but it was largely based on hearsay and rage. Here at last was concrete evidence of their duplicity. Mrs Berger was its proof.

Will too heard the broadcast and he was appalled. David, even more so, since he knew Mrs Berger and had shared her pain. In a way he felt responsible. He was, after all, part of the set-up that had so deceived her. He would not tell Will, but he would go to Jerusalem and sit by her side on a low mourning stool. As he had done when his grandmother had died, sharing with his mother the seven days of mourning. His father too, had sat on a low stool, for he had mourned her as a son. David told Will he was going to headquarters, which he did, but simply to report. Then he took the bus to Jerusalem.

Will decided to go out and walk. Just walk. He had fully expected a breakdown following Uri's death, but for some reason he was relieved. It was as if a great weight had been lifted. He was no longer burdened with hope. He walked. He wondered what song Uri had sung on his way to the scaffold. And why sing at all? Was a song part and parcel of a martyr's equipment? It was Uri's greed for martyrdom that now sickened him. What was its point? And how dare Uri cause him so much pain. He was now close to hating him. So he called 'Uri' aloud, again and again, and the name alone echoed the love he had borne him. He walked slowly, stopping to stare into shop windows, noting each particular, endowing each item with character, and letting it lead his mind away from himself and into places where the name 'Uri' had never been known. He passed a music store, and looked in at the display. He thought of the arcade shop in Cardiff, where a Mr Arthur Angle served musicians' needs. He supplied strings, bridges, mutes and resin. This was a similar shop, and a similar old man seemed to be its proprietor. He came to the shop door. 'Can I help you?' he asked.

'Just looking,' Will said.

'Come and have a proper look inside.' The man seemed friendly enough and Will was glad of company.

'I'm just fixing a new soundboard,' he said. 'Lovely fiddle, this.' He held up the violin that lay on the counter. 'Are you a musician?' he asked. The old man, too, was in need of company.

'I play the sax,' Will said.

'Jazz?'

'Jazz. Yes, when I can find a group.'

'Plenty of groups around,' the man said. 'Especially in Tel Aviv.'

'I used to play in one in Jerusalem.'

'Uri's lot?' the man asked.

Will nodded. He did not trust his voice.

'There he is,' the old man said. He pointed to a gallery of signed photographs on the wall behind the counter. 'My clients,' he said proudly. 'I've done work for them all.' He unhooked Uri's picture and laid it on the counter. 'Fine musician,' he said. 'He used to buy his strings here, and get his bow rehaired. Terrible loss,' he said.

Will looked at the photograph. 'He was a friend,' he managed to say.

'Foolish man. Threw away his life.' The shopkeeper was angry. 'And what for? For martyrdom.' He almost spat out the word. 'I'm sorry,' he said. 'But I've no time for that lot.'

Will picked up the photograph. The pony-tail draped over Uri's shoulder, almost touching the upper curve of the bass. He was holding the bow lightly over the strings and he was smiling. Will turned his face away. 'You're right,' he said. 'A waste of a life. I must go,' he said. 'Thank you for your time.' He needed to walk again, to walk and to watch and to witness in order to get his mind off his mind. 'Uri, Uri,' he whispered to himself as he walked, and the name and its rhythm soon tired him. Then he heard another name, his own, and looking around, he spotted Hannah sitting at the outdoor café table.

'Will', she was shouting, and she beckoned him to join her. He would be glad of company and Hannah would take his thoughts away from Uri. But as he sat down beside her, she said, 'I'm sorry about your friend,' and he wondered whether he would be dogged by Uri for the rest of his life.

'David told me,' she explained.

'A waste of a life,' Will said. 'He could have appealed, but he preferred martyrdom. I hate that word. It's sheer vanity, conceit, and it's futile.'

'You mustn't blame him,' Hannah said. 'He did what he thought was right. He was very brave.'

Whose side was she on? Will wondered. Was it possible that she was one of them?

'What do you think of the Irgun?' he asked directly.

'Very little,' she said. Which was true, though she was aware of her filial disloyalty. 'They are not good for us,' she added. She ordered him a coffee.

'Where's David?' he asked. 'Are you waiting for him?'

'Not particularly. But he knows he'll find me here.'

'I think he's very fond of you,' Will said.

She smiled. 'And I of him,' she said.

'We'll be going home soon. It's obvious. The Mandate isn't

working. And we're not wanted here. What will you do then?'

'He doesn't have to go. Neither do you. You're not in the army.'

Will hesitated. He hoped he'd not given himself away, together with David. 'The English, I mean. All of them. They won't be welcome here.'

'What about you?' she asked. 'Will you go?'

'I miss my family,' he said. 'Wales is my home. It's my Palestine.'

'You're close friends, aren't you?' she said. 'You and David.'

'Yes,' he said. 'I'd miss him if he stayed.'

'D'you have a bank job to go back to?' she asked.

For a moment he wondered what she was talking about. Then he remembered his fictitious calling. 'Yes,' he said. 'My old job. They sent me here, so it'll still be waiting for me.' He smiled to himself. A career in banking seemed to him ridiculous. As did his father's stint in the pits. He had no idea what he would do, except that he would have to come to terms with himself, that self so racked with bewilderment.

'Why aren't you working today?' she asked.

'We're given a pretty free hand,' he said. 'I'm on my way to see a client. That's probably what David's doing too.' He was glad he'd given himself an excuse to leave. He wanted to be alone, to go on walking, and hopefully to rinse Uri's name out of his ear. He finished his coffee. 'If David shows up, tell him I've gone to see a client.'

'Thanks for stopping,' she said.

He put some money on the table.

'The coffee's on me,' she insisted.

But by now David was close to Jerusalem. The bus journey had taken longer than usual. There were countless roadblocks and police hold-ups and David was impatient. He was not looking forward to his visit and he wished it over and done with. His sympathy for Uri's mother was real enough, but he could find no words to express it. He would hold her, he thought, and let her weep into his silence.

At last the bus pulled up into the terminal. He remembered the way to her apartment and he took his time. He idled a while in the souk, dodging the persistent vendors. He recalled the Seder table at Passover, and how, after the meal, his mother and grandmother would say, 'Next year in Jerusalem', as did most Jews in the Diaspora. But few of them meant it literally. For most, it was a spiritual metaphor. But for him, David realised, it was a reality. And a permanent one.

He made his way to Mrs Berger's apartment block. Her apartment faced a balcony, and was visible from the corner of the street where he stood. The door was open and he could see people coming and going. He waited a while and as he moved towards the entrance, he saw the figure of a man who looked familiar. Some instinct told him to hide. He peeped out from an opening and watched as Hannah's father entered the building. He timed his climb up the four flights of stairs, then he saw him emerge on the balcony and enter the Bergers' door. He couldn't understand what Hannah's father was doing there. Why had he come all the way from Tel Aviv so soon after Uri's death, unless there had been a positive connection? Had he known Uri? Had he been a close friend? Had he even been a co-conspirator? It was possible. Whatever the reason, he knew now that he couldn't afford to be seen, and that he had to get back to Tel Aviv. It worried him, Mr Wertman's appearance, in such a place and at such a time, and he wondered whether he was a little more than just a simple tailor who kept himself and his opinions to himself. He daren't ask Hannah. She would claim ignorance of the visit, and he might suspect she was lying. He would take no risks with her. He loved her, and he would marry her and respect her secrets.

The return journey to Tel Aviv was relatively unimpeded, and it was lunchtime when he arrived at the apartment. Will was glad to see him, and it seemed to David that he was in good spirits.

'Let's go out to lunch,' Will suggested.

'A good idea. We'll go to Jaffa. That Lebanese place. And give Abu a wide berth.'

They laughed to fortify their spirits, though each man was troubled on his own account.

The restaurant was crowded and noisy, which suited both of them for a private talk would be impossible. David was tempted to tell Will of his morning's encounter in Jerusalem, but he did not wish to involve Will in his own doubts, so he was glad that the noise absolved him of conversation. Will, for his part, was tempted to report his conversation with Hannah but that meant talking about Uri, and on that name he preferred to hold his tongue.

'Have you been to the bank today?' Will shouted.

David shook his head. 'We ought to put in an appearance,' he shouted back.

Then it was Will's turn to nod, and they laughed together and turned to the business of eating.

After the din of the restaurant, the streets were relatively quiet, and both men were content to maintain the silence between them. Together they went to the bank – in, through and out, their duty done.

That evening, David sat at the café table and waited for Hannah. He had decided not to mention his sighting of her father in Jerusalem. He suspected a connection with Uri Berger and he knew it was his duty to report such doubts to Headquarters. But should he mention my *zeyda*'s name to Coleman, Hannah would be involved, and her whole family. He did not want to put them in line for possible investigation. He tried to convince himself that her father was merely Mrs Berger's friend and that, as a simple friend, he had gone to Jerusalem to console her.

When Hannah arrived, he had no difficulty in putting his doubts aside. However valid they were, they were not for airing. He always marvelled at her beauty, but on that day it struck him almost painfully, as he realised how fraught with hurdles was their union. He rose to greet her, and held her gently.

'Let's walk,' she said.

Both knew that they would go to the river, and without words, they moved in that direction. They made for their tree, as inalienably theirs as was the café table. And as they lay side by side, she said, 'We're together for a time. And that's all we can be.'

'No,' he said. There was anger in his voice. 'It's not enough. It's not just for a time. I'm staying in Palestine. When the Mandate pulls out, I'm not going home.'

'What will you do here?' she asked. She was smiling, and David didn't know whether she was pleased with his decision or she thought it simply ridiculous.

'I shall marry you,' he said.

She kissed him. 'Staying here won't make you Jewish,' she said.

'But I could convert. Then your parents would accept me.'

'Conversion to Judaism isn't easy. Especially for a man.'

He felt helpless. And afraid. 'If I were already Jewish,' he said, 'would you marry me?'

'Tomorrow,' she said and she kissed him again.

Then he knew that all was well. That in her love, and in that guarantee, he was safe. And that was all that mattered. He stood and lifted her in his arms and swung her round in his joy. 'We will marry,' he whispered. 'You and I. It's possible.'

'How?' she asked.

'Be patient,' he said. 'And trust me.'

'Tell me. Tell me how,' she insisted.

He was sorely tempted, but he held his tongue.

'Tell me,' she said again.

'I'll find a way,' he said.

16

You didn't need Intelligence to guess where the Irgun would strike next. There were over thirty of them in Acre prison and five on death row. You knew where they would strike. And why. The problem was when.

It would be an audacious action, Coleman thought, and bound to fail. Acre prison was a fortress in a largely Arab town, an unlikely hunting-ground for the Irgun. It was surrounded by a cordon of British army camps. It was impregnable. Even Napoleon's army had failed to breach it. Nevertheless, he arranged extra security at the prison. And indefinitely. But Irgun Intelligence reported exactly what the British were expecting, so they wreaked havoc elsewhere. Assaults on railways, bridges and army camps. Moreover, the Irgun reverted to keeping the Sabbath holy, while the British still vetoed all Saturday leave. Acre prison remained a fortress, ringed with guards night and day. The Irgun decided it would have to wait. In any case, planning the prison assault would take time and meticulous preparation. Playing a major role in this strategy was the escape committee within the gaol itself and with whom the Irgun had several means of communication. Prisoners were allowed visitors – relatives, rabbis, doctors and lawyers – and through these sympathetic agencies coded messages were passed to the committee. Sometimes they were hidden in cakes or fruit, so that long before the assault was to take place the committee knew exactly what moves they should make to cooperate.

The head of the committee was one Yossi Weill. He claimed to be a religious man and was favoured with constant visits from a rabbi. The rabbi was no more a rabbi than Yossi was a devout. From the Irgun dressing-up cupboards, where British uniforms and Arab dress were stored, he'd selected rabbinical garb and a beard, and thus disguised, he came to administer to Yossi's spiritual needs. And to his hygiene, to which end, he presented him with a bar of soap, said something about cleanliness being next to godliness, muttered a prayer and left, his duty done.

Inside the soap, Yossi found a coded list of names spelling out the forty-one prisoners who were to be freed, and preparations for their escape. Other prisoners gorged themselves on cakes and swallowed the instructions to the escape committee. Where to place themselves, how to trail red herrings, mount diversions and always with an air of puzzled innocence.

The large Irgun contingent, dressed in British uniforms, was led by none other than my intrepid *zeyda*. He had tailored his uniform himself and it was a perfect fit. He was excited. The assault had been planned to the minutest detail, both in and out of the prison. There was no reason why it shouldn't succeed.

It was a Sunday. *Their* Sabbath. Over the weeks since Berger's execution, Coleman's seven-day alert had slackened. In the army barracks surrounding the prison, those soldiers who were not at morning service were besporting themselves on the beach, their rifles lying in the sand. Above the dunes, on the road that led to the prison, two trucks coasted down the hill towards the prison gates. Their arrival time was exactly as planned and, inside, the prisoners, each in his appointed place, waited for them. *Zeyda* led his men into the prison.

'Inspection,' he said to the sentry at the gates. He prayed that there would be no casualties. No more visits to weeping mothers. No more. They entered without interruption. Once inside, the 'inspection' went to work. Dynamite was laid against the wall that abutted the truck road and *Zeyda* himself lit the fuse. The prisoners stood back and waited to view their freedom. The wall crumbled and the noise was deafening. The soldiers on the beach heard the din, but most of them were in the sea, and it would take some time for them to collect their arms and return to action.

'Out,' Yossi shouted, and those chosen men leapt into the

bright summer air and into the trucks that would carry them to freedom. The gaping hole in the wall was an open invitation to escape, and altogether two hundred and fourteen Arab prisoners accepted it with pleasure. As they fled, they thought that the Jews were miracle-workers and they were grateful, and their gratitude endured over generations, until their great-grandsons and daughters joined the *intifada*.

It was not until they heard the explosion that the gunners on the watchtower realised something was amiss, and when they saw the massive escape they opened fire. Four of the liberators were killed as they made for the trucks. And three of them were captured, those three who would be at the heart of *Zeyda*'s story, the story that I am bound to tell. Avshalom Haviv, Meir Nakar and Ya'akov Weiss, three veteran Irgun fighters, were thrown to the ground as the trucks pulled away. They were roughly dragged back into the prison where they would languish until sentenced, and though they had killed nobody, any more than had their comrade Uri Berger, they knew that they would meet the same fate. And even as they lay there, beaten by the guards, they knew too that they would die sooner than appeal.

For the Irgun, pride in the success of the raid was muted by its own losses and by the capture of the three men. But elsewhere, everybody, including the British, seethed at the raid's audacity. From the House of Commons, enraged by such a catastrophic show of strength came the cry, 'We must get out of Palestine'.

David and Will relished that cry as it thundered over the airwaves, and secretly they rejoiced. Will ached to go home, even though, in the warmth of his family fireside, and in the censorious chill of the chapel, he would have to declare himself, to tell them what he feared he was. Or not tell them, which was equally painful. But David would not go home. He would relish his freedom from restraint. He would deliver his mother from her enforced quarantine, and he would whisper her maiden name, Levy, and her provenance into Hannah's ear. And then her father, Irgun or not, would welcome him into his family.

'They won't pull out for some time,' Will cautioned. They'll make sure they try those three prisoners in Acre. And they'll sentence them to death. And they'll make bloody sure that they hang before they leave.'

'They?' David asked. 'You keep saying "they". It's *us*, Will. You and me. We're part of the "they".'

'We have been,' Will said, 'but not any more. When they go, we can feel clean again. Both of us.'

David put his arm round his friend's shoulder. He would miss him, he thought. He had been a true friend, loyal and caring. He doubted that he would ever find an equal. Will did not respond to his gesture. On the contrary, he stiffened. But for the same reason David had shown his affection. He stiffened because he would miss that friendship. He stiffened with the memory of Uri; he stiffened in the name of love, a shivering name that overwhelmed him.

17

Will was right. The Mandate authorities were in no hurry to pull out. There was still unfinished business to attend to. Foremost among which was the trial, sentencing and hanging of the three Acre captives. The problem was timing.

A United Nations committee was scheduled to visit Palestine to study the problem, and to return to Geneva to propose a solution. The Mandate authorities made hasty preparations for the trial of the three men. As usual with Irgun prisoners, there would be no recognition of the court and thus no defence and no appeal, so that the trial took only one miserable day. It was the very first day of the UN presence in Palestine when the men were tried and sentenced to death by hanging. It was a move nicely timed to show the Mandate's authority. The hanging would be delayed until the UN committee was well on its way back to headquarters in Geneva. Meanwhile, Captain Coleman cautioned his men to be on the alert. He confined them to barracks unless they were called out on duty, and in such cases they were to go about in groups, or at least in pairs, and to be wary of kidnapping.

The Irgun was devastated. Not so much by the sentence itself – that was no surprise. It was its speed that was so threatening. Begin called his staff to his hideout. They were waiting for his call. So they came, Pinsker, Dror and Gad, and now *Zeyda*, who had been promoted to the elite in recognition of his valiant service in the Acre assault. They sat in a silent circle and Begin was the first to speak.

'Hostages,' he said. 'It's the only way. Hostages and threats. Gallows for gallows.'

Such a suggestion was radical enough and if carried out would no doubt invite horror and condemnation from the British. The

Haganah would fight it. They would do all they could to frustrate such a drastic move.

'There's no other way,' Begin said again.

'Who should we target?' *Zeyda* asked.

'Soldiers of course,' Gad said. 'Anyone in British uniform.'

'I think we should widen the net a little,' Pinsker said. 'The soldiers are on strict alert. They expect a kidnapping and we must not be seen to fail. I suggest any Englishman.'

'I agree,' Gad said. 'You know how the British are. They'll defend their own, whatever he's wearing.'

But *Zeyda* stuck out for soldiers. Begin agreed that a kidnapped soldier would merit ransom, a ransom of freedom for their prisoners, but he made it clear that he knew that there were difficulties attending such an abduction. 'We'll vote,' he said.

Zeyda was the outsider, but he yielded to their choice.

'There's no time to lose,' Begin said. Then he took *Zeyda*'s arm. 'Leave this one to the boys,' he said.

The three men took off in a borrowed car. They stopped at a phone box and Gad jumped out to make a call. Shortly he returned. 'They'll be ready,' he said.

It was early evening and Tel Aviv night-life was stirring. Clubs opened their doors. It was a good time to hunt down their quarry.

Zipporah and Hava were students at the Herzlia College and they shared a room in one of its hostels. Their fathers were active members of the Irgun, and they had schooled their daughters to follow the same course. The two girls were waiting outside the hostel gates. They looked like tarts of whom all parents would have been infinitely ashamed – except for their own, who would have been proud of them. They wore identical clothes: low-cut blouses and short skirts, fishnet stockings and high heels. The uniform of creatures of the night. They waved as the taxi slowed down and pulled up beside them. The rear door was opened and they bundled themselves inside. An onlooker would have been sickened by such an immoral display, and saddened at what nice Jewish girls had come to.

They drove around for a while. Occasionally they stopped at a bar and Gad went inside to case the joint. It was still early and many of the bars were almost empty. It grew dark as they drove round and more people came out to play. At last, Gad found a promising venue. The girls got out of the car and shimmied their way to the entrance. Dror and Gad followed them at a distance. Pinsker, who was driving, stayed in the car, though he left the engine running. Gad was excited. But nervous too. He had blown up bridges, raided army camps, wrecked railway lines. He'd covered the whole gamut of resistance battle. But never a kidnapping. He'd not been trained for that. And neither had Dror. He just prayed for luck. He knew the three condemned men. One of them, Haviv, was a close friend. They had grown up together in the movement. This kidnapping had to succeed, had to result in some reconsideration, even if it was only life. That would do. Alive, they could all escape and they could still work together.

The bar was a sleazy one, and the girls were suitably dressed. A few punters sat round the tables, each one hooked by the girls already there. A few lone drinkers leaned on the long bar. The girls eyed them.

'What about the one at the end?' Zipporah said.

'Promising,' Hava said. 'Drinks whisky. Smokes a pipe. I'll try him.'

'Good luck,' Zipporah said.

Hava slunk over to the bar and sat herself next to what she hoped would be her prey. She was not comfortable. It was a role that did not suit her. She had to keep the cause in mind in order to lessen her self-disgust. She smiled at him.

'What's your name?' she asked.

'Collins,' he said. 'Stewart Collins. People call me Stew.'

Promising, Hava thought. So was the pipe. So too the whisky. The marks of an English gentleman.

'Can I get you a drink?' he said.

'That's kind of you,' Hava said.

110

'What's your name?'

'Hava,' she said.

'That's a pretty name for a very pretty lady. And what will Hava be drinking?'

'Just a lemonade, please,' she said.

He called the bartender over. 'A lemonade for the lady. And another of the same for me.'

Hava sensed that he would do for their purpose, and she began to feel sorry for him.

But she thought of Meir, Meir Nakar, who had once told her he loved her, and she knew that this man would have to do.

The bartender brought their drinks, and the man took out his wallet. He unfolded it, and Hava noted a wad of English notes inside. He offered one of them as tender. The barman held it up to the light and placed it in the till.

'Keep the change,' Collins said. He noticed that Hava was eyeing his wallet. 'I have Palestine pounds, you know,' he said. 'Or do you prefer English?'

Then she no longer pitied him. She knew that she looked like a whore, and that she had come to a whore's market. But she deeply resented his easy assumption.

'English money will do,' she said. She tried a smile, but her face wouldn't oblige. Instead it flushed with shame.

'It's so hot in here,' she said, sipping her lemonade.

'My hotel's just near here,' he said. 'What do you say?'

'Let me finish my drink first.'

'Take your time, lady,' he said.

She sipped away. 'You aren't from these parts, are you?' Hava asked.

'No. I'm English. Just passing through.'

Hava sighed with relief. She slipped one hand behind her back and gave the thumbs up sign to Zipporah who she knew would be watching.

'I've just come in from Cairo,' he was saying. 'Back to London tomorrow.'

I wouldn't count on it, Hava thought. 'That doesn't give you much time to see our country,' she said. She sipped her lemonade again.

Collins raised his glass. 'Here's to a great evening,' he said.

Hava looked back at the door. There was no sign of Zipporah, but in her place, and with great relief, she saw Gad. She watched him come towards the bar. He winked at her as he passed, his sign that she should leave.

'Just going to the ladies' room,' Hava said. 'I won't be long.'

Gad took his place directly beside Mr Collins and gently pressed a gun into his back. Mr Collins shivered as he heard a hot whisper in his ear.

'I've a gun,' Gad hissed. 'Don't say a word. Just get up and walk towards the door.'

Poor Mr Collins felt his bowels melting. He stiffened to his feet and did as he was told. The bartender watched him leave and regretted the loss of a generous punter.

Once outside, Gad pushed his captive into the back of the waiting car. Dror, already in the back seat, helped drag him in. Then Gad wriggled himself in beside him, transferring the gun to Collins' temple, which was sweating with fear. Pinsker drove, slowly at first, so as not to draw attention, then he turned into a small road that led to Natanya, the site of their hiding place.

'What do you want of me?' Mr Collins sobbed. 'I've done nothing to harm you.'

'We know, sir,' Dror said. 'We need you, that's all.'

'But why? I've nothing to offer.'

'You'd be surprised,' Pinsker mocked from the driver's seat.

'Please, please, tell me.' Collins was almost weeping.

'Hostage, for God's sake,' Pinsker shouted.

Then the terrible truth struck him like an arrow. He'd read about the three men who'd been sentenced. The English newspapers had carried the story ever since the raid on Acre prison. He knew about the Irgun and its threats. He already felt a rope about his neck.

'You're Irgun, aren't you?' he said.

'Bull's eye, Mr Collins,' Gad said. 'What your rotten lot call terrorists.'

'But I'm Jewish too,' Collins screamed.

Pinsker brought the car to a shrieking halt.

'With a name like Collins?' Gad shouted as his hand hesitated the gun. With your pipe and your tweeds?' Then he laughed. 'There's no harm in trying.'

'It's not Collins. It's Cohen. I changed it for business reasons.'

Dror leaned over and whispered in Pinsker's ear. Then Collins started to sing 'Hatikvah'. The tune was off-key and he clearly didn't know all the words, but Dror and Pinsker were shaken. They didn't want to believe they'd made a mistake.

'That song's pretty well known,' Dror said. 'You don't know the words and you could have picked it up from the wireless. Tell us what festival we Jews celebrate next week.'

'The Passover,' Collins said quickly.

'You talk like a goy,' Pinsker said. 'We know it as Pesach.'

'I'm Jewish. I can prove it.' Collins was desperate. He opened his fly, and his unused, limp and circumcised member drooped on to his tweeds. 'Do I look like a Muslim?' he said, forestalling any more of their doubts. 'I promised my wife I'd be home for Seder night.'

Then the men had to concede.

'We're sorry,' Pinsker said. 'We all make mistakes.' He turned the car round. 'Go back and finish your drink,' he said.

'That lady will be wondering where I got to,' Collins said.

'She won't be there,' Gad told him. 'She's one of ours.'

They dropped him back at the bar.

'Shalom,' he said. 'And good luck.' Though he didn't mean it. He thought that the Irgun were a rotten lot, but he was grateful for his life. He skirted the bar and went straight to his hotel. He needed to ring his wife and tell her that he loved her.

The three men drove back to Begin's hideout to report their failure. They gave it in graphic detail. Begin was known to laugh very rarely, but at the end of their story he offered a chuckle. 'We must try again,' he said.

Zeyda, who had stayed with his leader, again questioned the choice of using civilians as hostages. And again Begin voiced his opinion that army hostages were too much of a risk.

'The UN Commission is here for another fortnight. The British daren't hang them while they're in the country. That gives us two weeks at the most. Next week is Pesach, I know. Perhaps the hostage business should wait till after the Holy days. Meanwhile, it's other business as usual.'

'What are you doing for Seder?' Gad asked.

'We shall go to my brother's house as usual, and possibly stay for the whole week. You know where to find me.'

'Seder at your place, Avram?' Dror asked *Zeyda*.

'The same as every year,' he said. 'Wives, children. We'll make it a Seder to celebrate.'

'In advance,' Gad said.

Zeyda loved this time of the year. It was a family time and he shared it with his comrades – his second family – and their children. As he walked back from Begin's hideout, he thought about his leader's preference for civilians. He would abide by it. But more than that. At Seder night, he would give them not one, but two English civilians on a plate. But it would take a bit of planning.

18

Every evening David took himself to their café table, but there was no sign of Hannah. There had been no news of 'illegals' landings and he feared that she might have lost interest. His missed her terribly. Then on the fourth evening, she was sitting there waiting for him. He held her in his arms.

'I haven't been able to get away,' she explained. 'It's just before our Passover and I've had to help with the preparations. But I've got good news.'

'Tell me,' he said.

'My father wants you to come to our Seder. You and Will.'

'Seder?' He feigned ignorance.

'Come,' she said. 'Let's walk. I'll explain.'

They held hands and made their way, as was their wont, towards the river.

'It's our Passover,' Hannah began. Then she told him the story of Pharaoh's cruelty to the Jews in Egypt and how God had visited ten plagues upon them, culminating in the slaying of their firstborn. Then the story of the exodus from Egypt and their journey to the promised land.

David knew the story as intimately as she, and he only half listened. His thoughts were in another place and at another time. He was at home in Bristol. And he was six years old. His very first Seder. All the family were there, as well as a stranger. It seemed to be the tradition to invite one every year. That one, he remembered, was his father's friend. He himself was the youngest at the table, and he was called upon to ask the four questions, and now he whispered them to himself in Hebrew, having lost not a single word. He remembered dipping his finger into a glass of wine. Ten times, to mark the terrible plagues, and then hiding the *afikoman*, that slice of matzoh without which the service could not continue. They'd give him a present when he pretended to find it.

'Why are you smiling?' Hannah asked. 'You look so happy.'

How could he tell her? But there would come a moment for that, he knew, and she would understand and forgive his deception.

By the time they reached the river, she had told him the whole Seder story. 'You will come, won't you?' she said. 'You and Will?'

'Of course,' he said. 'We'd love to.' They would be the so-called strangers at Hannah's table.

They walked towards their tree, but two couples were already settled under its branches.

'Doesn't matter,' Hannah said. 'I know a better place. It's up the hill. Let's walk.'

It was growing dark. There was a full moon, but it was shrouded in mist as if it forbade romance in its name. The stars too were hidden, and as they climbed it grew cold. At the top of the hill, from which there should have been a superb view, the river looked murky and the lights of Tel Aviv flickered dimly. There was a shepherd's hut on the crest of the hill, and when David saw it, he knew that the shrouded moon, the hiding stars and the dreary view would do nothing to hinder what was now, in his mind, an inevitable turn of events. It excited him, but he was nervous. He wanted more than anything to make love to Hannah but he remembered Captain Coleman's order during his Intelligence interview. 'Be careful where you drop your trousers,' he had said. On this spot, and in front of Hannah, was the last place he could drop them, for they would reveal that which he had been at such pains to conceal.

Hannah led him into the hut. He had dreamed of a more romantic setting but nature was in no mood to cooperate. There was no moon, there were no stars, but what worried him most was that he wasn't sure what he had to do. He'd had no practice, no experience, and he simply hoped that nature would show him the way. It was dark and chilly in the hut, two factors he

116

deemed in his favour. In such cold, they could not undress, and in such darkness, neither would see the other. He took her in his arms, and prayed to God to guide him.

'David,' Hannah whispered. 'I've never done this before.'

'I'll be gentle,' he said, though he had no idea of what he was talking about.

She laid herself on the floor and urged him towards her, as his body lost no time in telling him what he should do. And taught him the meaning of gentle.

'I love you,' he said, over and over again, donating a rhythm to their coupling.

'I'll find a way,' Hannah said. 'I'll find a way,' a descant to his refrain.

And when it was over, there was silence, but for the echoes of their vows one to the other. Afterwards, as they walked down the hill, the mist lifted and the full moon showed its face, bidding the stars to shine, as if, after some deliberation, it had decided to approve their union.

19

General Barker was worried. His three prisoners still languished on death row. In the prison yard, the gallows, never dismantled, were shrouded in tarpaulin. He itched to hang the men, but the tiresome UN team would have to leave before the scaffold could be unveiled. Already there had been wide criticism of the death sentences, even in Parliament itself, and God knows what the Irgun would be up to.

But suddenly, the Irgun had another problem on its hands. And so did the Haganah, and so, above all, did General Barker.

A few days before the Passover festival began, a dilapidated bullet-riddled ship was towed into Haifa harbour. It carried four and a half thousand Jewish refugees. With sad irony in its timing, the boat was called *Exodus* but it would be refused entry into the promised land. It had been hijacked. Seventeen miles distance from Haifa, it had been intercepted by the British cruiser *Ajax*, together with five destroyers. The boat was rammed, resulting in a hole in its side below the water-line. The vessel was boarded, and the refugees, unarmed except for bottles, cans and potatoes, put up a hopeless resistance. Three of them were killed and many injured. The passengers, as battered and as bruised as their carrier, viewed the promised land and despaired. The Irgun and Haganah, so seldom in agreement, joined forces to resist the immigrants' deportation, for it was clear from the three British vessels resting at anchor alongside the ship that a landing was strictly forbidden, except for a few unavoidable steps from one hellish boat to another. There was rioting on the quayside, but any protest was clearly futile. The rioters seethed with a rage that threatened to explode. A Major Malcolm Grey was in charge of the transfer. He was a kindly man who was not happy in this kind of work, but he'd been assured that he was to trans-ship the immigrants to Cyprus. Not too arduous a journey for those thousands who had already suffered a crossing laced with fear and hunger. He would land them in Nicosia and hope that in the fullness of time they could return. He watched as the cargo was roughly transferred. The wounded, women and children merited no special treatment. Army personnel were ruthless, giving no quarter. Even Captain Coleman, who viewed the transfer from a safe, untouchable distance, was appalled at their cruelty. And he was even more appalled when he spotted a group of members of the UN Commission on the quayside, with a full-frontal view of the shameful and disreputable army conduct. One of its members, aghast at the horror, said, 'The Mandate is finished. This is the best testimony of all.'

General Barker feared for his personal reputation. He wanted to go home, back to his farm in Shropshire. He'd had enough. But not quite enough. He first had to see those gallows unveiled.

The protesters stood helplessly at the quayside. The soldiers, fearful of their sublime rage, made no attempt to disperse them. They watched as the last of the immigrants boarded the third ship and as the shameful fleet sailed out of the harbour.

At mid-sea, without sight of coastline, Major Grey opened his sealed orders. There was no mention of Cyprus. He was to take his passengers to Port-de-Bouc, near Marseille. On the way back whence they came.

The *Exodus* tragedy resulted in a pall of depression among Jews. It seemed to have given the lie to the Passover story. The Exodus had taken place as it was written, but arrival had been denied. The customary joy in the festival was diluted as if the *Exodus* calamity had made a mockery of the Passover. *Zeyda* left Haifa, his heart full of rage, with a greedy appetite for revenge. Hannah and Joseph followed him. Their anger was no less than his, but revenge was no part of their agenda. They regarded the Mandate authorities with utter contempt and disdain, a disdain that was unworthy of revenge. They would soon be gone, and then, whatever its consequence, the state of Israel would declare its independence. They too had noticed the UN representatives, and they were glad of their presence and of their witness to so-called British justice. They surely had to recommend the Mandate's failure.

Miriam was waiting for them. All day she had listened to the Irgun illegal radio which had reported the *Exodus* event in detail. But she would not allow it to spoil her celebrations. 'We must rejoice, as we do every year,' she said. 'Otherwise, it's a form of surrender.' And she went about preparing their supper. Over the meal, she would not allow *Exodus* talk. Instead, she raised the subject of the Seder table and where everybody should sit.

'We're going to be eighteen altogether,' she said. 'Including the children. I think that Avram should sit at the head of the table with a "stranger" on either side of him, so that he can explain the Haggadah. And Dror's little boy will ask the questions.' She had arranged it all, and to prove it, she laid a sheet of the seating plan on the table.

'Where am I sitting?' Hannah asked.

Joseph scanned the plan. 'Next to David,' he said. He smiled. 'You'll like that, won't you?'

Hannah blushed and her father noticed. He ascribed it to modesty.

He smiled. 'Next to the suit I made him,' he said. The suit would be her neighbour. It did not occur to him that what was inside the suit was anything other than a stranger.

After their supper, Avram left the house. As was their habit, nobody asked him where he was going. Or when he was coming back.

'Be careful,' Miriam said, as she always said in the echo of the closing door.

Avram was going to Begin's hideout. He would have news from the deportation ships. One of their members, Chaim Levy, had managed to board, losing himself among the crowds of immigrants. Under his jacket, he carried his transmitter. Begin was waiting for his report. With him were Gad, Dror and Pinsker, come as much for company as for the bulletin. They needed to share their disquiet. They welcomed *Zeyda*, knowing he had come for the same purpose.

As yet, no report had come through. Begin sat at his desk and the receiver lay in front of him. He held a pencil in his hand and his notebook was at the ready. They sat in silence. After a while, the receiver began to crackle and Chaim's voice came through.

'I hope you can hear me,' he said. 'It's very noisy here and crowded. I'm in the third ship and I gather the other two are bursting at the seams. I've heard rumours that we are not going to Cyprus. God knows where they are going to send us. Some people are watching me. They think I'm mad, talking to myself.'

Here the line cut out, and Begin hastened to write down what they had heard.

'Not good news,' Gad said. 'If it's not Cyprus, it's Europe. Where else could it be?'

'Return journey,' Dror whispered. 'God help them.'

'I want to kill all of them,' Gad burst out. 'The entire British army.'

'You won't have to kill them,' Begin said. 'They'll go. The whole rotten lot of them.' Then, 'What's with the hostages?'

'It's arranged,' Gad said. 'Avram has a plan.'

'I don't want to know about it. I know too much already. When it succeeds, you can tell me. I had a visit from Mrs Weiss,' he went on. 'Ya'akov's mother. She visited the prison and she saw the three of them. She said they were in good spirits and full of hope. They're depending on you, she told me, though I'm sure they didn't say that. It was a mother's plea.' He looked at each one of his followers, his face a pall of pain. 'Those men must not die,' he shouted.

There was silence again. They stared at the receiver, willing it to come alive once more. They just sat there waiting. It was well after midnight. Begin urged his comrades to go home, but no one moved except Gad, who went to make coffee.

'Perhaps he's sleeping,' Pinsker offered.

'Chaim never sleeps on the job,' Begin said. 'Be patient. He'll be in touch.'

And almost immediately the receiver crackled.

'Chaim again,' his voice came through. 'I've been below. There are two large cages. About a thousand men and women lying almost on top of one another. The smell is sickening. Guards around each cage. A zoo smells better. Bad news. We are being taken to Port-de-Bouc near Marseille.' A crackle of 'Amen' ended the transmission.

'About nine days' sail from here,' Gad said. 'And in those conditions. God help them all.'

'I must inform our men in Marseille,' Begin said. 'Now go home. All of you. He's not likely to contact us again for a while. I'll have someone by the receiver. Night and day.'

The men left, separately, and went their own ways. The apartment was in darkness when Avram returned. They knew better than to wait up for him. But Miriam heard his key in the door and she called out to him.

'I'm back,' he said. He went straight to their bedroom and sat on the side of the bed.

'Bad news?' Miriam asked.

He needed to share it with somebody. It lay too heavy on his heart.

'They're not going to Cyprus,' he said. 'They're on their way to Marseille. Cooped up in cages. Many sick. Many injured. What has happened to our world?'

Miriam held him. 'Sooner or later they'll return,' she said. 'And nobody will be here to stop them.'

20

Over the next few days, little information came through Begin's receiver. Chaim, no doubt, was suffering with the others. Lack of sleep, hunger and the permanent stench, had all but stifled his reports. He managed only one piece of interesting news, which was the determination of all the passengers adamantly to refuse to leave the ships. On foreign soil, the British soldiers would have less authority and they prayed for the cooperation of the French. He himself would disembark at Port-de-Bouc. Further developments would be openly reported in the press.

The weary passengers had been at sea for five days and nights. No doubt, most of them were aware that it was the eve of Passover, the first Seder night, and no doubt they would have found some way to record it. Though they would have had no unleavened bread, no bitter herbs, no parsley, no *charoset*, no shankbone of mutton, no wine, in short, none of the symbols of the Passover celebration. All they would have was prayer, prayer that celebrated an exodus, that for them was going the wrong way.

'This *Exodus* business will put a damper on things,' Will said, as he and David were dressing for their evening out. 'Let's hope they don't take it out on us.'

'Well, at least they don't know we're in the army,' David said.

'We're British though, and maybe that's enough,' Will said.

They were nervous, both of them.

'I won't understand a word,' Will said.

'And I'll have to be careful not to explain it to you. It's safer for us both to keep our mouths shut,' David said.

'How do I look?' Will asked. He had on his his black chapel suit and he looked like an undertaker.

'Fine,' David said. 'A bit dark though. Take one of my brighter ties. Liven it up a bit.' He, too, wore his suit, the one Hannah's father had made. Will admired it. 'It looks fine,' he said.

They had been asked for seven o'clock and it was almost time to leave. The streets were practically empty, but they did not hurry. Rather, they dawdled, still nervous.

'I think this is a mistake,' Will said suddenly. 'We don't belong there.'

'We're the strangers at their table,' David said. 'It's part of the tradition. Don't worry. We might even enjoy it. Come on. We don't want to be late.'

And although they were on time, they were the last to arrive. The apartment was crowded. Miriam greeted them and introduced the guests. 'You already know my family, of course,' she said, 'but this is the first time for your friend.'

Will gave a little bow. 'Thank you for having me,' he said, recalling a phrase he had used time and time again at each visit to relatives in the valley.

'This is my brother Joseph,' Hannah said. She gave a quick blushing glance at David. They had not seen each other since the night in the shepherd's hut and she blushed, as he did, at the recollection. Not so much a recollection. More a reliving, since their loving had never been absent from their minds. Then *Zeyda* introduced his friends and their families. Dror, Gad, Pinsker, their wives and children.

The long festive dining table stretched almost the length of the room and adjacent to it was a trestle-table, laid for the little ones. Each seat was backed with a white cushion, and the table was strewn with symbols that Will couldn't fathom, but which brought a lump of nostalgia to David's throat.

'Shall we begin?' *Zeyda* said when they were all settled.

Miriam, who was seated at the end of the table, lit the two candles and made a blessing. At every stage of the service, Avram turned to the 'strangers' at his sides and explained the meaning of each symbol of the feast and how each token of sweetness is

124

tempered by bitter herbs to depict the sufferings that were the prelude to freedom. Then Dani, Dror's youngest son, was called upon to ask the four questions. All over the world, little Jewish boys were asking the same questions. Most of them would not understand the Hebrew words of the enquiries, but certainly, whether they understood them or not, they would not listen to the answers. They were waiting to hide the *afikoman*, that middle piece of matzoh without which the service could not continue and for which presents had to be given on its discovery.

Will was feeling more at ease. As long as he was not called upon to participate, he was comfortable. David, on the other hand, was troubled. His thoughts were at home, and at his mother's table, and he had difficulty in sealing his lips from the prayers and blessings that he recalled by heart. Occasionally he wondered what all these strangers were doing at his table. And as he looked at Hannah, reliving their union, he was acutely aware of his duplicity. He was tempted to stand up there and then and declare himself so that he would be a stranger no longer. But one glance at Will, Will the innocent, stifled his tongue.

The service continued with the allusion to four types of children, the wise one, the wicked one, the simple one and the one who does not know how to ask. Then came the story of Pharaoh's cruelty in Egypt and the ten plagues that God visited upon them. The children around the table were suddenly aroused. Here at last was something they could do. They could dip their fingers into their wine glasses, and spill ten drops on to the table, for the pleasure in their wine must be diminished by the memory of the suffering of the Egyptian people. Drop after drop recalled the plagues, those of blood, frogs, lice, flies, cattle disease, boils, hail, locusts, darkness and the final savagery, the slaying of the firstborn. The children shivered with the horror of it all and then licked their wine-soaked fingers to comfort themselves.

A cheerful song followed the plagues. Its tune was familiar to Jews everywhere, but David dared not join in the singing. With Will, he availed himself to be taught the chorus, '*Dayenu*', it is enough, and this he sang with all his heart. He knew that the song was a prelude to the meal and he remembered how his grandmother had then stood and recited that part of the Haggadah which was the heart of the thanksgiving. 'In every generation, each one of us must regard himself as if he himself had gone forth from Egypt.' Then she had sat down and there was a silence. As a young boy he knew that what she had said was very important but he didn't know why. But now he knew its meaning and with a shocking understanding. He thought of the *Exodus* immigrants who were being sent back to where they came from and for the first time he fully understood his grandmother's admonition.

The meal was about to be served. Miriam and Hannah moved to the kitchen, while the men at the table left to wash their hands. This was the cue for the children. They removed the *afikoman* from the Seder plate. They had already decided on its hiding place. Behind the picture on the sideboard. They rushed back to their seats as the men returned.

'What's all this giggling?' *Zeyda* asked, and he ruffled the children's hair as he laughed with them. He seemed in a good mood. He sat and put his arms around the two strangers.

'How do you like our Seder?' he asked.

'I'm enjoying it very much,' Will said. They were the first real words he had spoken and he meant every one of them. Family was important to him and he saw the evening as a rehearsal for his homecoming. Within the bosom of his family he could become himself again as he had been before the Uri days, before that painful disturbance of his nature. It would be as it was before. It had to be.

David too expressed his delight in the evening. 'We are honoured to be your "strangers",' he said.

'It is our custom,' *Zeyda* told him. He filled their glasses. 'Let us toast our brothers and sisters on the *Exodus*,' he said, whatever his strangers might be thinking. But they too raised their glasses.

'May God look after them,' David could not help saying.

'Amen to that,' the men said and they drank.

The first course of the meal was a hard-boiled egg, which was to be dipped in salt water.

'Again the paradox,' *Zeyda* explained. 'The egg is the symbol of spring, growth and joy, and the salt is to curb our enthusiasm.' He laughed.

Hannah had rarely seen her father in such a joyous mood, and she was hopeful that one day he would welcome David into the family.

The egg was followed by chicken soup and matzoh balls. Exactly the same menu as David remembered as a child. Then came the chicken itself, and David knew that fruit compote would follow. Which it did, as it possibly did at every Seder table in the world.

The children were restless, and their mothers urged the concluding grace.

'Where's the *afikoman*?' *Zeyda* shouted with feigned anxiety. 'It has disappeared and we can't go on without it. Everybody look for it,' he appealed. 'A present for whoever finds it.' The children rushed to the sideboard. They were too tired to pretend to be looking. They wanted the reward so they could go home to bed.

'We've found it,' they shouted together and they put it back in its original place, and hung around *Zeyda* for the pay-off. He handed out small packages to all of them. They tore them open. Inside each was an embroidered *yarmulka*. They tried to hide their disappointment, and again *Zeyda* laughed.

'Oh, I've forgotten these,' he said, and he took from his pocket a generous handful of pounds, and divided the coins between them. That was more like it, the children thought, and they were ready to go home. Their mothers agreed not to wait for the final grace and they made to take their leave.

With the women and the children bundled away, only the men were left at the table, together with *Zeyda*'s family. It fell to

Joseph to read the grace after the meal. The table felt suddenly like a day-to-day family table. Dror, Gad and Pinsker were the extended family, and had been so for many years. They hoped that Joseph would not dawdle on the grace. They had work to do, a job they did not relish, but which they knew had to be done.

Joseph began the grace with a psalm. A song of Ascents. There followed a thanksgiving for food and deliverance. A silver wine goblet was the centre piece of the table, and into this glass Joseph poured wine. Then Hannah rose and opened the apartment door as Joseph repeated the promises from God. An exodus from Egypt, a deliverance from bondage. And above all, to be His chosen.

It was then *Zeyda*'s turn to explain Hannah's move to the strangers. 'The goblet that my son has filled is Elijah's cup. God has promised to send the prophet when the time of redemption is come.'

Hannah returned to the table and the door was left open.

'Let every man sit under his vine and under his fig tree, and none shall make them afraid,' Joseph said. It was a call for peace, and a fitting end to the thanksgiving.

The men rose and drained what was left of their wine.

'We must go,' David said. 'It has been wonderful.'

'A little schnapps to see you on your way,' *Zeyda* said. He had warmed towards his strangers and, like his comrades, he did not relish what he had to do. Moreover he hoped the brandy would numb the pain they were about to undergo. And God forbid, he prayed, much worse than mere pain.

At first David and Will refused. 'We've drunk enough,' they said, but they were persuaded when the other men offered to join them.

'We'll walk with you a little,' *Zeyda* said. His voice broke and he covered it with a laugh. 'A little fresh air will do me good. Come,' he said to his friends.

And so, after David and Will's farewells and thanks, the men escorted the strangers out of the open door and into the street below. Then subtly, and with minimum transition they went into formation. It was a choreographed movement, repeatedly rehearsed, with two of their comrades standing in for the kidnapped. As they walked, *Zeyda* slipped in between David and Will, while Dror and Gad fell into step beside each man. The quartet intact, Pinsker dawdled on ahead. A few yards away, a car was parked, the sole car on the street. *Zeyda* was laughing and joking with his captives. His laughter was loud, hinting at desperation. 'The fresh air is good,' he said.

When they reached the car, the quartet slowed their pace. Will and David wondered why. And wondered further when they felt a gun in their backs. And then stopped wondering as, in a terrifying flash, they understood everything. They had been duped by warmth and hospitality. And though they knew, they still asked. 'What are you doing?'

There was no answer. Pinsker opened the back passenger door and David was shoved inside. Then *Zeyda* hauled Will after him. He sat between them, fighting his regrets. Gad and Dror tied the men's wrists and placed a bag over their heads. Then they jumped into the front seat.

'Let's go,' Gad shouted.

Pinsker drove.

'My friend's Jewish.' A muffled cry came from inside Will's bag.

'It's not true,' David shouted. Now, more than at any other time, was no time to declare himself. He would not risk leaving his friend.

Pinsker was laughing, recalling his failure with Mr Collins.

'All of a sudden everybody's Jewish,' he said.

'What are you going to do with us?' Will's voice trembled.

'You're hostages.' *Zeyda* spelt it out for them. He was glad they could not see his face. 'They've sentenced our men to death. The three of them.' He could say no more.

So Gad finished his sentence. 'If they hang,' he said coldly, 'if your people hang them, we will do the same to you.'

'Gallows for gallows,' Dror said.

Zeyda felt the two men shiver on either side of him, and he prayed that they would be spared.

The hooded men had no idea where they were. David tried to tot up the distance they were travelling. There were three stops, presumably at traffic lights and many twists and turns in the road. Then, after about half an hour's drive, the car came to a stop and he heard the ignition silenced.

'Where are we?' he dared to ask.

'It doesn't matter to you,' Gad said. 'We've arrived.' They sat in silence for a while.

Then Dror alighted and shone his torch into the darkness. Two sentries were waiting there, as had been arranged, and in the light of the torch they hurried towards the car. They dragged David and Will outside.

'Over to you,' David heard Dror say, and then the car started again and he heard it purr down the road and out of earshot. He felt someone take his arm and he was pulled forward. Will likewise. He prayed for the hood to be removed. He wanted to see his friend again.

The Irgun had chosen the site of their hiding place in an abandoned diamond factory on the outskirts of Natanya. Over the past weeks, in anticipation of a kidnapping, they had cleared out a cellar in the factory. It was windowless and entirely underground. On its roof was a ragged lawn sprouting a few rusting bushes. A trapdoor, camouflaged with ivy, led to the cellar.

David and Will were pushed inside. The binding was loosened from their wrists and the hoods taken from their heads. They blinked in the torchlight, then fell into each other's arms. For a moment the relief of their togetherness offset the fear of their dire situation. Both managed a smile. They looked round at their new accommodation, while the sentries stood at the door directing their torches. The chamber was clean and measured about three square metres. Two mattresses lay on the floor covered with blankets. In one corner was a large canvas bucket

130

and in another, two canisters of oxygen with nose-masks hanging on the bottle necks.

'What are those for?' David whispered and he wondered why he was whispering. He seemed to be colluding in their conspiracy.

'You'll find out soon enough,' one of the sentries said.

'What's it for?' Will shouted.

'There's no point in shouting. No one outside can hear you.'

There was a low table between the two mattresses, presumably for dining, and on it were two books. David picked them up. One was a Bible, which he welcomed. The other, the Irgun manual, which he thought he would find faintly resistible.

Suddenly the torchlights dimmed.

'We're leaving you now,' a voice said. 'You must be tired. You've had a long day.'

It was said kindly, and somehow David and Will felt less threatened. But only for a few seconds, for when the sentries withdrew the cellar was in total darkness, and the dire implications of the kidnapping stunned them into silence.

'I'm frightened,' Will said after a while. 'What's to become of us?'

'They'll never do it,' David said.

'Who do you mean by "they"?'

'Both of them. The British and the Irgun.' He tried to inject some confidence in his voice, though in his heart he was as frightened as Will. He groped for Will's hand and together they felt their way towards the mattresses. The cognac had begun to make him sleepy and he yearned for an escape from their terrible reality.

'Let's sleep,' he said. There was no point in suggesting that things would look better in the morning, for there would be no light to comfort them.

'We'll sleep,' he said, 'and when it seems like morning, we can start screaming.'

21

It was a silent drive back to Tel Aviv. The men did not rejoice in their kidnapping success. None of them had relished the task. Halfway home, they stopped at a telephone kiosk so that Gad could inform Begin of the event. From the car windows, the men watched Gad's face as he talked. It was solemn. At one point he covered his eyes as if he did not want to see what he was saying. Shortly after, he returned to the car.

'I gave him the names,' he whispered. 'And that they worked in a bank. It will go out on the radio in the morning.'

That would make it real, what they had done, the men thought, and it disturbed each one of them. No word passed between them. When they reached Tel Aviv they left the car separately and in different parts of the city.

Pinsker drove alone. He would have liked to drive around for a while and try, though in vain, to lose himself in a town he knew so well, but he dared not risk drawing attention to himself, so immediately after he had dropped his last passenger, he parked the car and slid into the alleyway that led to his home. He hoped that Sarah was not waiting up for him. Like all Irgun wives, she would be in bed waiting for the sound of his key in the lock, and then she would allow herself to go to sleep. He would creep into the living room, and sit for a while, trying not to think of the unthinkable consequences of what he had done.

Dror took the long route to his apartment. He was in no hurry to face the familiarity of his home, its furniture, its knick-knacks, its pictures, its cushions that Aviva had embroidered with such skill, the litter of children's toys, all those tokens of a family life, which passed for real. But tonight there was a different reality, one that would be confirmed in the morning broadcast. Only a while ago, though it seemed like years, Dani, his youngest, had asked the first question. 'Why is this night different from all other nights?' In the morning the radio would answer his question, and he would never want to ask it again.

Gad, on the other hand, took the short cut. He was anxious to get home. His new reality was unbearable and he needed to get back to the old. To his familiar armchair and desk, his bookshelves, his kitchen table. Every known object that would annul the past few hours and turn it into an illusion. As he opened his door, he called his wife's name. Dahlia would hear him and she'd come into the kitchen and they'd talk about the Seder and though he would tell her nothing, she would bring him comfort.

Zeyda on the other hand, didn't want to go home at all. For in truth, he was frightened of Hannah. Over the past few weeks he had watched her and had noted her happiness with pleasure. He did not know its cause and it didn't concern him – until Joseph's teasing at her table placing. 'Next to David,' he had said. 'You'd like that, wouldn't you?' He had watched them both at the Seder, his daughter and the stranger, and he had caught the odd loving glance between them. He didn't know that those few signals were enough to justify his fears, but there was something between them. He felt it in his bones. So he was afraid to go home. Hannah and Joseph would be in bed and Miriam would pretend to be sleeping. She would ask no questions but the morning would come and with it, the announcement from the illegal Irgun radio which was never turned off. Its dire bulletin would resound from the kitchen. Then he would pretend to be asleep until Hannah and Joseph had gone off to work and he could postpone for a little while longer the confrontation that he so feared. He slipped quietly into bed beside Miriam, feigning not to disturb her pretend sleep. He closed his eyes, hoping to induce some form of slumber, some path to oblivion. But vague images blocked such a path and rattled him. He saw his strangers sleepless in their cell, perhaps reaching out to each other in the dark and in silence, their fears beyond words. And their hopes likewise. He saw the oxygen bottles, and he caught his own

133

stunted breath. He saw the rope at the ready, in the boot of Pinsker's car, and he stifled a scream. As it grew light, he felt Miriam leaving the bed and, as the images faded, he eased himself into sleep. A merciful and very deep sleep which would have taken a thunderclap to disturb. And when it came, at seven o'clock in the morning, he knew that sleep would tease and dodge him for the rest of his life. He heard Hannah screaming, then the rip of the bedcovers. He was relieved that he was still clothed. Nakedness would have underlined his shame.

'Where is he?' Hannah was shouting. 'Where have you hidden him?'

Then he knew that she loved the stranger and that she would never forgive him.

'It's the cause,' he managed to say, as if that explained everything.

'Bugger the cause,' Hannah shouted. 'Tell me where he is?'

Wearily *Zeyda* got out of bed. 'I shall never tell you,' he said as gently as he could. 'Our men in Acre must not hang. It's the cause,' he said again. 'Please try to understand. Sometimes we have to do things we prefer not to do. But we must. It's for *your* future too, Hannale.'

He made for the door, but Hannah blocked it. 'Please, please,' she begged like a child.

He could have wept for her and he could find no words. So he shook his head and gently urged her aside.

'Papa,' she said to his back. 'I love him.'

He dared not turn to look at her. 'It's the cause,' he said to himself, and in its name he had lost his daughter. 'It's the cause,' he shouted, and he left the house swiftly like a thief who had stolen his family.

He made straight for Begin's hideout. His leader would have returned to Tel Aviv. There might be more news from the *Exodus*, and he would wait there to hear the reaction of the Mandate authorities. As he expected, Pinsker, Dror and Gad were already there, all of them bereft of sleep.

'I didn't hear the announcement,' *Zeyda* confessed. 'I was avoiding the family.'

'So were we all,' the other men said.

'Then listen,' Begin told them, and he switched on a tape.

'This is Radio Irgun,' they heard. It was Shimshon's voice, that cultivated almost BBC accent which was such an irritant to the British. It was a kind of mockery.

'Two British citizens were taken hostage last night,' he said. 'Their names are given as David Millar and William Griffiths. They are bank employees. The Irgun warn the British Mandate that if their men in Acre prison are hanged, the same fate will meet the two hostages. Gallows for gallows.'

'That's clear enough,' Gad declared.

'We have to wait for their response,' Begin said.

'Is there any more news from Chaim?' Pinsker asked.

'Nothing. They're still en route. They should reach the port in a few days. Then there'll be news in plenty,' Begin said.

'As to the hostages, it may be some time before we get the Mandate's reaction. We must just wait and see.'

22

The Authorities were in a quandary. The Irgun broadcast, though half expected, had shaken them. They had been called to General Barker's office. All the senior officers of the Organisation were present, together with Captain Coleman and those from Intelligence.

'Those bloody stinking Jews,' was General Barker's opening gambit. Having defined the premise of the talks, further discussion would relate to that context.

'They've got it wrong,' he said, 'and we have to decide whether to come clean or not to come clean. Millar and Griffiths are not civilians. They are honourable sergeants in the British army. They are Intelligence, with the bank as their cover.' He announced these facts as if he were divulging highly secret information, though everybody in the room was aware of them. He was stalling. He clearly did not know which way to turn. He was a man loath to ask for anybody else's opinion but in this case, he would have welcomed some suggestions even if he chose to ignore them. If any suggestion appealed to him, he would turn it around as if he himself had thought of it.

'We have a number of choices,' he said. 'We can keep quiet, and let them believe the facts they have broadcast. Or we tell the truth. There is also another angle,' he said. 'I gather this Millar fellow is a Jew-boy. How he was sent to Palestine in the first place is beyond my understanding. He must have slipped through the net. We could come out with the fact that Millar is a Jew. That might stop them in their tracks. As you see, there are a number of options. Have any of you got anything to say? Captain Coleman,' he shouted. 'You know the men well. What's your opinion?' As he spoke, he picked up his pen and started to doodle as if Captain Coleman's opinion was of no consequence. But he listened carefully.

Captain Coleman was glad to be called upon. One didn't as a rule volunteer an opinion to General Barker.

'First of all,' Coleman said, 'we're not supposed to know Millar is Jewish. We never *were* supposed to know. I think to expose Millar as a Jew, would be a very dangerous move. It would put Will – William Griffiths – in deep jeopardy.' He thought of that young Welshman who had yet to acknowledge what he truly was, that anxious innocent boy who had stirred his heart. 'It's out of the question,' he almost shouted. 'It would be like hanging him ourselves.'

'I agree,' another officer felt free to voice an opinion. 'We would be betraying Griffiths.'

'Yet we can't deny that Millar is a bargaining chip,' General Barker intervened. 'They would let him go perhaps. Then we'd only lose one.'

'Millar's no bargain,' Captain Coleman insisted. 'The Irgun would turn against him, against the idea of a Jew working in Intelligence. He'll go the same way as Will.'

'I agree with the Captain,' another officer offered. And a mumble of 'So do I,' came from the body of the hall.

It was clear that General Barker was out-voted, and he had to accept the men's judgement. But in truth it didn't really matter to him one way or the other. He was determined to hang the three men in Acre prison. Of that there was no question. He'd be damned if he'd be blackmailed by the Irgun and if it cost the lives of two of his men, especially if one of them was a kike, that was part of the deal. Whatever their religion. But there still remained the question of rank. 'I firmly believe,' he said, 'that we should squash this idea of two British civilians. I want to honour them, and to declare that they are two loyal sergeants in the occupation army, who are working in Intelligence. I know that that bastard Begin will gloat over his scoop but we owe it to our captured men to tell the truth about their honourable calling.' He listened to the garbage that spilled from his lips. He did not wonder what the men looked like. They would remain faceless to him, and unknown and unrecognised, they would have to pay the price. Yet a search must be set in motion. A thoroughly organised search throughout the country. He knew it was futile. The men could be anywhere. But the authorities had to be seen to be caring of their men. 'I shall draft a bulletin for broadcast,' he said. 'I will appeal for information, though I expect little response.'

'Not everyone is on Irgun's side,' an officer ventured. 'The Haganah must surely disapprove. They might well be helpful.'

'I thought of that,' General Barker said, 'and I already had it in mind to make an approach.'

He hadn't, of course, but it was a good idea. 'Now get going,' he said. 'Contact the regions. Every single man you can spare. Off with the lot of you.'

The men shuffled out in silence, keeping their thoughts to themselves. But all of them knew that, without the cooperation of the Haganah, the search was pointless.

Zeyda, fearful of going home, was still holed up with Begin and the others, in the hideout, and it was there that the kidnappers listened to the official broadcast from Mandate headquarters. They had expected a total denial of the Irgun bulletin, so they were astonished when the announcer coldly confirmed the hostage taking. And not only that. The Irgun details were wrong and the bulletin set out to correct them. The men could hardly believe their ears.

'The Irgun have reported the kidnapping of two hostages,' the announcer said. 'The authorities name these men as David Millar and William Griffiths. Both men are sergeants serving in His Majesty's forces. They were on secondment to Intelligence at the time of their capture. A curfew has been imposed throughout the country and a thorough search for the men is under way.'

No mention was made of the gallows threat. They would not reveal it, in the hope that the sergeants would be found.

Begin actually jumped for joy. 'Sergeants,' he yelled. 'And two of them. What a bargain. Now they daren't hang our men.'

But Gad thought his leader was being naïve. 'I wouldn't count on it,' he said. 'Hanging the hostages is a last resort, and I hope to God we're not driven to it.'

'Amen to that,' *Zeyda* said and he meant it. His thoughts were now totally confused. The news bulletin had carried a ray of hope, that Hannah, on hearing it, would abruptly fall out of love with such an impostor, with a spy who had patently used her for information. And he wondered with fear what Hannah might have told him. But she was a loyal girl and he doubted whether, even in the throes of what she considered to be love, her tongue had loosened. He was hopeful and now he was less afraid of going home.

He met her at the apartment door. She was going out.

'Where are you off to?' he asked.

'I'm going to the Haganah,' she shouted at him. 'I'm going to help them find him.'

'Did you hear the wireless? The government broadcast.'

'Yes. I heard it,' she said.

'The men were sergeants. In the British army. Our enemies. How can you say you love such a man?'

Easy, she thought. A mere flashback to the shepherd's hut was enough to guarantee her love for David. His rank and his Intelligence calling were irrelevant. The latter entailed subterfuge, and that she understood.

'It makes no difference,' she told her father. 'We shall find them, and the Irgun will know once and for all that their way, *your* way,' she insisted, 'will never work. More than that, your way is criminal.'

She pushed past him and ran into the street. He watched her as she turned the corner, and he feared that he might have lost her.

23

The Haganah movement was led by three men who, in the future, would play a major part in the post-Mandate government of Israel. David Ben-Gurion would become its first Prime Minister, Moshe Dayan, a hero of the Six Day War, and Yitzhak Rabin, a great peace-seeking leader who would not be allowed to die in his bed. According to Mandate rules, the Haganah resistance was as illegal as the Irgun. But unlike the Irgun, they were willing at times to negotiate. Their activities were confined to sabotage and the rescue of illegal immigrants. Where possible, they avoided violence and they regarded the kidnapping of the sergeants as immoral as it was unnecessary.

'It's sheer madness,' Ben-Gurion said. 'It will wipe out all sympathy for our resistance. We have to find them.'

Dayan suggested that the search should be divided regionally, so that the whole country could be covered. 'We won't want for volunteers,' he said.

And so their search began.

Hannah found Joseph at the Haganah centre. Like Hannah, he had dodged the curfew, and was waiting with many others for his search orders. Hannah sat by his side.

'How do you feel?' he asked.

'I love him,' Hannah said. 'Nothing has made any difference.'

She was silent for a while, but Joseph guessed what was going through her mind.

'Don't even think about it,' he whispered. 'It would destroy our whole family.'

But Hannah had been tempted. She held information for which the authorities would have been deeply grateful. She could have told them at what time the men had been taken and from what precise point. She could have told them, name by name, of their kidnappers. They would have been arrested, and the army, with their 'usual practices', would have tortured them into revealing the hostages' whereabouts. It would have been so easy. But Joseph was right. It would destroy the family. So she sat quietly beside him and waited for her orders.

The army search concentrated on the Mea Shearim quarter of Jerusalem. It was the residential and commercial area of very orthodox Jews and was known to harbour many in sympathy with the Irgun. Indeed, in the past, Irgun fighters had been found there, in hiding from the authorities. The area was cordoned-off with barbed wire, and every single dwelling was thoroughly searched. Most of the residents congregated in the streets. Their regular mode of dress paid no respect to the climate for, though the sun was beating down, the men wore their long black kaftans and their broad black hats, some even with sable trimmings. They fingered their beards while their sons tugged at their ringlets and joined them in prayer.

The search lasted the whole day and the sun had begun to set when the last of the soldiers left the quarter. The residents returned to their houses to find them ransacked. Failure had nurtured rage. Furniture was overturned, drawers littered the floor with their contents scattered. Crockery had been wantonly smashed. Even the floorboards had been lifted. Each house was strewn with the debris of British fury. The army had had high hopes of Mea Shearim and their frustration was boundless.

Every day and night throughout the following week, the country was scoured. Tiberias, Jaffa, Jerusalem, Tel Aviv, even Acre itself. Every kibbutz, every moshav, known to be Irgun-prone, each one was searched, and the soldiers tried to ignore the grins of satisfaction in their wake. The Haganah search was as thorough, and often they worked together with the soldiers. And all to no avail. The Irgun radio issued no more bulletins. Instead they broadcast music but as an introduction to each work, the announcer gave its title. 'Gallows for Gallows.'

Despite the curfew, there was still café life during the few curfew-free hours of the day. Talk across the tables was concerned almost exclusively with the hostages. The general opinion was that the three prisoners in Acre should appeal, thus saving themselves from the rope and the British from losing face. Then the hostages could be freed. On the whole there was little sympathy for the Irgun and their thoughts turned to the parents of the two hostages whose days and nights must be being spent in suspended breath, and hope.

Because of the search, Hannah, like Joseph, had willingly been given leave from their teaching posts. Both of them searched all day and sometimes most of the night. Hannah never went home. She did not want to face her father. She spent her sleeping hours at the Haganah centre. Occasionally she would take a break and go to their café and sit at their empty table. She would think of the shepherd's hut, and wait for him.

At times, she lost all hope. Again she was tempted to go to the authorities and again she shrank at the unspeakable consequences. Yet if the worst were to happen, she would never again speak to her father. And Joseph too would have difficulty looking him in the eye. The hostages had to be found, if only to keep her family together.

A pair of soldiers passed by her table. They smiled at her, and she gladly returned their greeting. They must have read her thoughts.

'We'll find them. Don't worry,' one of them said.

'I wish you luck,' Hannah said. 'We all do.'

24

David was the first to wake. It took him a little while to fathom where he was, and the 'where' spelt out the 'why' and he shut his eyes again. It was dark anyway. He felt the face of his watch as if it were Braille, so he had no idea of the time. But he was careful to wind it, as he did every morning. Even if he couldn't see the time, he knew that it was reliably passing on his wrist.

A sudden shaft of light pierced the trapdoor and he took advantage of it to look at his watch. Seven o'clock. It must be morning. It was the moment to start screaming.

The swift opening of the door had woken Will.

'Hello?' he shouted. Then in full recollection of where he was, he whispered, 'David?'

'I'm here,' David said.

The door closed.

'I've brought your breakfast,' the guard said. 'And two torches. Use them sparingly,' he said, 'and make the batteries last.'

'For how long?' Will asked, then regretted his question.

'It's up to the others,' the man said.

But when David shone his torch, they saw that the carrier was a young man, no more than twenty or so.

'What's your name?' he asked.

The man did not answer. He set the tray down on the table and, without looking at either of them, he made a quick getaway.

'I'm hungry,' Will said. It was normal to be hungry first thing in the morning, whatever one's circumstances.

They looked at the tray. Two cups, a thermos of sweet coffee, two rolls, two hard-boiled eggs and two tomatoes. It was adequate. David noted that it required no cutlery.

'First we'll eat,' David said, shining his torch over the tray.

143

'Then we'll decide what to do.' He spoke as if they had choices. It was too soon to lose hope.

Each man made the meal last as long as possible. It was an event, and they feared there would be few of them during the long day. Yet fearing the worst, they dreaded any event at all.

When they had finished eating, Will tidied up the tray. It's what he would have done at home.

'Have you a pen or pencil?' David asked.

There was a pencil permanently placed in the breast-pocket of Will's chapel suit. It was part and parcel of the style, and had never been used. Will looked at it, relieved that the lead was not broken. He handed it over.

David picked up the Irgun manual, and drew a short vertical line on the first blank page. Such a boring book had to serve some purpose. It would serve as a prison wall on which he could chalk up the number of days of their confinement.

'Day number one,' David said.

Will shivered. He had a sudden thought of Uri. Had he chalked up his days on the wall of his cell? There must have been over thirty of them in all. And as he was chalking up his last day, did he start singing?

'That's what Uri would have done,' Will said. It was a relief to give sound to his name.

David kept his torch on the book. He did not want to look at Will's face. He knew it was ticking with fear.

'We'll get out of here, Will,' he said. 'I'm sure the whole army is looking. They'll find us.'

'How?' Will almost shouted. 'We don't even know ourselves where we are.'

'We were going north. About thirty miles. We can't be far from Natanya,' David said.

Will lay down on his mattress.

'Don't do that,' David said. 'We must exercise. Otherwise we'll just get depressed.'

'I'm depressed already,' Will said. 'I'm going to start

screaming.' And before David could stop him, Will started. It was not a sustained scream. It paused, rhythmically, for breath. It was urgent, piercing, a hyena's mating cry, a cry that would have shattered eardrums.

David put his hands over his ears until his friend had disgorged his fear and frustrations.

'We can't be heard,' he said. 'They've made sure of that. This is some kind of cellar. Or a bunker. Let's not waste our energy.'

'But we've got to do something,' Will said. 'We can't just sit here and stare at each other.'

Both men wanted to talk. And about the same subject. Both were afraid. Yet there might be some relief in dealing with their confinement, airing their hopes, and their fears.

It was Will who first broke the ice. He approached the matter obliquely. It was too soon for direct surmise.

'What d'you think the army are doing?' he asked.

'Looking for us,' David said. 'I'm certain of that. And searching high and low. The Haganah too. They'd certainly help.' He thought of Hannah. She would have recruited the whole movement to find them. She would recall the shepherd's hut, as he himself did at every waking moment. That memory sustained him and it saddened him that Will had no similar thought that made survival imperative.

'How long will the army continue their search, d'you think?' Will was pessimistic. He had little respect for the army and its indifference to suffering. Its treatment of Uri had been a mockery of human rights. He did not expect military compassion.

'They'll give up looking,' he said. 'We're not worth all that much to them.'

'They'll look until they find us,' David said. 'They can't be seen to fail.' He was irritated by Will's despondency. There must never come a time to lose hope. 'We've been here barely a day,' he said. 'You can't expect miracles.' He put his arm round Will's shoulder. 'Cheer up. In time we'll be free. You've got to keep thinking that.'

'Your Hannah knows that it was her father who kidnapped us. All she has to do is to go to Headquarters. They'd arrest him. And the others. And get the truth out of him.'

'It's her father,' David shouted. 'Would you betray *your* father? In any circumstances? She'll beg him, plead with him. Tell him she'll never speak to him again. But she'll not betray him. Never.'

'Did you suspect nothing?' Will asked. He was calmer now. 'You saw the family often enough.'

'As far as I knew,' David said, 'Hannah is a teacher. So is her brother. And her father is a tailor.' He would not mention his sighting of Hannah on the Jaffa seashore. Nor of her father at Uri's mother's apartment. Will would have been appalled at his friend's lapse of duty. And further appalled at the dire consequences his lapse had landed them in. So David held his tongue. But he knew in his heart that, in view of their present predicament, he had betrayed his friend.

'You have to tell them you're Jewish,' Will said suddenly. 'You've got proof. And you know lots of Hebrew. You knew that Seder service by heart. They'll let you go.'

'I'll never tell them that. Never!' David shouted. 'And you must promise me never to mention it. Ever. Do you promise?' He gripped Will's shoulder. To tell them about his mother would have been the most monstrous betrayal of all. 'Do you promise?' he asked again.

Will nodded. 'If that's how you want it,' he said.

A sudden light pierced the trapdoor, and the guard, led by his torch, entered the chamber.

'Is there any news?' Will asked. He was fearful of the answer.

'I've come to see how you are doing,' the guard said. 'Is there anything I can bring you?'

'Some paper,' David said. 'And pens. We want to write home.'

'Of course,' the guard said. 'But who will post your letters?'

'It will give us something to do,' David said. 'And who knows? We may post them ourselves when this is all over.'

'Is there any news?' Will asked again. 'Tell us. Please.'

'There's nothing to tell,' the guard said, and he left quickly, blocking the slither of light from the trapdoor.

'We'll keep a diary,' David said. 'Both of us.'

'But there's nothing to write about,' Will said. 'We don't do anything. Nothing happens. What can we write?'

'We'll write about what we're thinking. Our true and private thoughts. It will help us,' David said.

Will smiled for the first time. 'D'you promise not to read mine, if I promise not to read yours?'

'It's a promise,' David said.

Shortly the guard returned with the required pads of paper and two pencils. 'Give my regards to your parents,' he said. He spoke kindly and without a trace of mockery.

As soon as he had gone, both torches were flicked on and the men began to write. The cellar was silent and the pencils made no sound on the paper. But the words they wrote roared with passion and rage.

'I think continually of Hannah,' David wrote. 'She is looking for us. And she will find us. I'm sure.' He paused and read what he had written. Seeing her name, each letter spelt out on the paper, made her real, and he was comforted. He rested his pencil and doused his torch. In Will's light, he watched his friend as he wrote. His tongue was curled over his upper lip, like a child trying out his letters. His jaw jutted and his cheeks were clenched as if what he wrote disturbed him.

'I must try not to quarrel with David,' Will had written. 'I will never find a better friend, but sometimes I want to hit him. He is so stubborn. I fear for us both.' Then he too doused his torch and rested. Tomorrow he would write to his parents and try to tell them about Uri. Just Uri's story. No more than that. It would be a beginning.

25

All the English papers led with the hostage story. Opinion was undivided. There was a candle-lit vigil outside the Foreign Office. 'Free the sergeants', the crowds shouted, or 'British out of Palestine', to vary their protest. Men, women and even children voiced their concern. And of course, the remnants of the banned British Union of Fascists, always eager to find a respectable cloak for their innate anti-Semitism. But most of their gangs were painting walls with 'Down with the Jews', or throwing bricks through Jewish shop windows in the East End. There were marches to Trafalgar Square, with the same bannered legends as there were in the streets of Tel Aviv and Haifa. Everybody, for whatever reason or motive, wanted the British out of Palestine and the sergeants freed. But a pair of stricken parents wanted it more than their own lives.

Mr and Mrs Griffiths travelled by bus from the Welsh valleys, and Mr and Mrs Millar took the train from Bristol. All were heading for London. They had an appointment with Richard Crossman MP, who had raised the subject of the hostages in a crowded House of Commons.

'We have never ceased to be appalled by the activities of the Irgun terrorists in Palestine,' he said. 'We cannot tolerate this latest act. The taking of hostages is a crime against humanity. It is the very worst form of blackmail.'

Crossman was personally concerned with the situation and he had invited the sergeants' parents to call on him. He knew that there was little he could do for them, except to show them his support.

Throughout the long journey from the valleys, Mr and Mrs Griffiths exchanged few words. Words of hope were as inexpressible as words of despair. Mrs Griffiths had prepared cheese

148

and tomato sandwiches for the journey, together with a thermos of tea. But neither of them had any appetite. 'On the way home perhaps,' were some of the few words that Will's father could cope with.

The Millars on the other hand, were in deep debate. They faced a dilemma. By Judaic law, their son was Jewish. He had never hidden that fact, but at the same time he didn't flaunt it. It was more than possible that the Mandate authorities did not know of his origins. Was now the time to inform them? Both parents knew that such information might well save their son's life, but both knew too that it would put his co-hostage in even greater jeopardy. And although, throughout the journey, they discussed the pros and cons of such a revelation, they had each decided from the very beginning that, whatever the cost, they would reveal the truth that might save their son.

On arrival at the House of Commons they were ushered into a waiting chamber. Mr and Mrs Griffiths were already seated there and their presence threw the Millars into some confusion. They had not expected to share the audience. Yet they greeted each other with affection. The mothers hugged each other and the fathers clasped with both hands.

'We mustn't lose hope,' Mrs Griffiths said, words she could not release on the bus, but which now comforted her. And her husband echoed them with the same relief. After that exchange there were no further words. For such an exchange, one word was far too many and a thousand not enough. So they waited, staring at the floor. In a while, the door opened and a uniformed attendant stood there.

'Mr Crossman will see you now,' he said.

Still they sat there, all four of them, unwilling to face what might be a dire verdict.

'He's ready for you,' the attendant said. 'I'll show you the way.'

Then they had to rise, and they followed him numbly as if to the scaffold.

'I'm so glad you could come,' Mr Crossman said, as they were led into his room.

If he was glad, the parents thought, then he must have good news to impart, and they eagerly took the seats he offered them. There was a tea-tray on the table and the pot was covered with a hand-knitted pleated cosy.

'Shall I be mother?' Mr Crossman asked with a smile, a smile that froze suddenly when he realised that in this company 'mother' was a loaded word. He started to pour. 'Milk?' he asked. 'Sugar?' Then he passed the plate of biscuits around. Anything to delay the news that there *was* no news and that there was very little he could do for them. They waited politely until he had completed his ploys of adjournment.

'Is there any news?' It was Mrs Griffiths who reminded Mr Crossman why they were there.

'No developments, I'm afraid,' he said. 'Though we're in touch all the time.' He listened to the empty echo of his words. 'We must not give up hope,' he added lamely.

The parents stared at each other in disbelief. Had they come all this way to be told absolutely nothing, but to hang on to their hopes?

'What exactly are you doing?' Mrs Griffiths dared to ask.

'Behave yourself,' Mr Griffiths whispered in his wife's ear.

'Yes. What exactly?' Mrs Millar took her side. 'Are they going to hang those three prisoners?'

It was a supremely brave question. And a direct one, and the others marvelled at her courage. For that was the nub of the matter, and until Mrs Millar had spoken, it was unmentionable.

'The UN investigation committee is still in Palestine. Nothing is likely to happen while they remain in the country.'

'When do they leave?' It was Mr Griffiths' turn. His wife had given him courage.

'It depends on the progress of their investigations.' Mr Crossman was afraid to tell them that the UN would be out of the country within the week. And that once their backs were turned, the Mandate authorities would have no scruple. He personally feared the worst. 'But we keep in touch with them all the time,' he added helplessly. He felt deeply for the parents of the boys, but now he wished they would go home.

'There is something you ought to know,' Mrs Millar said suddenly. Though disturbed by the Griffiths' presence, she had decided to speak out.

'Something I'm not aware of?' Mr Crossman asked.

'I don't think so,' Mrs Millar said.

'Our son David is Jewish,' Mr Millar spoke on his own confident account. 'My wife is Jewish, and by Jewish law, so is our son.'

'What about our Will?' Mrs Griffiths sobbed. She had immediately seen the consequences of such information. 'Our Will is a simple Christian soldier.'

Mr Crossman was perturbed. 'Do the authorities know of this?' he asked.

'My David has never denied that he is Jewish,' Mrs Millar said, 'but I doubt that as a soldier in the British army in Palestine, he would have broadcast it.'

'They couldn't have known,' Crossman said almost to himself. It didn't add up at all. It was his duty to inform the authorities. He could do that straight away and possibly receive some response. He wished the parents would leave so that he could do what had to be done.

'This information is crucial,' he said, 'but it might take time to investigate. I think it's best for you to go home and wait for my response. I assure you that I shall be in touch as soon as I have news of their reaction.'

'What about our boy?' Mrs Griffiths said again.

'This news affects your son too,' Crossman said. He tried not to envisage a single death warrant. He stood up. 'I'll get on to it right away.'

His guests then had to stand.

'Thank you for seeing us,' Mr Griffiths said. It was mere courtesy, for he was thanking him for nothing.

'It's me who has to thank you for coming,' Crossman said. 'I'm with you all the way.' And he meant it, every word injected with his sense of helplessness.

As soon as they had left, he was on the hot line to General Barker. He waited for an astonished response to his news. But Barker was unimpressed.

'We know about that,' he said. 'Have known since the start. But it must never be known that we know. If we were to declare it now it might free him, but it would send Griffiths to the gallows. We cannot do that. We can't even think about it. The UN Committee, as you know, are still here. When they leave, we will inform you of our decision. Meanwhile we are searching high and low.' He was clearly anxious to get off the phone. Interference from Parliament always irritated him. Crossman especially, with his constant criticism. Jew-lover, he thought. Always meddling. But the call had irked him. He was not sure he'd made the right decision. So he called his close associates together, not for their opinions but for their support. Nevertheless, he would hear them out, feigning interest.

'How is the search going?' he asked, when they were gathered together.

'We've drawn a blank,' Captain Coleman said. 'And it's not for want of looking. We've more or less covered the whole country. We're running out of places to look.'

'Or anyone to ask,' another officer said. 'Nobody knows anything. And I think it's genuine. Most of the Jews hate this business as much as we do.'

'We could commute to life imprisonment,' one timid voice ventured.

'That will look like surrender,' General Barker said. 'Moreover, it would set a precedent. Kidnapping could then be in order.'

'I hate to say this,' that same timid voice ventured further, 'and you're not going to like it, but I have this nagging feeling that if the hostages were officers, like us, we wouldn't hesitate. We'd commute.'

In his heart, General Barker agreed with him. But he had to make a stand. 'That's a disgraceful thing to say,' he said. 'The life of every enlisted man is precious. We make no distinction. But we have to come to a decision.'

Then an officer, cut from the same cloth as General Barker, shouted, 'I don't understand why we're messing about. Three lousy Yids. Hang them. Why are we wasting our time?'

'Have the prisoners been thoroughly questioned?' another officer asked. 'We could offer them life in exchange for names. They must know who the kidnappers are.'

'Good idea,' said the former. 'Get the names out of them. Then we can hang them anyway.'

'They've been questioned,' General Barker said. 'And we've carried out the usual practices, short of killing them. But they won't cooperate. Let's just get on with the search,' he said. 'If by the time the UN Committee has returned to Geneva the search has failed, we'll meet again and come to a decision.'

The officers left the room. They knew what that decision would be. General Barker had already made it. The three men in Acre prison would hang. And bugger the consequences.

26

Nowadays Miriam was often alone in the apartment. She liked to think she was holding the fort, but a fort that seemed in her eyes to be crumbling. Joseph was rarely at home. Occasionally he would snatch a meal standing at the kitchen table, then go out yet again on the search. And God knows where he slept at night. She hadn't seen Hannah since the kidnapping and she feared that while Avram was at home she was not likely to see her for a long time. Even Avram was rarely in the apartment. She presumed he spent his time with his leader and his co-kidnappers. Or alone, sifting his tangled thoughts. In the many years of their marriage, she had never questioned his comings and goings. Nor had she ever offered an opinion. Despite the political differences within the family, its tight-knit unit had never been threatened. Until now.

From the beginning she had been aware of Hannah's attraction to David. Indeed, she herself had once seen them at the café table. She had noticed the spring in her daughter's step and her sudden glow. Their friendship had concerned her, for she knew that nothing could come of it. She hoped that as the end of the Mandate approached, if it ever did end, their friendship would wind itself down. It was Hannah's first love, and painful, but in time she would recover. But only if he were, through circumstances, obliged to leave. If he should leave her on his way to the gallows, Hannah would never recover. And never again would she speak to her father. Something had to be done. Some words must be spoken. Some questions must be asked, and some opinions must be offered. Miriam was nervous, for she was the only one who could ask those questions. She would have to play a role totally unfamiliar.

She was preparing supper in case any of the family needed to eat. She heard the key turn in the front door. It was Avram. He used to call out her name, but recently he had come in silently and gone straight to his workroom, where he stayed for a long time. But Miriam heard no sewing-machine whirr. Just silence. She knew that he was troubled. He knew the damaging price he had paid for the cause and he must have wondered whether such damage could ever be repaired. When finally he came into the kitchen, Miriam offered him a glass of lemonade, his favourite drink.

'We're losing our daughter,' she said. She wouldn't bother with questions and there was no point in opinions. It was enough to face him with the facts.

He did not look at her. He simply put down his glass and left the kitchen. And out of the apartment, leaving the door ajar, as if he did not want to close the subject. He just wanted time on his own, to still his nerves. He walked around the city until he was tired, then he made his way to Begin's hideout, needing rest and company.

Dror was there, Pinsker and Gad. Their presence pleased but did not surprise him. But there were others there, seated at the table. Hannah's people, the leaders of the Haganah. They gave him a cursory glance as he entered. He was known to them, as were his children, and because of that and at this time, they felt sorry for him. *Zeyda* sat in the corner. He was unnerved by their company.

'You have to let them go,' Ben-Gurion was shouting.

'Or tell us where they are,' Rabin said. 'Then you won't be seen to lose face.'

Then Begin shouted too. 'D'you think I worry for a second about losing face?' he spluttered. 'I worry about losing far more than my face. My country above all.'

'No good will come of it,' Dayan said. 'Think for one moment. The repercussions will be terrible. Not only here, but in England too. Already Jewish cemeteries have been vandalised.'

'You tell me nothing I don't already know,' Begin said.

There seemed to be little else to say. Dayan turned to the others. 'Are you all of the same mind?' he asked.

'We have no choice,' Gad said.

'But you don't intend to hang them. Honestly?' he asked.

'We have made our position very clear,' Begin said. 'Gallows for gallows.'

Ben-Gurion placed his hand over Begin's. 'Please, Menachim,' he said. 'I beg you. Please think again. Think of the harm it will do to all of us. There'll be dire consequences.'

'Of course. We expect that. But you and your lot, you think only in the short term.'

'You will have blood on your hands,' Ben-Gurion said.

'In the short term, yes,' Begin agreed. 'But history will absolve me.'

Ben-Gurion stood up. He saw no point in further attempts at persuasion. 'You're a megalomaniac, my friend,' he said. 'How in God's name can anybody talk to you?' He motioned his friends to leave.

They left separately and went in different directions. It did not for a moment occur to them to shop Begin's whereabouts to the authorities. If he was found, they would torture him into submission. And when that failed, they would shoot him in the back, as they had done to others in the resistance, claiming that the prisoner had been shot while trying to escape. Though Begin could never be a friend, they respected him for his dedication. Besides, Jew did not betray Jew. They were deeply disappointed, but there was nothing more that they could do. They just had to continue with the search.

Ben-Gurion's visit, and his nagging attempts at persuasion, had left Begin's men angry and more determined than ever.

'We must not waver,' Begin said. 'We must sit it out. Who knows? In the end, we might win.'

It was what they had to think, but in his heart *Zeyda* knew that he had already lost.

The others left. They went back to their wives who had no

need to ask questions. But *Zeyda* stayed with Begin. Both men were glad of each other's company.

'The *Exodus* should be landing at Port-de-Bouc in a couple of days,' Begin said. 'Anything could happen, and it might change the situation here. It might cause delay.' He paused. 'I have to tell you, Avram,' though it seemed he was talking to himself, 'I would not be happy to hang the sergeants. I don't want them found, but I want them to live. I have enough blood on my hands.'

Zeyda didn't know what to say. He began to pity his leader. He was floundering in a morass of his own making. So were they all.

'Shall I make coffee?' *Zeyda* asked.

'No. Go home to your wife and children. They need you there at this time.'

How could he tell Begin that whoever needed him, it was certainly not his family. He doubted that Miriam would even speak to him. She hadn't asked questions. She hadn't voiced an opinion. She had just simply stated the facts, and they were more hurtful than any question. But he would go home to her. He had left the door ajar and she certainly would not have closed it. He would go straight to his workroom and sit at his machine, with his head in his hands, while outside the door, Miriam would accuse him with her silence.

He wished Begin well, and left. When he arrived at his apartment, he found the door closed. Not only had Miriam given him the facts, she had stated an opinion. In a rush of melancholy, he put his key in the lock. He called her name from the door.

'I am here,' she answered. A cold announcement of her presence. She was there to judge him, and he had no defence. 'The cause, the cause,' he said to himself, and it echoed like cannon in his heart. He expected her to block his way to his workroom. He felt himself on trial but she made no move to stop him and the free passage she gave him made him feel even more like a prisoner. In all their years of marriage, he had never laid a finger on her, but at that moment he wanted to strike her. Because what she had said was true. They were losing their daughter and it was of his own doing.

'She loves him,' Miriam whispered.

'What d'you expect me to do?' It was no question and he did not look at her.

'Free them. Let them go. And don't tell me it's the cause,' she yelled at him.

'That's what it's all about,' he said, and he went to his room and shut the door.

She listened to his silence within, and he listened to her silence without. And below those silences, their marriage was buried.

27

This is what Will Griffiths wrote in his diary. 'I am so frightened. I just don't see how we can survive. Unless the army finds us, we are condemned. Even if they don't hang the prisoners, the Irgun will kill us. Because we could shop them and they would be finished. I shall try and write home tomorrow. David is writing. Probably about Hannah. I wish I could write about Uri.'

And this is what David Millar wrote. 'We are doomed. I'm afraid. The Irgun dare not spare us. They know that we would shop them if we were free. I hope this thought has not occurred to Will. Sometimes I fear that he will lose his mind.'

That morning, when he woke, David chalked up their fifth day of confinement. He was not feeling well. His breathing was shallow and he felt weak. When he'd first seen the oxygen cylinders he'd thought they were a joke. But now he saw them as a necessity. He unhooked one from its hanger and placed it over his nose. He breathed deeply and in a while he felt a little better. Will was still sleeping, peacefully it seemed. He too would be needing oxygen. He hoped that the mask would not further rattle his friend's already frayed nerves. He heard Will stirring, and then a groan. He flicked on his torch and unhooked the second mask. He waited for Will to raise his head.

'This will help,' he said, as he fixed the nozzle on Will's nose. Will screamed. He was still half asleep. He'd been dreaming about the noose and now it seemed to be slipping around his neck.

'It's all right, it's all right,' David calmed him. 'It's only oxygen.' But it was a lot more than 'only', David thought, and he wondered how much longer they could survive. He was relieved when the trapdoor opened and the guard entered with their breakfast. He was glad there was a witness to their distress, one who could perhaps help them. The guard put the tray on the table, looked at them both, and hurried away. He seemed frightened and David was hopeful that something would soon be done.

'I'm not hungry,' Will said. 'And I'm beginning to smell. How many days is it?'

'This is our fifth,' David said. 'You've got a little beard. Suits you.' He tried a laugh. 'I smell too. I just imagine myself in a hot bath and then I feel better.' But he didn't feel better. His mind was too numb to stretch to such a vision. 'We must try to eat,' he said. He shone his torch on the tray. He noticed an extra item. Two large oranges. 'There's more to eat today,' he said.

Will looked at the tray with scorn. 'They're fattening us up for the kill,' he said.

'Stop it,' David shouted. 'You mustn't think like that. They'll find us.'

'If we're not dead by then,' Will said.

David could have struck him. 'Listen, Will,' he said as kindly as he was able, 'you mustn't give in. Don't you see, if we give in, they've won. We've got to be strong. We've got to be polite to them. Even friendly. That'll make it harder for them to get rid of us.'

'*You* be friendly and polite,' Will said. 'I hate them.'

The trapdoor opened again.

'They're coming for us,' Will said.

It was the guard who'd brought their breakfast. He was followed by another man who was carrying a black bag.

'I'm a doctor,' the man said. 'I've come to see how you're doing. Now let's have a look at you.'

The guard shone his torch, first on David. The doctor knelt by his side, opened his shirt and placed a stethoscope on his heart. His listened a while, then placed the instrument on David's back. Again he listened. David watched his face but it showed

160

no concern. Then with another instrument he took David's blood pressure and it was then that concern registered. But he said nothing. He simply moved towards Will and conducted the same procedure. When he had finished he said, 'I'm sorry I disturbed your breakfast. I'll leave you to it.'

The doctor's good manners threw Will into a rage. He rushed to the trapdoor barring his exit.

'What's happening out there?' he yelled. 'Are they going to hang the prisoners – for God's sake, you miserable piece of scum, what's happening?'

'Will,' David said. 'Leave him be. He's only doing his job.'

The guard urged Will back to his mattress. 'Calm down,' he said. 'Eat something. You'll feel better.'

Will allowed himself to be led. He sank down on to his mattress. David went to his side. He couldn't be angry with him. Will had simply voiced his own frustrations. 'It'll be all right, Will,' he kept saying, but he was saying it to himself, and with little conviction. He lifted Will's mask to persuade him to eat. He urged him to the table and peeled him an orange. As they ate they felt better, until they heard movement above the trapdoor. Any sound outside their cell was ominous. Footsteps were the worst; they were threatening. But this sound was more than footfalls. It was as if furniture was being moved. The hostages trembled. Both feared that the doctor had found them barely well enough to hang, so the sooner it was done, the better. Neither man voiced this fear, but when the trapdoor opened again, they clung to each other. The guard was obliquely framed in the slither of light. 'Time for a little fresh air,' he said. Will fell to his knees at David's side. 'Our Father,' he stuttered. 'Our Father which art in Heaven . . .'

David pulled him quickly to his feet. 'Not that,' he said. 'It hasn't come to that.' He prayed that he was right, that indeed it was only fresh air that was being offered and no more.

'Come,' he said. He took Will's hand and led him to the trapdoor.

'Follow me,' the guard said. He climbed a number of stone steps, ten in all, David counted, and he gauged that their cell was very much underground. Unfindable. At the top of the steps was a wide corridor, wide enough for a table and two armchairs. And at the end of the corridor was an open window. Fresh air. It opened on to nothing but a high brick wall. On its edges patches of sky could be seen and in the eyes of the hostages, their new location was paradise. They sank into the armchairs.

The guard put their breakfast tray on the table together with their pads and pencils. 'Now you can eat,' he said. 'And write home. And breathe.' He smiled at them.

The men returned his smile. It could mark the beginning of a connection which the guard would find disturbing to break.

'Thank you,' David said. 'You are very thoughtful.'

The move lightened their spirits. It was like a reprieve. They even began to think of their future. David with Hannah, and Will in the bosom of his family. Both began to write. Both recorded their move and their glimpse of the sky. Neither began a last letter to their parents. Perhaps now it would be unnecessary.

They were allowed to stay in their armchairs for the rest of the day, but at night they were returned to the cellar. This procedure continued for the next few days until David was about to chalk nine days on his calendar. On the tenth day, they waited to be called, and they collected their pencils and pads ready for the move. But the guard brought their breakfast tray to the cell and left without saying a word.

'We've had our air ration,' Will said. 'What can that mean?'

'It may be good news,' David said. 'They may be close to finding us and the Irgun won't take any risks.'

'Perhaps the British have already hanged the others,' Will said. 'Don't sit there and tell me not to lose hope,' he almost shouted. Then casually he asked David the time, though he was aware that knowing the time was irrelevant to their situation. David looked at his watch. When last he had looked, it was because he had woken in the night, and by the light of his torch it had read 2 a.m. Now, to his horror, it registered the same time. 'I've forgotten to wind it,' he said.

Then Will lost control. 'You bloody fool,' he said. All at once it seemed to Will that knowing the time made the difference between living and dying.

'I'm sorry,' David said.

'Sorry, for God's sake. Is that all you can say? You're useless. You can't do anything. You can't even save yourself. All you've got to do is to drop your bloody trousers and you can get out of here. Why don't you do it, you idiot?'

'And leave you here?' David put his arm round Will's shoulder. 'Will,' he said. 'We're friends.'

Then Will calmed himself a little. 'Sorry,' he said. 'I just lose hope sometimes.'

David said nothing. There was little hope that he could offer. The thought crossed his mind to write his letter home. But that would be a final abdication. He would wait, and try to hope. But he knew that he too was close to breaking. Had he been alone, he would have wept aloud. And Will would have done the same. But each knew that they were dependent on the other. Tears were not a source of reliance. So they began to laugh. Both of them and at the same time.

'We're stuck with each other, I'm afraid,' David said.

Their laughter faded as they reached out to hold each other's hands.

28

After nine gruelling days at sea, the passengers of the *Exodus*, distributed in three ships, approached the harbour of Port-de-Bouc. As his vessel neared the jetty, Chaim Levy jumped ship, his undercover assignment over and done with. He was not surprised to find the pier overrun with the press, villagers and certain notables. They had come to view the show-down.

There was going to be trouble. It was known that Ernest Bevin, the British Foreign Secretary, had tried to persuade the French authorities not only to welcome the Jews but to force them to disembark. The French, never Jew-lovers, hated the British even more. Three years earlier the British had thrown them out of Syria and Lebanon and here, on the shores of Port-de-Bouc, was a god-given gift of revenge. So for the time being, the French shelved their anti-Semitism and they offered the weary travellers asylum. But they made no effort to assist their disembarkation. They didn't have to. Despite the dire conditions of their habitat, the travellers refused to leave the ships. The world's press descended on the little port, and Begin read their reports in his hideout. Most were thoroughly anti-British, accompanied by the opinion that the Mandate rule in Palestine was over and that the army should pull out. Begin was hopeful. With world-wide anti-British feeling running at fever pitch, it was unlikely that they would dare hang his three Acre prisoners. In his mind, much depended on the fate of the *Exodus* passengers. He prayed that they would be allowed to return so that the British could leave with a certain dignity, in view of a final act of compassion. But he knew that all that was wishful thinking. The British were too intransigent and loss of face would never be tolerated.

His comrades-in-arms were gathered at the hideout. Talk was exclusively about the *Exodus*. The subject of the sergeants was scrupulously avoided. Between breaks for coffee, they discussed the choices facing the British authorities. They spent time applauding the French, mocking the failure of Ernest Bevin, wondering when Chaim would come home. After some hours of skirting around the issue, Begin called a halt. 'I am not wavering in regard to the hostages,' he said. He must have sensed some vacillation among his followers. If the sergeants had to hang, they wanted it over and done with.

'I pray that they will spare our men in Acre so that the sergeants can be released. Believe me, I don't want to see them hang.'

'Is there news from the prison?' Dror asked.

'They're bearing up, I'm told. They've been tortured of course, but they have been silent. They are brave men. Rabbi Levin has organised a visit. I hope to hear more from him,' Begin said.

The rabbi was Begin's friend but neither he nor Begin understood why, and it was possibly only because of the many years that they had known each other that the connection was sustained. The rabbi had little respect for Begin. He was sickened by his tactics but he respected his dedication and his religious bent, for, despite his trespasses, Begin was a true man of God. When Begin needed his assistance as a prison visitor, the rabbi was always ready to oblige. But it was a painful duty. Most of the prisoners on death row were Begin's men, and he comforted them as best he could. Despite the pain of his visits, his faith had never been shaken. But he was angry, angry because of the lies that were spread about the men's final moments. They were lies, all lies. He himself had witnessed their very last moments. The men were not brave. They were terrified. Some even wept with fear. When tortured, they had given names, and gladly. All the names that they could think of, and some mere inventions. And had they known of Begin's whereabouts, they would have happily divulged his hideout. They were not cowards. They were simply human. They did not shout 'Long live the Irgun' on their way to the scaffold. Neither did they sing. They hated the Irgun with a passion. They cursed themselves for having been part of it. They didn't want to die. Any of them.

165

They all wanted to appeal, but they knew that appeal was frowned upon and all were frightened to challenge the Irgun. They were dragged to the scaffold practically on their knees. They had pleaded for life and their guards had laughed. Neither did the prisoners on death row sing the 'Hatikvah' as the rope trembled. Only one prisoner sang. Just one. Uri Berger. Uri had walked to the scaffold with his head high and a song of hope orchestrated his steps. But only Uri. The only one. Rabbi Levin had witnessed that too, and he had marvelled at the man's courage. Uri Berger was different from the rest. His belief in God and in the Irgun was unshakeable. To witness such heroism was to change one's own life.

Rabbi Levin was always wary of visits to those who were about to die. Even if that death were natural, in a hospital bed or in a loving home, he was never easy as he intoned the final prayer, 'Hear O Israel' . . . At such a moment his faith was threatened and he wondered what was the point of it all. But here, in the prisoners' cell, waiting for a death that was most unnatural, it seemed almost obscene to be calling on a God who had let it happen in the first place, or at least a God whose back was turned. He had no doubts that the prisoners would hang. The authorities were simply waiting for the UN investigative committee to return to Geneva. Then, whether or not the hostages had been found, the hangman would be called. His heart was heavy as he entered the condemned men's cell.

They were housed together, the three of them, and each man was in chains. They had clearly been tortured. Their faces were bruised blue, and their bare feet blister-burnt. They did not greet him when he entered. His role smelt of death and could bring no comfort. He sat himself on a cot between them, and he said nothing. Every word was a lie in this place and he would respect the prisoners with his silence. Then one of them spoke. Haviv.

'I don't want to die, rabbi,' he said. 'It was all a mistake.' His voice was bereft of any emotion. Or perhaps he had never been disturbed by feelings of any kind – until now – and he was unable to express them.

'What was a mistake?' the rabbi asked.

'The Irgun,' he said. 'I curse the very day I joined it.'

'Then why don't you appeal?' the rabbi asked. 'You could be given life. In time, you might even be released.'

'Appeal, he says,' Nakar interrupted him. 'We dare not. It's not allowed.'

'Who says?' the rabbi asked, though he knew full well.

'Begin,' Weiss said. 'Begin and his lot. We are ordered not to recognise the court. Therefore we can't appeal.'

'And if we did,' Nakar added, 'we would be outcasts. Our families too.'

'But is it not better,' the rabbi said, 'to live as a pariah, rather than to die as a martyr?' He began to wonder why Begin was his friend.

At last the men broke down. All three of them.

'They'll have to drag me to the yard. I'm not going quietly,' Nakar sobbed.

'Save us. For God's sake, save us,' Weiss begged.

'I'll do what I can,' Rabbi Levin said. He hated himself for giving them false hope. For there was nothing he could do. He clasped them all in his embrace. 'God bless you all,' he should have said, but he saw no point in it. The men had just spoken out their truths, and lying no longer played a part in this cell. So he said nothing. He simply hugged them. He loved them for their honesty, which for him was the finest form of heroism.

'We are all afraid,' Nakar said.

'You are entitled to fear,' the rabbi said. 'Do not be ashamed. You are human, after all.' He did not want to leave them. He wanted to stay by their sides till their last moments. He would go with them to the scaffold, but, respecting their honesty, he would not pray. He would make himself watch the drop, then he would leave and go to their mothers and tell them that their children had died bravely. Then he would find a quiet place and settle down to pray, and with all his might and passion, he would curse his merciless God.

167

29

Hannah was distraught. She had not had a full night's sleep since the search had begun. And never in her own bed. Joseph had tried to persuade her to go home, that no good could come of a quarrel with their father. Hannah refused to see him. She hated him and she was prepared to take the consequences. But she missed her mother. When all this was over, and she dared not think about the meaning of the 'over', she would see her mother again.

In one of the short breaks that she took from the search, she made her way to their café. She would sit alone at their table and find solace there, and hope that soon David would join her. She was surprised to find their table already occupied and it angered her, for she considered that space reserved. A woman sat there with her back to the street, and Hannah had it in mind to ask her to move. To tell her that that place was bespoke. As she approached the table, she rehearsed the eviction summons. But she'd seen the woman's coat before, and the sloping shoulders triggered a painful familiarity. She rushed to the table. 'Mama,' she cried.

Miriam turned and rose, and simply held her without a word. They remained in an embrace for a while.

'I knew that this was your table,' Miriam said. 'I've seen you here with David. I hoped you'd come again. I miss you, Hannah.'

'I've missed you too, Mama. Terribly. But you know I can't come home.'

She expected her mother to mount a defence of her father but Miriam offered no excuse on his behalf. 'It's a sad time for us,' was all that she said. Then, after a while, 'How is the search?'

Hannah began to cry. Not only for David, but for her mother's understanding and love.

'You must keep looking, Hannah,' Miriam said.

'Where? Where?' Hannah pleaded.

'I don't know how those Irgun people work,' Miriam said. She spoke with such disdain that it was difficult to imagine that she was married to one of them. 'There's nothing I can do for you,' she said. 'Nothing I can tell you. He tells me nothing.' She could not even call him by his name. 'The house is quiet,' she went on. 'Joseph comes sometimes. He gives me news of you. Will you come to this table again?' she asked.

'Of course,' Hannah said. 'I'll send a message to you through Joseph. Soon, soon,' she added and she hugged her mother again. 'You've given me strength.'

They sat together for a while, drinking their coffee, talking of the past, because the present was unsafe and the future unmentionable. Occasionally they smiled. Hannah was grateful that her mother did not say 'We must not give up hope'. That's what everybody said, as if hope was there in the first place. To hold on to hope acknowledged the possibility of failure and that Hannah would never do. What she must never give up was her certainty of finding him, and it was that force that propelled her through her days and nights of searching.

'Where are you looking today?' Miriam asked.

'Natanya,' Hannah said. 'The army have been there, but not the Haganah. Natanya's a hotbed of Irgun supporters. They won't be much help. But today, maybe we'll be lucky. Maybe you'll bring us luck, Mama.' She rose. 'I have to go. Our bus leaves soon.'

'I'll sit for a while,' Miriam said. 'I like this table. It feels more like home than the apartment.'

'Is it all my fault, Mama?' Hannah asked.

'It's nobody's fault,' Miriam said. 'Sometimes people cannot help themselves. Go,' she said, 'and good luck.'

They kissed again and Hannah rushed away. Miriam looked after her until she had disappeared. She thought of Mrs Katz, she who had lost her son and her husband to the Irgun. Did she curse the cause? Miriam wondered. And Mrs Berger. Did she spit on its name? And all those wives who waited for the sound of the latch on the door and whose hearts beat with fear in its endless silence. She thought of other wives too, and other mothers, far away, their tears on the telegram, the same tears, the same pain as Mrs Katz and Mrs Berger's. Pain that had nothing to do with any cause. Only of loss. She prayed for the lives of their children, and for Avram's life too, though she wanted no further part in it.

Other members of Hannah's group were waiting at their pickup. Joseph among them.

'I've seen Mama,' she told him. 'She was sitting at our table. Mine and David's.'

'Mama having coffee?' he asked.

'She was hoping I'd come there. It was so wonderful to see her.'

'How did you find her?' he asked.

'Sad. Sad about everything. She doesn't mention Papa's name.'

'He's hardly at home,' Joseph said. 'I think he's ashamed.'

'And so he should be,' Hannah said. 'If anything happens to David or Will, I'll never speak to him again.'

'Sometimes I'm a bit sorry for him,' Joseph said.

'Spare your pity. He knows exactly what he's doing. And he truly believes that it is right,' Hannah said.

'We used to be such a close family,' Joseph muttered, almost to himself.

Just then the truck drew alongside them. A dozen of them in all were waiting, with no idea of what they would do or where they would go in the streets of Natanya. When they were settled inside, Joseph pulled out his pocket chess set and laid it out to play with Monty, his chess partner. And in this manner they whiled away the journey. Hannah sat at the back of the truck, alone. She needed to gather her thoughts and to recall her mother's words. She wondered where she had gone after she'd left the café. Although they were her friends, Miriam would have avoided other Irgun wives. Indeed she must have felt those friendships fraying. In all, she must have sensed her isolation, and Hannah imagined her walking alone along the streets, wary of returning to an apartment that was no longer home. I must see her often, Hannah decided. She needs my support.

'The army has done Natanya,' Shlomo said. 'Twice.' He too, like Hannah, was a teacher, but in a high school. He was the oldest in the truck and he was looked upon as the leader.

'We'll go to the outskirts of the town,' he said. 'There are lots of old buildings that used to be factories. Good hiding places. We could try them.'

When they reached Natanya, they found it a ghost town. Apart from groups of soldiers, the streets were empty and many of the shops were closed. The army search had not left a stone unturned. Many residents, known Irgun sympathisers, had been arrested. Some were caught listening to the illegal Irgun radio. The mayor of the city had been manacled and taken in for questioning. Natanya had been thoroughly combed, and it seemed to Hannah that there was little point in combing it further.

'We'll drive out of town,' Shlomo said.

The group had been searching for almost twenty days, and most of the nights, and they were losing heart. All of them, except Hannah. 'Perhaps we'll be lucky today,' she said.

'You say that every time,' one of them said. 'What's next after Natanya? Is there anywhere left where we haven't looked?'

'Just drive on,' Shlomo said. 'Out of the town.'

There were fewer soldiers on the streets as they approached the outskirts. After a couple of kilometres, they faced an army post, and their truck was halted by two soldiers. One of them came over. A young man of twenty or so, wearing a British corporal's uniform.

'What's your business here?' he asked.

'We're Haganah,' the driver said. 'We're looking for the sergeants.'

'You and the whole British army,' the soldier said with a smile.

'We were here last week. Here and in the town. All these old factories up to the woods. You'd think it would be an obvious place. But we had no luck. If you want my opinion, I think they're somewhere in Jerusalem. Needle in a haystack town. I've got to check your truck anyway,' he said. 'Army orders.'

'D'you want us out?' Shlomo asked.

'No. Don't bother. I'll just peek inside.' This he did, cursorily.

'I wish you luck,' he said, as he waved them on. 'We need to find them.'

Shlomo told the driver to turn back. There seemed no point in retracing the army's search. The soldier guided them into a U-turn. 'Good luck,' he shouted again.

As they drove past the post, Hannah asked, 'What kind of factory was that?'

'An old diamond factory,' Shlomo said. 'It's been shut up for years.'

And so they returned to Tel Aviv, disheartened. 'I'm taking the night off,' one of them said. 'I'm going to have a great supper and then a long sleep.'

'So must you all,' Shlomo said. 'We'll be in touch tomorrow.' They went their separate ways.

'Let's have supper together,' Joseph said. 'We can go to the chess café.'

Hannah was glad to be with her brother for a while. Although she saw him every day on their searches, they spent little time together.

'Let's do that,' she said. 'A good supper, and then a long sleep.'

The café was empty of diners, but the chess-playing section was crowded. Hannah wondered why everybody was not out looking for the hostages and she resented the fact that people could carry on with their lives as if nothing was out of the ordinary.

It was a self-service café, and they helped themselves from

the counter. When they were settled, Hannah said, 'I don't want to talk about Papa. I don't want to talk about David and Will. I want a night off from all of it. And I don't want you to talk about it either,' she added. 'I don't want speculations, I don't want opinions. I just need to hold on to my own certainty.' So Joseph said nothing and he was grateful for her request for silence. In any case, he wouldn't have known what to say. At least not to Hannah. His mouth was full of words, but he could find no listener. He needed somebody with whom to share his personal involvement in the kidnapping. But that was for no one's ears, for to divulge it would spell the undoing of his whole family. And he had other words too, and again those he could not utter. For in truth, he had lost hope. Their searches were fruitless and by now pointless. The men would never be found. Not alive anyway. The Acre prisoners would hang, and David and Will's corpses would at last be found. So he did not resent the silence that Hannah had requested. He set to eating his supper. After a while, he stroked her hand and smiled at her.

'Can we talk about the food?' he asked.

She laughed. 'Yes,' she said. 'It's terrible. It always is. But it's cheap, and if you're hungry, it'll do. I wonder what Mama is eating,' she said. She had opened the can of worms and Joseph took the advantage.

'You must try and understand Papa's position, Hannah,' he said. 'He daren't even give us a hint of where they are. From his standpoint, they must not be found. The hostages are the Irgun's sole bargaining ploy. Their blackmail if you like, their only hope of saving the Acre men.'

'I understand all that,' Hannah said. 'What's so sad is that there is nothing that we can do about it.'

'If you understand,' Joseph said, 'how come you can't go home? Live there. Like before.'

'We have a father who puts his cause before his children,' Hannah said. 'That's why I can't go home.'

There was little more to say and they finished their meal in silence.

'Perhaps that soldier was right today,' Joseph said. 'Perhaps Will and David are hidden in Jerusalem.'

'He called it "needle in a haystack town",' Hannah said. 'And in any case, it's been covered.'

'Where *hasn't* been covered?' Joseph was disconsolate.

'Jaffa,' Hannah said. 'It's such an unlikely place. Laughable almost. I'm sure the army hasn't bothered to look there.'

'Shlomo has,' Joseph said. 'With another group. About a week ago. He thought like you. So unlikely, it was an obvious hiding place. With enough bribable stallholders to help with the search. Believe me, if they were there, they would have been found. I'm thinking of pulling out of the search,' he added.

'You can't do that.' Hannah was angry. 'We've got to go on looking.'

'I know. I want them found as much as you do. I just don't want the Haganah to find them.'

'What difference?' Hannah asked. 'The army or the Hanagah.'

'If the army were to find them,' Joseph said, 'that would have nothing to do with us. But if we were to find them, Papa would never forgive us.'

'Then we'd be quits, wouldn't we?' Hannah said.

30

A few days later it was *Zeyda*'s birthday. Every year, that day was a cause for celebration. It was the family custom to spend the day at Degania, the kibbutz where *Zeyda* had spent his childhood and had met and married Miriam. A day for nostalgia, for renewing of old friendships, for catching up on gossip, and for keeping one's lips firmly sealed. For as far as the kibbutz knew, *Zeyda* was a simple tailor who had set up a shop in Tel Aviv.

On such a day, *Zeyda* would close his workroom, Miriam would pack up home-made cakes and biscuits, Joseph and Hannah would take leave from school, and the whole family would board the bus going north to the Sea of Galilee. It was always an exciting ride and Joseph and Hannah recalled how loving and tender their parents were on such a day. But this year would be different. No mention was made of the day. Miriam made no preparations and both children were out on the search, and because of his family's indifference *Zeyda* pretended to have forgotten that it was his birthday at all. Nevertheless, he shut up his work place, and early in the morning he took the bus north, empty-handed and alone. Nowadays he found himself alone so often and it was a state he did not favour. For despite his stubborn allegiance to the cause, he considered himself to be a family man. Having been brought up on a kibbutz, the notion of family was deeply ingrained. He was saddened by the fraying of that kinship and he wondered whether it could ever be whole again. He looked forward to renewing old friendships at Degania, but he was ashamed of being alone. He could be honest about his children. They were searching for the sergeants, and the kibbutzniks would approve of that. But Miriam was another matter. After some thought, he decided to enlist her in the search as well. It was probable that she'd wanted to do that from the start and that only a slither of loyalty had kept her at home. He had no doubt that the main topic of conversation on the kibbutz would be the fate of the sergeants. Degania was solidly behind the Haganah and he would have to agree with their opinions. He would have to close his ears and condemn his own cause, for their antipathy to the Irgun was loud and clear. It would pain him, but he would weather it for the sake of old friendships and the shared memories of his childhood.

It was a curfew-free day. There was no logic in the army's curfew arrangements. They varied from day to day. But they could be reimposed at any time. Jews of no particular allegiance had joined in the search. The kidnapping had become a humanitarian issue that had nothing to do with politics.

The bus was full. Avram found a seat at the back, and alone, he huddled by the window. He was in no mood for sergeant discussion, a topic that hummed indignantly from the front seats. Even the driver put in his shekel's worth. 'Terrible, terrible,' he kept saying. 'We have to find them.' The bus wound its way along the coast road. At every stop, Herzlia, Shefayim and Yakum, it picked up other passengers bound for Natanya, which seemed, thanks to Intelligence, to have become the central focus of the search. But Avram wasn't worried. Even a direct search of the diamond factory would yield nothing. The cellar had been too carefully camouflaged and, from the outside, looked like part of the neglected overgrowth of a disused factory. He gave a thought to the hostages. In his heart he knew that the Acre men would hang and that the sergeants would pay the same price. When the bus stopped at Natanya he turned his face away but he could still see how most of the passengers left, on their way to a fruitless search. It was a relief when the bus turned inland, away from any reminders of his kidnapping journey and he was able to look out of the window and wait for his first sight of the Sea of Galilee. He thought of those childhood friends of his who had grown up on the kibbutz, and who, for their own reasons, had chosen to stay.

On arrival, he was afforded an enthusiastic and warm welcome. His friends were disappointed that he had come alone, but they applauded the reasons for his family's absence. Which led inevitably to a discussion of the hostage situation. As Avram had expected, they abhorred the kidnapping, but found it typical of Irgun's lunatic strategy. *Zeyda* heartily agreed with them. He could not do otherwise. He offered the opinions of his Haganah children as if they were his own, and as he listened to them out of his own mouth, he heard how wrong-headed his children were. He was glad that they were elsewhere. They would have silently poured scorn on his blatant hypocrisy.

Zeyda's closest boyhood friend on the kibbutz was Zvi. He remembered the day Zvi married Ruth, a townee, whom he'd met on a kibbutz errand to Haifa. His friends, including himself, had been wary of the match. A city girl could not easily adapt to kibbutz life, but within a few weeks of the marriage, Ruth had become as if kibbutz born. They had three children, all boys, grown up now, like Avram's and, like Avram's, in the Haganah.

'They're in Jerusalem,' Zvi told him, 'joining in the search.'

'It's as good a place as any,' Dan, another old friend, offered. 'But I think that they are already dead. The Irgun know very well that their Acre boys are going to hang. They're not going to be polite about it.'

'I agree with Dan,' someone said. 'I think they're dead.'

'I don't think so,' Avram said, and with some confidence, for only the day before Begin had told him that the hostages were well and were constantly monitored by a doctor.

'I wouldn't put anything past those hooligans,' Dan said.

'Can we change the subject?' *Zeyda* asked. 'That's all anybody talks about. Everywhere you go. And I'm frankly sick of it. In a few days' time, when the UN Committee leave, things might change.'

'They'll change all right,' Gideon said. 'As soon as their backs are turned, the Acre men will hang. And so will the sergeants, if they're still alive. And then there'll be chaos.'

Avram rose from the table. 'Enough,' he said. He was smiling. 'Show me round the farm.'

'We have a new crèche,' Zvi said proudly. 'Twenty-seven babies. Come. Ruth still works there. She wants to show you.'

Zeyda was glad that the conversation had turned. He was not good at dissembling, especially in the company of people whom he admired, and for whom he held a long-standing affection, and a shared history that should override their politics.

Zvi took his arm. 'It's always good to see you. D'you ever regret leaving the kibbutz?' It was a question he asked every year.

'Sometimes,' Avram said. 'But Miriam wanted to go. She wanted to try something different. The idea of Tel Aviv excited her, but mainly she wanted more privacy. There's not a lot of that about on a kibbutz.'

But again he was lying. Miriam would have been happy to stay on the kibbutz. And for always. The children too. To leave had been his decision, and his alone.

It had come about quite accidentally. The kibbutz often took on outside work in order to supplement its income. Plumbers were always in demand, as were electricians. And occasionally tailors. Once, Avram had been asked to go to Tel Aviv. One Gad Freedman wanted a suit for his brother's wedding. *Zeyda* gathered up his measure, his chalks, pencils and samples, and took himself off to Tel Aviv. Gad Freedman was an engineer and at the time that was the only information *Zeyda* was given. But during the course of their meetings, and there were many, far more than was sartorially necessary, *Zeyda* learned that the engineering profession was merely a front and behind that front lay a dedicated and obsessional political pursuit. It was Gad Freedman, over the frequent tailoring visits, who introduced *Zeyda* to the Irgun movement, and to its aims and principles. *Zeyda* was hooked. He knew that his future could no longer lie in the kibbutz. He had to become a soldier of the Irgun. He would dedicate himself to the cause, and the matter of such dedication had no place in Degania. So he had taken his family to

Tel Aviv, and his tailoring became a front in the same way as engineering was covering Gad Freedman. Gad was his mentor and guide, roles that had led to a lasting friendship.

'We miss you though,' Zvi was saying.

They had reached the crèche. A crèche is the pride of any kibbutz for it spells continuity. It was a new building, or rather an extension of the original, that basic hut where Joseph and Hannah had been cared for in their infant years. Ruth welcomed them both. She had worked at the crèche since the birth of her own three children and, until she'd left the kibbutz, Miriam had worked alongside her.

'Where's Miriam?' Ruth asked straight away. They had been good friends in the kibbutz days.

Yet again, Avram had to repeat his invention, and as he spoke he saw Miriam at their kitchen table, steeped in silence. This is the saddest birthday I have ever spent, he thought.

Ruth was proud of her crèche, and she toured Avram around the cots, calling each child by name, as well as those of their parents, the girls and boys who had grown up with his own children, and he wondered about those children of his and he was disturbed. Had he not been called to Tel Aviv that day, had he never met Gad Freedman, had he not been seduced by Gad's ideas, and had he not been infected by his zeal, he would still, to this day, be in Degania, and probably with grandchildren of his own. But he did not regret his move, though he was now aware of the big price that he would probably have to pay. It was the cause. Gad had taught him that word, and had urged him to honour it and keep it holy. Against that word, all else was secondary. Even family. He recalled how Mrs Katz had cursed the word. Mrs Berger too. And now Miriam and his children. But whatever happened to him, he convinced himself that he would leave his family a legacy of freedom. For after the cause, freedom would be the effect. Of that he was convinced.

It was time for the birthday tea. They gathered around the long table in the dining room. In its centre was the birthday cake. Josh, the head cook, baked it every year, as he did for the birthdays of every kibbutz member. Josh too was a boyhood friend. He had always worked in the kitchens. He had been a skinny child, and despite his profession he had remained lean and gaunt. Though numerous attempts had been made by his fellow kibbutzniks to marry him off, he was, at the age of forty-four, still unattached. Josh was a confirmed bachelor, a rarity on any kibbutz. He was the confidant of many women, and even men took their problems to him. He loved children, especially babies, and he visited the crèche almost every day. The children called him Papa Josh, and nothing pleased him more. He sat by Avram's side. 'Tell me about Joseph and Hannah,' he said.

'They're on the search,' Avram said, hoping that that would explain everything.

'Apart from that,' Josh said. 'Are they still teaching?'

'Yes. Both of them.' It was one of the few statements of truth that he had made since his arrival and he repeated it, relishing it to himself.

'Any signs of marriage?' Josh asked.

'You're a right one to ask,' Avram teased him. 'I could ask the same of you.'

'One day I might surprise you,' Josh said.

'Tell me,' Avram urged.

'First I have to surprise myself. Then I'll tell you,' Josh laughed. 'I'm sorry you left us,' he added.

And at such moments, *Zeyda* was sorry too. For most of all he missed the daily companionship and the carefree banter. The cause did not allow for that. 'Carefree' was an unknown word in their lexicon, and 'banter' was rare. But he had not lost his appetite for it. Nor his skill. Banter did not require practice. Even if long repressed, it could quickly recover its pitch. He noticed that Zvi was standing. 'I don't want a speech,' *Zeyda* said. 'Not again. It's the same speech every year,' he laughed. And he reeled it off for them. 'We're all sorry you left. Why don't you come back? We need a decent tailor.'

'You forgot something,' Zvi said.

'And you miss my terrible jokes,' Avram provided.

They all laughed. 'Happy Birthday,' they shouted.

With much huffing and puffing, *Zeyda* blew out the single candle on his cake. Josh sliced it up and handed it round. It was the same procedure every year. And at that moment Avram and his family, when they were present, each one of them experienced a moment of regret. This year Avram, on his own, felt it acutely. He wondered where he truly belonged. And for the first time since his meeting with Gad, he thought that perhaps he had made the wrong choice. The idea frightened him. His wavering was not good for the cause. He was anxious to get back to Tel Aviv, to go to Begin's hideout and spend time in his company in order to reassure himself.

'It's getting late,' he said. He thought that if he stayed much longer he would have to become a kibbutznik once more. His friends had already packed a parcel of the kibbutz crops for him to take home. Tomatoes, beans, spinach, carrots and plums. He saw himself handing the goods over to Miriam and she would wonder how, without a family to feed, she would use them. The kibbutz gifts would only serve to widen the rift between them. Nevertheless, he accepted them with grace. 'Miriam will be overjoyed,' he lied.

Before leaving, as was his wont every year, he went to the kibbutz cemetery. It lay on the outskirts of the settlement. The founders of the kibbutz, those very first pioneers from Eastern Europe, were buried there. Those who had drained the swamps and fought malaria, had planted crops where nothing had ever been grown before. And his father. One of them.

He laid a pebble on his grave, as was his custom on each of his birthdays. His mother lay beside his father, her tomb, like his, strewn with pebbles. He sat on the ground between them, and slowly, and in whispers, he poured out the sergeants' tale. He knew that they would not have sanctioned what he had done, but he had to tell them, and as he spoke its reality frightened him. Yet he did not regret what he had done, nor its possible dire consequences. He would learn to live with them, even if he had to do it all alone.

The sun was beginning to set over the lake, and he stood on the shore and watched its descent, as he had done every night as a child. And later on, with Miriam at his side – the most painful recollection of all. He refused to admit to himself that it was all over between them. Yet he could find no reason to hope that it would be otherwise.

When the homeward bus reached Natanya, he once again turned his face away. From the street tannoy, he heard the announcement of a curfew from midnight. He thought that perhaps the army were calling off the search.

'No luck?' the driver asked, as new passengers boarded.

'They'll never be found,' one of them said. 'Begin should be shot.'

Zeyda was enraged by the remark, but he held his tongue. In his eyes, Begin was a saviour, the only leader who could guarantee Israel's future independence and that belief was unshakeable. He turned his face away from the coast road, but in shutting it out, he could not help but recall the journey he had made with the hostages almost a month ago. He remembered looking carefully at David's suit. He'd been pleased with his workmanship, and while its wearer sat blindfold and trembling he had even fingered the material and found it good. Then he'd done likewise with Will's chapel suit. Hard-wearing was its only quality. He recalled their arrival at the diamond factory, and his relief that the task was done. And then the silent drive back to Tel Aviv. He travelled that ride over and over again, until the bus pulled into the Tel Aviv station.

When he entered the apartment, he called Miriam's name, as he had done regularly over the years. But this time, he did not expect a response. He hoped that she was out, which would account for her silence, but he saw her place a plate of food on the table before leaving the kitchen. At least she had not withdrawn her feeding services. But she had withdrawn her company, for the table was laid for one alone. *Zeyda* had no appetite. He went straight to his workroom and sat at his bench and listened sadly to her silence outside. While Miriam did likewise, and with equal sorrow.

31

David staggered off his mattress, flashed his torch, slipped off his mask, and recorded their twentieth day in hiding. He had no idea of the time, and he knew it need not be the twentieth day. It could be the middle of the night of the nineteenth, or indeed the twenty-first, if he had overslept. He looked at Will who was still sleeping, his mask fixed firmly over his nose. He was careful not to disturb him. Will awake was a volcano waiting to erupt, for by now he had lost all hope of rescue. And David had little enough hope left himself to dissuade him. Their sorties into the so-called open air were now less regular. Only occasionally were they allowed the armchairs, open window and patch of sky. He felt completely disorientated and longed for the breakfast tray to appear to confirm that whatever day it was, it was certainly morning. Again the thought occurred to him, as it did every day, that the time had come to write his letter home. The thought was painful enough, but to put it into words would have meant a total loss of hope. Nevertheless, he could not help thinking of the words he would write, of how he would frame his farewell message. But that thought evoked such an offensive bout of self-pity, that he quickly dismissed it. He would refuse to contemplate those words until it was made abundantly clear to him that they would be his last.

He noticed that Will was stirring and he dreaded that once again, out of habit, he would ask the time, if only to remind David of his negligence. Then he would lose his temper, and after a while he would be calm, and then he would apologise and they would embrace each other in their common peril.

He heard movement outside the trapdoor, the movement of furniture, and he had hopes that day of a glimpse of the sky. After a while, the guard lit his way into the cell and David knew it must be morning. But he had brought the tray with him. They were to eat in the cell. David wondered what furniture had been moved, and to what purpose. And when he saw the breakfast tray, for the first time steaming with hot food, he knew that there had been a change in their circumstances. His first terrible thought was that the Acre prisoners had been hanged, that the Irgun were arranging their revenge, and that the lavish spread, though unrequested, was to be their last meal on earth. On the other hand, it might simply indicate a change of diet and that the prisoners still languished in Acre prison while negotiations continued. That was the theory he would suggest to Will, though his bowels melted in fear. But Will, when he awoke and saw the tray, thought the very worst and he would not be comforted by any alternative.

'Our last supper,' he said and he mouthed the beginning of the Lord's Prayer. This time David made no effort to stop him. It struck him that the prayer was direly appropriate. The *Shema* was ready on his own lips, that traditional farewell of a dying Jew. But he stifled it. He would first have to write his letter home.

'We might as well enjoy it,' David said, sitting himself at the table.

Will finished his prayer and rose from his knees and joined him. He was resigned. Words of hope or despair were now pointless. The prayer had censored them all. But it had done nothing to allay fear. Will was trembling. His hand quivered as he lifted the food to his mouth and as he swallowed, the tears flowed. David stretched out his hand and Will gripped it to steady himself. The meal was eaten in total silence. They waited for the footsteps that would herald their end. Both men wished they would come quickly so that the waiting could be over and done with, for neither man could stand the uncertainty for much longer. David took out his pad and pencil, and Will did likewise. 'Dear Mum and Dad,' they both wrote. And then the trapdoor opened.

'I've got to finish my letter,' Will shouted.

But it was only the guard come to collect the tray. 'I'm not stopping you,' he said. 'You can finish it upstairs. Fresh air today.' Even this offer was fraught with fear, for what if the fresh air that he referred to was simply the backcloth to the gallows, and the patch of sky their last look at heaven. Still, they would not continue their letters. For the time being 'Dear Mum and Dad' would have to do, and if there were no more time, that declaration of love would be enough. 'Dear Mum and Dad', those words would be their sole legacy and their loving power would sustain their parents through the grief of their unspeakable loss.

'Follow me,' the guard said.

They unhooked their masks and puffed their way to the door. Once in the corridor, they breathed deeply and sank into the chairs, exhausted. Neither man spoke. Both craved sleep, but neither would risk a rude awakening. Whatever their fate, they would not allow themselves to be caught napping. They would not be robbed of a final act of resistance.

The day passed in near silence. Lunch was brought and even supper, and when the guard told them it was time to return to their cell, it was almost a relief. It was like going home, for the cell was familiar, with its sparse furnishings, its fading torches, its sheer friendly confinement. Even its thin and threatening air was bearable and felt almost safe. On entering they unhooked the masks, and fell on the mattresses overcome by the fatigue of fear and despair.

The following morning, if it was morning, David chalked up their twenty-second day, hoping that it was accurate. He had a feeling that his birthday was close, or perhaps it had already passed, for he had no idea of the date. But whatever the date, he knew that he would soon be, or already was, twenty-four years old. He recapped on his short life and he owned that he had achieved little. Except for that one monumental discovery. He had found love. That could well count as a life's achievement. He comforted himself with thoughts of Hannah. Positive thoughts, which helped to convince him that he would survive.

And he decided that if he did survive, he would declare himself immediately on his release. He would let it be known loud and clear, that he was a Jew, and bugger the army and Intelligence. He would go to Hannah's father and forgive him, and he would persuade Will to do likewise. Then, in the presence of Hannah and her family he would tell them about his mother and his grandmother. He would tell them, too, of his circumcision and his bar mitzvah and that as a child he had asked the four questions at the Seder table. And he would recite them in Hebrew. And when all that was done, he would ask Avram for permission to marry his daughter. He relished such a scenario and he played it in his mind over and over again, and in time his fear dissolved. Now it was his job to transfer that sense of hope and anticipation to Will, and he wondered what fair future he could promise him. His life, that was all, but that would be more than enough. He hoped that Will would go on sleeping for a while. He looked at him, his still face, the mask but a footnote to its serenity and he felt a surging love for him. For his unwavering friendship, his loyalty, and even his occasional bloody-mindedness. Wherever they lived, they would be friends for life, for their long lives, David decided, as he daydreamed his own way into freedom.

He waited for the breakfast tray to prove that it was morning, and he whiled away the time rehearsing his confession to Hannah's father and his request for her hand in marriage.

When the guard opened the trapdoor, he almost believed that he would be freed but when the tray was laid on the table, he told himself that perhaps it would be tomorrow or the next day. There was no doubt in his mind that very soon he would walk to freedom. He went over to Will's mattress and gently shook him awake. 'Breakfast, Will,' he said. He waited for Will to stir, for that moment when he would wonder where he was, for that moment when he would realise his state, that moment when he would want to go to sleep again rather than face his terrible reality.

'Breakfast, Will,' he said again.

'I'm not hungry,' Will muttered and turned himself over. He would not admit to appetite. He would not acknowledge that there was a breakfast tray, for then he would have to face the reality of where he was, in a cell under the earth, waiting – or not waiting – to die. It was easier to go back to sleep.

David shook him again. 'You have to eat,' he said.

'Why?' Will mumbled.

'To go on living, that's why.'

'For how long?' Will asked with a certain logic.

'Till you're an old man,' David said. 'Till you're married, with children and grandchildren.'

Will actually laughed. He was thinking of Uri, and the notion of marriage was faintly ridiculous. In any case, Uri was dead. He would never be his Hannah, the thought of whom kept David fighting for his life. Indeed, unlike David, he had no life-belt of a daydream to keep him afloat. He might as well go back to sleep. Now David shook him more roughly and he pulled his blanket away. 'Get up,' he almost ordered. 'I can't keep hoping on my own.'

Will sat up suddenly. 'You've no right to depend on me,' he said. 'It's not fair.'

'You're my friend,' David said. 'Friends depend on each other.'

Will rose slowly and went towards the table. He stretched out his hand and touched David's shoulder. 'I'm sorry,' he said. Then after a pause, 'Perhaps they'll let us have some fresh air today. How many days is it now?'

'Twenty-three,' David said. He wasn't sure, but this was no time to sew doubts of any kind in Will's mind.

'Over three weeks,' Will said. He stroked his face. 'How's my beard?' he asked. 'Suits you,' David said. 'How's mine?'

'You look like a rabbi,' Will said.

They stared into each other's faces. They had become their own mirrors. The lines that had furrowed around Will's mouth, David assumed, had furrowed on his own and Will fingered his sunken cheeks like those he saw on his friend's face.

'We're neither of us pretty,' Will said.

They smiled at each other and resumed their breakfast. Then both picked up their pads and pencils. 'Dear Mum and Dad' they read and both men put them aside.

When they heard footsteps again, they were not afraid. It was simply the guard come to collect the tray. But when the trapdoor opened, there was someone else with him. For he was closely followed by the doctor, the sight of whom made Will tremble and mouth yet again the Lord's Prayer. But he was angry too, as well as frightened and he was not going to go gently. 'Have they hanged them?' he shouted. He raised his fists as if he were prepared to fight, to kill even, such was the rage inside him. There was no answer from either man. The guard collected the tray and the doctor held open the trapdoor to ease his passage. The guard had come and gone without a single word. Not even a glance at the hostages. He seemed as frightened as they were.

'They've hanged them,' Will whispered.

Then the doctor spoke. 'How are you today?' he asked.

'How d'you bloody well expect us to be?' Will said.

'They're not yet hanged,' the doctor told them.

That should have brought some relief, but for the 'yet', the word that erased all others.

'Let's have a look at both of you,' the doctor said quickly. He opened his bag and took out his stethoscope, then his blood-pressure gauge and a little felt hammer.

These he laid aside in readiness. 'Who's first?' he said, cheerfully.

Will put himself forward. He wanted the farce over and done with. 'Suppose there's something the matter with me,' he said, 'would you recommend treatment?'

'Let's see, shall we?' the doctor said. He was uneasy, and the men noticed how his hand trembled as he fixed the stethoscope in his ear. Will's heart began racing in fear. He was glad of it. The doctor might find him in real need of treatment that might, in its course, prolong his life. But the doctor found nothing amiss. 'Relax,' was all that he said. Then he took Will's pulse and with his hammer he tested Will's reflexes. Then his blood pressure.

'How am I, doctor?' Will dared to ask.

'You'll live,' the doctor said.

Was there some hope in that diagnosis, David wondered. Or was it just a standard remark that doctors always made to patients who were not on the verge of dying.

'Next please,' the doctor said, and he smiled.

David put himself forward and was subjected to the same procedure.

'Will I live too?' he asked, as his pulse was taken.

The doctor looked him squarely in the face. 'I sincerely hope so,' he said. 'Both of you.' It was a remark that placed him squarely on the sergeants' side.

But Will wasn't satisfied. He wanted more reassurance.

'Please,' he begged, 'tell us what's happening outside.'

'I know no more than you do,' the doctor said.

Then Will blew. 'You're lying,' he shouted. 'They're hanged, aren't they? You're just afraid to tell us.'

The doctor closed his bag and rose.

'Will,' David said. He put his arm around his shoulder and felt it trembling with rage. He was frightened that his friend would go to pieces.

But Will was in the process of pulling himself together, of gathering the courage to speak out, to say those words that would most certainly condemn him but would at least save the life of his friend. He gathered them in his mouth. And then he released them, leisurely and without panic.

'My friend's got a terrible pain in his groin,' he said. 'He's too shy to tell you about it but it wakes him up at night. You'd better look at it.'

David was appalled. Will was putting the rope round his own neck. And all in the name of friendship. 'There's nothing the matter with my groin,' he shouted. 'Will's only trying to detain

190

you. He hopes you'll give us some information from the outside.'

'I've told you, I know nothing,' the doctor said again.

'Then you might as well go,' David told him.

The doctor picked up his bag and made to leave. Will was furious. He emptied his mouth of what was left of his words, words he was reluctant to utter, but all the other words had failed. He plucked the doctor by his sleeve and whispered in his ear, a hoarse whisper, loud enough for David to hear. 'My friend's Jewish,' he hissed. 'I think you ought to know. I think the Irgun ought to know. My friend can prove it.'

The doctor looked worried. He turned to David. 'Is this true?' he asked.

'Of course not.' David even managed a laugh. 'Do you think I'd be here if I were Jewish? Will's only trying to delay you. He'll say anything to keep you here.' He laughed again, hoping to donate some authenticity to his false claim.

The doctor hesitated. He was not a happy man. He made a quick calculation. If Will were telling the truth, the whole hostage strategy would be put in jeopardy. Yet if he didn't report it, he would have it on his conscience for the rest of his life. But it would never be known that Will had spoken. There would be no witnesses, for the men would surely die. It was easier for him to accept David's less complicated denial.

'You're right,' he said to David. 'But I can't stay. In any case, as I've said, I know no more than you do.' And indeed he was telling the truth. The Irgun hierarchy was a tightly knit unit. Even the guards outside knew nothing of the progress of events. They just guessed that the UN investigative committee would have to leave the country before the Mandate would make any decision. And the Irgun's decision depended on the Mandate's move.

'I'll see you again,' the doctor said. It was the only hope he could give them.

When he had gone, there was silence for a while. Then Will said, 'I meant it for the best, David. One of us must survive, if only to tell our story. Otherwise, nobody will ever know. I meant it for the best,' he said again.

'I know,' David said, 'and you are a true friend. But wherever we are going, and in whatever way, we are going together.' He put his arm round Will's shoulder. 'If necessary we are both Jews, you and I.'

They clung to each other, and sank down together on to their cots, and lay in each other's embrace for a long while.

32

When *Zeyda* woke in the morning after his visit to Degania, he found himself still in his workroom. He had fallen asleep at his bench. He went into the kitchen. His breakfast was set on the table, but there was no sign of Miriam. He was hungry, and slightly ashamed of his appetite. He picked up the newspaper and began to eat. Over the weeks the hostage report had slowly moved from the front page to a small column on the back. There was nothing to report. Except the nothing. 'The search for the sergeants continues', was all it said. He wondered where Miriam was, and with a sinking heart he feared she might have left him. He could not envisage how he could live without her. She would have been happy to stay in Degania. The children too, and the thought troubled him. He had to admit to himself that he'd been selfish and that the move had finally cost him his family. It was too late now to pull out of the cause. The cause had become an addiction and the pains of withdrawal would be too severe. He decided to go straight to the hideout, for another fix, as it were. Hopefully Gad would be there, the reminder of his life-changing conversion and he would be comforted.

But there was little comfort to be found in Begin's den. Gad, Dror and Pinsker were seated at the table. Begin's head was in his hands. The mood was black as if the men were in mourning.

'What's happened?' Avram asked. At worst, the Acre prisoners could have been hanged. Or worse still, the sergeants had been discovered and they would have talked, and now all their lives would be in danger. And they would be hanged with the rest of them.

'I've had news from Port-de-Bouc,' Begin said. 'They're trying to keep it out of the papers.'

Avram was at pains to hide his relief. 'What news?' he asked.

'The British gave an ultimatum,' Gad said. 'Disembark or you sail on. They didn't mention Germany, but that's where they're going. To Hamburg. Back where they came from.'

'It's unbelievable,' Pinsker said.

'What can we do?' Avram asked.

'Nothing,' Begin said. 'We can only pray for them. I think it may well affect the Mandate's decision,' he said without a pause. 'Its reputation is none too clean in England, and the UN Committee's report will dirty it further. I doubt that they will risk further approbation by hanging our men. I'm hopeful,' he said. 'Though it's a high price to pay for their magnanimity. I gather there's a farewell reception at Government House this evening,' he added. 'The UN people leave tomorrow. The next few days are crucial. We must all be on our guard. I suggest you each arrange an escape route.'

Avram thought of Degania and his friends there. If, when learning of his Irgun involvement, would they love him enough to hide him? His presence would put the whole kibbutz in danger. He would not ask them to take that risk. He wondered where Gad would go. And Dror and Pinsker. Perhaps they could help him. Though he knew that it was not good to know where anybody was. And in no way could he involve his family, even if they were prepared to help him. He was on his own, and he was frightened.

'Are they still searching?' Begin asked suddenly.

'I think they've given up,' Gad said. 'The Haganah is still out looking.'

'I know,' Begin said. 'The guard reported their presence at the factory. He was laughing. "A close shave", he said. I think from now on, Natanya is safe.'

'Will we . . . ?' Avram started. 'It doesn't matter.'

'What is it, Avram? What's troubling you?' Begin asked.

'If our men are hanged,' *Zeyda* started, 'are we —'

'Yes, we are,' Begin said. 'It's what we have threatened. The gallows will not be all of one colour, Avram,' he said gently. 'It's the cause.'

194

That word again, and coming out of the mouth of one *Zeyda* regarded as the saviour. 'So be it,' he said.

Shortly afterwards, the men left separately and on different routes. They were depressed. The news from the *Exodus* was heartbreaking. The British was a nation on whom it seemed proper to wreak revenge. And that, the men feared, would come soon enough. Each man was thinking of the sergeants. The two had rarely been out of their minds since the kidnapping. And each man knew that the hostages were going to die. Nothing could save them. Even if the Acre prisoners were reprieved, the risk of releasing the hostages was too great. They had to die, and the men dreaded the task that would fall to them. Begin would insist that no others be involved, that those who abducted them would see to their dispatch.

Zeyda returned to his apartment. He hoped to find Miriam there, though he wondered whether her absence was preferable to her accusing silence. He called her name anyhow, as he opened the door.

'She's out,' he heard Joseph say.

He was relieved that he would not be alone. It had been a long time, ever since the search had got under way, that he and Joseph had been alone together. He didn't know what they could talk about, but he would be satisfied just to be in his company.

'Where is she? Where has she gone?' he asked.

'I don't know,' Joseph said. 'Probably shopping. Do you want some coffee? I've just made it.'

'Thanks,' Avram said, and he sat at the table. 'How's the search going?' he dared to ask.

'Let's not talk about it,' Joseph said. 'Is there any news from the prison?'

'We're all waiting,' *Zeyda* said. Then he told him about the *Exodus*. That was a subject on which no Jew would argue. Joseph was appalled. 'Back where they came from?' he said.

'D'you hate the British as much as I do?' Avram asked.

'Yes,' Joseph said. 'I hate them with all my heart. But I don't want to kill them. I just want them to leave.' He passed his father a cup of coffee.

'How is Hannah?' *Zeyda* whispered.

'How do you expect her to be?' Joseph said. 'She's in despair. No good will come of it, Papa,' he almost shouted. Then in a whisper, 'Our family is crumbling.' He put his hand on his father's arm. 'Papa, I think Mama's left you.'

Avram stared at him. 'How do you know that?' *Zeyda* was angry and his voice was breaking.

'She told me that it was difficult being with you. Not able to talk. She worries about Hannah.'

'Where has she gone?' Avram asked.

'I think she's probably gone to stay with Mrs Katz. She wanted to go back to Degania, but she couldn't, because there was no way she could explain why she had come. How was your birthday by the way?'

'Lonely,' *Zeyda* said. Then after a pause. 'D'you regret our leaving Degania, Joseph?'

'I think we would all have been happier there. Certainly we wouldn't be in the mess we are in today. We would have done what you yourself did, Hannah and I. We would have married kibbutzniks, had children by now, given you grandchildren. Tell me, Papa, do *you* have regrets?'

Avram had been dreading such a question. He could not lie to his son. 'In view of everything that has happened,' he said, 'and is going to happen, I regret it with all my heart.'

Joseph saw tears in his father's eyes. He had never seen his father cry before. Except once when Mrs Katz's son, Dov, had been killed. That was part and parcel of his regret.

'Then why did you do it, Papa?'

Zeyda had no answer that would satisfy anybody. Not even himself. He risked that filthy word. 'The cause,' he said. It was a Pavlovian reaction, as if he had been brainwashed. Joseph knew that there was no point in argument. He poured his father more coffee, and tried not to pity him.

'D'you think I should go to Mrs Katz?' Avram asked. 'What do you think I should do?' He was like a child asking a parent's advice.

Joseph would not lie to him. 'She won't welcome you,' he said. 'Leave it for a while. Let's see how things turn out.'

But *Zeyda* knew that things could only get worse and he sensed that Joseph knew it too. He wanted to hide, not from anyone who might be looking for him, but from himself, for he did not like what he had become. What frightened him most was what he might be called upon to do. He had killed in his time, but at a distance, and people whom he had never known. People who were not made of flesh and blood, but were mere symbols of the enemy. But he knew the flesh and the blood of David Millar and Will Griffiths. For one of them he had made a suit, and both of them had sat at his table. It was hard to label them as the enemy. 'Where can I find Hannah?' he asked suddenly.

Joseph sounded hopeful. 'Do you want to tell her where they are?' His father was wavering. 'You could tell her,' Joseph urged. 'Nobody need know that the information came from you.'

My *zeyda* was appalled. The cause, that safety net, had trapped him again. 'We don't want them found,' he shouted. 'D'you hear me?' He felt himself in harness once more. 'And they'll never be found,' he added.

'Are they already dead?' Joseph shouted too.

'No. They're well. They're alive. And they'll stay alive as long as our own men in Acre.'

They sat in silence for a while. *Zeyda* held Joseph's hand. 'Joseph,' he said, 'tell Mama to come home. We all need her here.'

'*You* need her, you mean,' Joseph said. 'But it's you who have sent her away.' He gathered up the coffee cups. 'I must be off,' he said. 'We're still looking, you know.'

'Where are you looking today?' Avram asked.

'Why should I tell you?' Joseph said, and he was gone, leaving his father disconsolate at the table, reaping the sour oats that he knew he should never have sown.

33

The farewell reception at Government House was mere protocol. There was a feeling of relief on all sides. The UN Committee sipped politely at their cocktails and could not get out of the country soon enough, and their hosts, smiling and plying them with drinks, could not wait to see the back of them. The following morning they would be gone and General Barker could get back to the business of law and order, to let those in the Irgun know, once and for all, that the Mandate would not be blackmailed. Time to return to discipline, to trials, whether or not recognised, to the gradual sieving of the dregs on death row, starting with the three prisoners who had caused all the trouble to begin with.

The following morning he called together his chosen entourage. They settled in his office, and from the determined set of his features, they knew that a decision had been made.

'They're going to hang,' the General said. No preamble, no request for discussion.

'And about bloody time,' one of the officers said.

Captain Coleman shifted in his seat. 'What about the sergeants?' he asked.

'I don't think the Irgun will carry out its threat,' the General said, displaying an ignorance beyond belief. After all his years of service in Palestine, he should have learned that the Irgun was to be taken seriously.

'I'm not too sure of that,' Captain Coleman insisted. He was thinking of Will. He would like to have seen him again. 'I think the Irgun will hang them,' he said.

'They're barbarians,' an officer gave his opinion.

It was too much for Captain Coleman. 'And we're *not*?' he shouted.

There was a sudden and appalled silence in the room. And a distinct smell of treachery.

'What exactly does that mean?' General Barker asked.

'Well, we hang without much compunction.' The Captain knew he could not now withdraw.

'We are law, and we are order,' the General shouted. 'We have that right. Now I must ask you to apologise, not only to me, but to your fellow officers, whose courage and integrity you have sorely doubted.'

For a moment, Captain Coleman envisaged his future. At best, a dishonourable discharge. A pariah among his so-called friends. An idle and desperate stroll down civvy street. It was a high price to pay. Too high, he decided. He would apologise, and he would mourn Will in sad secret.

'I'm sorry,' he said. 'I was caught off guard. It's because I know the men. I know them personally. I myself recruited them into Intelligence. For a moment, I allowed myself a personal involvement. I'm very sorry,' he said.

But he was not sorry at all. And never would be. He would nurture dreams of General Barker hanging from a eucalyptus tree.

'Accepted,' General Barker said with a certain reluctance, for it was obvious he would have preferred a court martial. But he was anxious to get on with the business in hand.

'Do I have your unanimous approval of my decision?' he asked.

There was a general murmur of approval in the hall.

'Then I shall get on with it,' he said. 'But I want this kept quiet. Secrecy is of prime importance. I've no doubt it will come out eventually. The Irgun has its spies everywhere. But the longer we keep it unknown, the better. You can dismiss,' he said. 'Don't forget. Keep your mouths shut.'

As the men filed out of the office, the General detained Captain Coleman, and when they were alone he said, 'You have dangerous thoughts, Captain. Personally, I don't like them. I think they are corrupt and unworthy of an English officer of the Crown. If you cannot scrub that filth out of your mind, then the least you can do is to keep it to yourself. I will not have my other officers contaminated. You may go.'

The dismissal was abrupt and reeked of contempt. Captain Coleman controlled himself by staring at General Barker's neck, imprinting its image on his retina for all time, so that occasionally, when he called Will to mind, he could circle it with a rope and almost make it real.

When he was alone, the General telephoned the prison, and was put through to the Warden's office. Colonel Hackett answered the phone. 'Hackett speaking,' he said. 'Yes, General. What can I do for you?'

General Barker slightly resented the Colonel's familiar tone. An arrogant tone, inferring that a mere colonel could do the General a favour. 'It's something you can do for all of us,' the General said coldly.

'I'm waiting,' the Colonel said.

'I want this to be kept highly secret; it should only be conveyed to those who will be involved. And the fewer, the better. Everyone must be sworn to secrecy.' He paused then, giving time for his orders to register. 'They must hang. Tonight. Those are my orders.'

'I understand, sir,' Hackett said. 'I must tell you, sir, it will be a relief.'

'For all of us,' General Barker said. He put down the phone. It's done, he said to himself. And with not a hint of scruple.

Colonel Hackett went to work immediately. He began by recruiting an execution team and swearing them to secrecy. He decided to wait till it was dark when the scaffold cover could be moved without being seen. The prisoners would be told at the very last minute. No last visitors would be allowed. The prisoners' mouths must be taped, but their legs must not be chained. The warders involved would wear slippers. The whole procedure must be carried out without a sound. He gave these orders to the men in a whisper, as if in rehearsal for the real performance, and the men tiptoed back to their quarters and waited for darkness to fall.

Shortly after he'd given Colonel Hackett the orders for the execution, General Barker had instructed his driver to take him to Acre prison. Hackett had been told to wait for his arrival. For General Barker, there was nothing like a good hanging and, although he was a busy man, he rarely missed one. He regarded them as a treat, as a reward as it were, for his good government.

His car drew up at the prison as darkness fell. Inside Colonel Hackett assembled his men. He himself was wearing slippers as he led the guards along the corridor of death row. As quietly as possible, they opened the cage that housed the three condemned men. Haviv, Nakar and Weiss were sleeping and the Colonel was surprised at how peaceful they looked. He felt sorry for them.

'Gags first,' he reminded his men.

They moved towards the beds. Haviv was the first to be woken, and he shouted. 'It's over. It's the end.' He started on the *Shema*, but the gag stifled the prayer.

Nakar had woken. 'I want a rabbi,' he whispered. But that plea too was gagged. 'Plenty of rabbis where you're going,' one of the guards whispered.

By then Weiss was awake and he was given no time for a plea of any kind, for the warders were hovering over him, the gag at the ready. Soon they were all trussed and ready for transport. Each man was taken by two guards. They were propelled into the corridor and led towards the door of the prison yard. Not a sound was heard. Once outside, each prisoner was guided to the scaffold. General Barker stood at attention at the base of the gallows. His uniform jacket glistened with his medals, tokens of his courage in the line of fire, though the scaffold was the most perilous line of fire that he had ever confronted. As the men climbed the steps, he saluted, and he kept that position until it was all over. He meant it as a gesture of farewell, and coming from such an authority they should be honoured. He watched as the noose was placed round each man's neck. He grew excited and his saluting arm trembled. This was the best part, the fore-play as it were, with its promise of sublime climax. He relished it for a while as the guards gently adjusted the ropes. Then he took a deep breath. His face assumed a rictus grin, and as the men dropped, so did his saluting arm in the exhaustion of post-coital joy.

It was all over. Soon, when it was known, three more mothers would be weeping and cursing the cause. They would join an army of innocent mourners who would shiver in the cold absences that would haunt them for the rest of their lives.

34

Avram was woken by a knock on the apartment door. 'Miriam?' he called. For a happy moment, he thought she might have returned. But then he was worried, for what was she doing knocking at the door in the middle of the night. 'Miriam?' he called again as he opened the door.

It was Gad standing there in the semi-darkness, wondering why his friend was expecting his wife at such an ungodly hour.

Avram was confused. 'What is it?' he asked. He feared he might have bad news of Miriam.

'Begin wants us straight away,' Gad said.

Avram went to get his coat, slipping it over his pyjamas and fearing dire tidings.

'What's happened?' he asked, as he settled into Gad's car.

'He didn't say,' Gad said. 'But I fear the worst.'

And since both men feared the same, neither of them put it into words. So it was a silent drive to the hideout. The sun rose meanwhile and by the time they arrived, it was light.

The regulars were gathered there. Dror and Pinsker. Both silent and both ignorant of why they had been called. Begin's head was in his hands, and they all knew it was a time for grieving.

After a while, Begin spoke. 'I've had a message from Acre. From our trusty guard,' he said. 'They've gone, our comrades. Hanged in the dark. In silence. They're trying to keep it quiet. We will get our own business done first, comrades, after which I intend to announce everything on our radio. I mean everything. We must make our plans.' Then he laid out the details of the operation. Each man was given a precise role, and he urged that there should be no overlapping. 'I have tried to be fair to you all,' he said. 'None of you will relish this job, but it has to be done. I suggest you leave here late afternoon, and arrange to arrive at the factory as the sun begins to set. I wish you all Godspeed,' he said.

The men dispersed, trembling. Each one of them had hoped that it would not come to this point. It had seemed such a very last and distant resort that it was unreachable. But now their orders were clear, and to comfort themselves a little they thought of the three hanged prisoners, all of them close comrades. It was on their behalf that they would execute the plan. It would be a just revenge in their names.

Zeyda went straight home. For the first time he hoped that Miriam would not be there. He could not bear to face her, in case the mere thought of his mission betrayed him. But thankfully he found himself alone. He had eaten nothing since he had risen, but he had no appetite. He would sit quietly and try to take his mind off his mind until Gad came for him. The hours crawled by. He wandered on to the balcony overlooking the streets. An ordinary day, with people going about their business, women shopping, children playing, and a group of men loitering on the corner, all of them sublimely ignorant of what was going to happen on that day and he was tempted to shout it out loud, but he himself did not wish to hear it. He waited. He hoped to catch sight of Miriam perhaps, coming into the drive of their block. And many women did so, burdened with shopping, curfew-shopping to be on the safe side. But not one of them was Miriam. For a while he managed to dislike her a little for giving him so much grief. But that quickly passed. He understood that she had had to leave him and that no repair was possible.

He went back to the kitchen and he heard the newspaper slip through the letter-box. He rushed to view its headline.

'The UNSCOP Commission departs,' he read. There was a picture of the Chairman of the Committee shaking hands with General Barker, both smiling at each other as if they were old friends. In the background, groups of people were laughing and drinking and a portrait of the king was clearly visible on the wall.

But there was not a word in any part of the paper about the prisoners in Acre prison. And not a word about the hostages. It was as if Acre and Natanya were already history, to be reported or distorted at will when the Mandate authorities considered the time was ripe. He longed for Gad and the others to come for him so that he would not feel so entirely alone.

He was hungry. He felt he should eat something. A little nourishment to tide him over the ordeal he was facing. But the thought of food sickened him. He was restless, and he decided to go down into the street and wait there for the sight of Pinsker's car. He walked to the shop on the corner, an ironmonger's, and he feigned an interest in its window display while watching out for the car in its reflection. He was fascinated by the sight of the latest vacuum cleaner and he thought that he might buy it for Miriam. It was a thought that belonged to normal times and for a while he half dreamed in those times, until he saw Pinsker's car pull up behind him and remind him of his present reality. But he was glad of company. He slipped into the back seat beside Dror. Pinsker, as usual, was driving, with Gad by his side. None of them spoke. There was only one topic of conversation and that was unutterable. They weaved their way through the streets and then were suddenly halted. Not by soldiers, but by a traffic jam. Irate drivers were hooting, but to no avail. The road was blocked by a protest march, the head of which was making its way towards them. A policeman motioned the drivers to pull over to the side, to allow the march to pass. Pinsker idled on the kerb, and they watched the march go by.

It was an orderly procession, a solemn and silent one. But the banners said it all. 'Free the sergeants', they read. One after another. Home-made banners, do-it-yourself banners, quickly run up, with their simple and clear message. There was no need to shout it out. Their letters stung in the eye. The march was so silent, one could hardly hear its footsteps and was all the more telling for that. Spectators on the street stopped and stared, their silence signalling their approval. *Zeyda* watched from the car window, hiding himself a little in fear of what he might see. But it was unavoidable. For the first time in almost a month, he caught sight of Hannah. Joseph walked by her side and they shared a banner between them. 'Free the sergeants' it pleaded like the rest of them, and his heart turned over. I am on my way to murder the man you love, he said to himself and he knew that never again could he look himself in the eye.

He was relieved when the tailend of the march shuffled by, and the traffic was able to move once more. The march and its banners had shaken the others in the car. Gad shifted uncomfortably in his seat and Pinsker revved the engine to release whatever he was feeling. Dror put his head in his hands.

The coast road was a scenic one but it held no interest for the travellers. They maintained their silence until they reached Natanya. On the outskirts of the town they stopped. It was still light, and Gad suggested a meal in an off-street café. But Dror said that they could not risk being seen. Neither could they remain stationary.

'Let's drive round for a while,' Dror said.

Pinsker lost his cool. 'Let's get it over and done with, for God's sake,' he said, and he revved the engine once more and turned towards the outskirts of the town. On reaching the factory they parked the car on a dirt-track alongside. Pinsker turned off the engine, and the silence was terrifying.

'Shall we go?' Gad whispered.

But no one moved. They simply stared at each other. Then not able to bear the mirror of their own fears, they turned their faces away.

35

When David had woken up that morning, he hadn't bothered to record the numbered day of their confinement. He didn't care any more. His daydream scenario of freedom had faded and, although he was at pains to hide it from Will, he had almost lost all hope of rescue. He adjusted his mask over his nose. Nowadays, he was rarely without it. They hadn't breathed fresh air for a long while. It was possible that in time they would die of simple suffocation. Again he thought of writing home, but in his heart he still clung to the idea of survival. The letter would have to wait, and he would take the risk that one day it might be too late to add an extra word. He waited for the guard and the breakfast tray. He was relieved that he was hungry, proof that the will to live still clung to him. Will was sleeping. His look of innocence pierced David's heart. He would not wake him until the guard arrived. But Will was already stirring and mumbling in his after-sleep.

'I'm starving,' he said, and David was happy that Will too, even after such a long and uncertain confinement, was envisaging a future. David helped him up from his mattress.

'Perhaps we'll get some air today,' Will was saying.

For the first time in many days, Will had not asked David for the time. At last he seemed to have forgiven his friend's negligence. Or perhaps he had forgotten it, as the best way of dealing with what had irked him. They sat at their table and waited for the guard.

'Where are we?' Will suddenly asked.

David feared that his friend was losing his mind. He himself had occasional lapses of memory. He ascribed them to the almost continuous dark and airlessness of their cell. A little fresh air would clear the mind and, like Will, he hoped that day for a glimpse of the sky. Then the guard entered the cell, and, as if on cue, invited them into the corridor to take their breakfast.

Both men rushed to the trapdoor, doffing their masks on the way. They were no longer afraid. The guard could be trusted. The fresh air that he promised would be no more than fresh air, and there would be nothing to pollute it. They sank into the armchairs and started on the cooked breakfast that he had provided.

Although they did not speak of it, both men sensed a positive change in the air, which accounted possibly for their attitude and sudden change of mood.

'We don't need to write that letter home,' Will said. 'I feel it in my bones.'

David was infected by his confidence. 'It will be a good day,' he replied.

They were on a high, both of them, as if a merciful shot of morphine had raised their spirits. They ate with appetite and relish and when the guard cleared away their tray, they felt the need for conversation, a need unheeded for a long while.

Both David and Will were private people, and though they were close they were wary of confiding in each other. It was not that they had no wish for such confidence, but they were shy of revealing themselves. It was easier to confide in a stranger or in someone you could be sure of never seeing again. It was, perhaps, this subconscious thought that had wriggled beneath their optimism. In all the days of their confinement, they had never been unaware of their peril and, despite their present hope, that awareness still lingered.

David was the first to unveil his feelings. 'I think of Hannah all the time,' he said. 'We are betrothed, you know.' He did not wait for a response from Will. He did not want his disclosure interrupted. 'You know the river Yarkon,' he went on. 'There's a hill that rises from its banks. At the top of the hill, almost hidden by trees, there's a shepherd's hut.'

Will leaned forward. He was wondering where the story would lead. It seemed as if David was dreaming and that what he was about to say was fantasy. But David's expression was earnest and care-worn yet bright with the need for confession.

'I went there once,' David was saying, 'not long ago. Maybe yesterday, I can't remember. I was with Hannah. I love her, Will, and I am going to marry her. We kissed on the hill and it seemed quite natural that we should enter the hut. I was a virgin, Will. And so was Hannah. We made love to each other, my friend. So we are betrothed.'

Will was confused. He wanted to be happy for David, but the chapel was on his back, that black forbidder. In his Welsh mining village, what his friend had done was called *rude*. There was no other word for it. Silly young boys would sometimes do it up the mountain and, coming down, would be forced into wedlock.

'Will you be a father?' was all he could say.

David laughed. 'I sincerely hope so.'

'I'm glad for you,' Will said.

David welcomed Will's response. He had not relied on a reaction of any kind. It was enough for him that he was unburdened. Now the blurring of his daydream would clear, and pave his way to freedom. He sank back in his chair, exhausted. 'I'll sleep for a while,' he said.

But Will was restless. He was troubled by David's story and troubled too because he knew that it would soon be his turn to confide. He looked at his friend and envied his ease. Perhaps the unfolding of his own story would grant him the same relief. He managed to sleep for a while, and was woken by the guard with the lunch tray.

'The day seems to be passing very quickly,' David said. He noted that a cloud had misted their patch of sky, but he did not let it trouble him. Nor did the lavish spread on the lunch tray disturb him. It was just another pointer to an extraordinary day.

They had finished, and the tray had been removed. 'Your turn,' David said.

Will plunged straight into the deep end. 'David,' he said. 'I think I am a homo.'

David was vaguely familiar with the word. He remembered a boy at school. His name was Brian. The prefects called him 'nancy boy', and they'd laughed. And David had laughed too, though he didn't know why. Brian walked like a girl, with mincing steps, and his wrists were always aflutter. It was at that time that the word 'homo' was bandied around. But later he had learned that you didn't have to walk like a girl or flutter your wrists to be a nancy boy. Will walked like a man, and his wrists were still. He simply loved men. He preferred them to women, and that was nothing to laugh about.

'I think I was in love with Uri,' Will said. 'I had feelings for him that I've never had for anyone else before. I had a girlfriend once, in our village. Two, in fact, but I never felt for them like I did for Uri. Somehow they didn't fit. It was Uri who made sense to me.'

'Why does it trouble you?' David asked.

'How can I tell my mam and dad?' Will said.

David heard that as a hopeful sign. Will could still envisage a confrontation with his parents. 'They'll understand,' he said, 'because they love you. And you'll find another Uri. You'll fall in love again.'

Will said nothing for a while. Then, 'Do you feel awkward with me, David?' he asked.

David smiled. 'Why should I?' he said. 'It's loving that matters. The target is irrelevant. You will be happy again, my friend.' He stretched out his hand to hold Will's in his own. The sky was no longer blue. A dark cloud had stained it.

'It's going to rain,' Will said.

It grew dark, and shortly the guard came and told them that it was time to return to their cell. He opened the trapdoor and led them inside.

'Sleep well,' he said as he left. Something he had never said before, but the hostages did not find it amiss. It was simply part and parcel of an extraordinary day. They reached for their masks and their torches.

'My batteries have run out,' David said.

Will flicked his switch. 'So have mine,' he said. 'We'll ask the guard to renew them in the morning.'

So they lay down in the dark, stretching out their arms to each other.

'See you in the morning,' Will said.

36

A morning that would not come for either of them. They woke suddenly, blinded by the harsh light that filled their cell. Four dazzling torches picked out their mattresses and a voice told them to get up. A familiar voice, one that had been heard recently, a voice that had explained the four questions, a voice that had once suggested soft grey flannel.

'Tell Hannah I loved her,' David shouted.

'Our Father which art in heaven,' Will's voice was resigned as he knelt down to pray.

Gad and Dror waited. Begin had told them not to hurry, and to be as gentle as possible. Those two had been ordered to be the executioners. *Zeyda*'s role was to be that of the witness. It was Begin's way of being kind to him. But to be a witness was the hardest of all. A witness would not be allowed to forget. It would be his responsibility to report. To be a witness was to bear a cross for ever. When Will rose, full of prayer, 'fit and season'd for his passage', Dror approached. He placed his wrists on Will's shoulders. Then, with his bare hands, he strangled him. Will offered no resistance, his only protest a rattled gurgle as life drained out of him as he slumped to the floor.

Gad waited for a moment. Perhaps David had a prayer too. He stared at him and saw how he viewed his friend's body and how the tears flowed freely down his cheeks. Then David stared at *Zeyda*. 'Why is this night different from all other nights?' he asked. The first question of the Seder service. Then he lowered his head, and in a crystal clear voice, he intoned that traditional dying prayer. '*Shema Yisrael, Adoni Elohainu. Adonoi Echad.*'

Dror grinned. 'Worth a try,' he said. 'Any goy could pick up those words, and use them in a tight situation. Let's get on with it,' he said.

But *Zeyda* was stunned. No non-Jew could have uttered that prayer with such authority and in an accent so impeccable. He had to pretend that he hadn't heard. That those words played no part in his witnessing. Then it was Gad's turn as executioner. *Zeyda* watched, marvelling that he was so adept in his role, skilled even, and working untroubled by an ounce of scruple. That mentor of his who had changed his life, whom he had loved and almost worshipped, that wrapper of necks, that strangler. Now for the first time, and in an avalanche of relief, he began to hate him and everything he stood for.

David's body slumped silently to Will's side.

'It is done,' Dror said. 'Let's move.'

Between the three of them they carried the bodies out of the cell and into the fresh air the hostages had craved. They bundled them out of the corridor and towards the car. *Zeyda* was left to place the bodies in the boot while the others returned to the cell to remove whatever evidence remained. Pinsker sat idly at the wheel, in sublime indifference. He wanted to pretend that he had nothing to do with any of it.

It was Will *Zeyda* laid first in the boot. Tenderly and with infinite care. The chapel suit that had once so offended his tailor's eye now moved him to tears.

David was the second burden, and burdensome enough for the deeply troubled witness. He laid him gently on to Will's body and then succumbed to a temptation that he knew he should have resisted. Slowly he opened the fly on David's trousers. He paused to admire his skill in button-holing. Then the dead penis lay exposed. As circumcised as his own. He rebuttoned quickly and closed the boot of the car. Then he rushed to the side of the track and threw his heart up.

Dror and Gad returned and once more they all got in the car. Pinsker drove. He had his instructions. He drove west, to Umm Ulexga and there, in a eucalyptus grove, they unloaded the bodies of the two sergeants. It was *Zeyda*'s assignment to string them up, as the others bore witness. This he did because it was what

Begin had ordered, but it was the last order of Begin's that he would ever obey.

When it was done, Gad said, 'Let's eat, for God's sake. I'm starving.'

'I'm not hungry,' *Zeyda* said. He hadn't eaten all day. It was his Yom Kippur, his Day of Atonement.

Early next morning as she was preparing for the search, Hannah switched on the resistance radio. 'This is Radio Irgun,' she heard. 'In retaliation for the hanging of our three heroes of the revolt, the two British sergeants, David Millar and William Griffiths, were last night given the same treatment. Their bodies hang in the eucalyptus grove of Umm Ulexga.'

The streets outside were silent. It seemed that the whole of Tel Aviv was still. Nothing could be heard but the sound of Hannah screaming.

37

There. It is done. The story has been told. I have kept my promise.

The aftermath of the story varies, as does the story itself, depending on the narrator. But I know for a fact that *Zeyda* lived only a short while after he had put the ropes round the hostages' necks. He joined a unit of the Haganah and fought in the 1948 War of Independence. An Arab bullet caught him offguard, an unlikely stance for *Zeyda*. Witnesses thought he took unnecessary risks, as if he was indifferent to whether he lived or died which, in the light of his troubled conscience, was understandable.

As for Miriam, she was shattered with grief and she returned to Degania to serve out her fraught widowhood. Joseph married Zelda, a comrade in the Haganah. They had two children, the eldest of whom, Seth, was my father. Alas, Joseph was killed in the Six Day War in 1967. He had already told Seth *Zeyda*'s story and my father wrote it down by way of a memorial. Ten years later my father left the promised land, that for the most part had failed to keep its promises. He was a physicist, and he settled in London in a university post. In that same year, he married my mother who was a lecturer at the same university. Two years later I was born. It was not until my twentieth birthday, as a present I suppose, that my father gave me his written version of *Zeyda*'s tale.

And Hannah? A mystery remains about what happened to her. Joseph told my father that she had simply died of a broken heart. But my father, being of a sentimental nature, offered a more hopeful version. He claimed that Hannah was pregnant with David's child and that shortly after his death she went to live with David's parents in Bristol, where the child was born. But my version is the true one, for it is the result of my diligent research. First of all, there was no baby. Hannah moved to Jerusalem and, in a moment of near-madness, possibly due to her despair, she turned ultra-orthodox and moved into Mea Shearim. By arrangement with the elders, she entered a loveless and unconsummated marriage with a Talmudic student. She shaved her head, according to tradition, and wore a wig. Three years later, at the age of twenty-four, hairless and full of rage, she died. Her husband survived into old age, having refused all his life to fight in any battle. He spent most of his time at the Wailing Wall, praying to God, sticking obscene notes into the crevices, and occasionally a dirty picture, all the while praising God and cursing everybody. That's more or less Hannah's story.

And here am I, born gay, with no issue, up to my neck in the *intifada*, with no one left of *Zeyda*'s blood to whom to tell his story. It saddens me that the troubadour line has come to an end. So I was obliged to tell *Zeyda* that, despite my deviations, his story was now in the public domain, and that I, as his great-grandson, had honoured my pledge. I went to Israel.

I suppose I have distant relations still living there, but it was not my purpose to visit them. I had cemeteries in mind. My first visit was to the British military cemetery in Ramallah. I had some difficulty in finding the sergeants' tombs. The caretaker could not help me. Or would not, for he shrugged off my request with scorn. Perhaps he'd been told that those graves were of little matter and that they should not be advertised. Or perhaps he was an old Irgun member who was ashamed. But I was determined to find them. I walked the long rows of crosses, row upon row. Eventually I found them. Side by side.

'Sergeant David Millar' and 'Sergeant William Griffiths' the legends read. Crosses marked their graves. I noticed that on David's tomb, someone had painted the Star of David. Probably *Zeyda*. His remorse. His apology. I laid a pebble on his grave, the Jewish token of remembrance. On Will's too. I left the cemetery taking care to tell the caretaker that I had found the graves and that I would let others know where they were, since there was a great deal of growing interest in the sergeants' story. He was not a happy man.

It was a day for communing with the dead, and I made my way to the old Jewish cemetery on Trumpeldor Street in Tel Aviv. I found *Zeyda*'s grave without difficulty. The legend was decipherable, but the grave was largely overgrown. That saddened me. I put down my pebble. I counted just four others. He'd had few visitors. I sat on the ground beside him.

'I've told your story, *Zeyda*,' I said. 'I think I told the truth of it. You were wrong, you and your lot. And they're still wrong. They're in danger of destroying what you wished to create. We came here to find a safe place, but we are not entitled to make that place unsafe for others. If we could respect that, we could live together in peace.'

I love my great-grandfather. I love him for the terrible price he had to pay. I love him for his dedication, his zeal and for his sheer bloody-mindedness. I love him above all, for his doubts and uncertainties. So rest, *Zeyda*. Rest in peace.'

Now you can order superb titles directly from Abacus

☐	Brothers	Bernice Rubens	£8.99
☐	I, Dreyfus	Bernice Rubens	£6.99
☐	Milwaukee	Bernice Rubens	£6.99
☐	Nine Lives	Bernice Rubens	£7.99
☐	Our Father	Bernice Rubens	£7.99

The prices shown above are correct at time of going to press. However, the publishers reserve the right to increase prices on covers from those previously advertised, without prior notice.

───────────────── ⟨ABACUS⟩ ─────────────────

Please allow for postage and packing: **Free UK Delivery**
Europe; add 25% of retail price; Rest of World; 45% of retail price.

To order any of the above or any other Abacus titles, please call our credit card orderline or fill in this coupon and send/fax it to:

Abacus, PO Box 121, Kettering, Northants NN14 4ZQ
Fax: 01832 733076   Tel: 01832 737527
Email: aspenhouse@FSBDial.co.uk

☐ I enclose a UK bank cheque made payable to Abacus for £.......

☐ Please charge £ .... to my Visa/Access/Mastercard/Eurocard

Expiry Date ☐☐☐☐   Switch Issue No. ☐☐

NAME (BLOCK LETTERS please) . . . .

ADDRESS . . . .

. . . .

. . . .

Postcode . . . .   Telephone . . . .

Signature . . . .

Please allow 28 days for delivery within the UK. Offer subject to price and availability.
Please do not send any further mailings from companies carefully selected by Abacus ☐